AN ACT OF GOD

ALSO BY STEPHEN FRANCIS

Into the Lion's Den

A DANIEL MILLER THRILLER

AN ACT OF GOD

STEPHEN FRANCIS

This edition published in Ireland 2019 by Unicorn Publishing

Kindle edition published by Unicorn Publishing

Cover and printed matter formatting by Design for Writers
Inset photography by Simon McDermott

ISBN (HB)   978-1-9162361-3-4
ISBN (TPB) 978-1-9162361-4-1
ISBN (E)   978-1-9162361-5-8

ABOUT THE AUTHOR

Stephen was born in 1968 and lived most of his life on Dublin's Northside before moving even further north into the adjoining county of Meath, where he lives with his wife and two children.

He graduated from Kevin Street DIT, Trinity College Dublin, and Dublin City University with a diploma, degree, and Master's in physics, respectively. He is a classically trained musician (tuba), and an avid watcher and player of tennis, the latter, though, only when injuries permit.

Stephen is the writer of two published novels: *Into The Lions' Den* and *An Act Of God*, which chronicle contract agent Daniel Miller's path through the events of the mid to late 20th century. He is writing the third Miller thriller entitled, for the moment, *Where Angels Fear To Tread*.

For My Family

'The best weapon against an enemy is another enemy.'

- FRIEDRICH NIETZSCHE

PROLOGUE

TEMPERATURES HAD SOARED AND BATHED Rome in a sweltering summer heat, bringing with it a tide of renewed hope, optimism, and opportunity that had displaced more than a decade of fear, intimidation, and hate which had fed an ideology that had thrown, at first a continent, and then the world into yet another war.

But Father Felipe Hernandez did not share the joyous mood openly displayed by the majority of those who'd survived. The dying declaration of a frail man's lifetime of experiences had haunted him ever since it'd been uttered. 'We are born without sin, a pureness that becomes eroded each day we live our lives.'

With the evening sun setting at his back, he hurried along the narrow, twisting streets, his feet sore from pounding the cobbled passageways. He stubbed his toe and stumbled slightly, quietly cursing his new shoes and tight-fitting cassock before quickly offering a penitent prayer. He pulled a handkerchief from his pocket and patted the dust from his sweating brow. He tightened his grip on the leather-bound envelope given him by his master and walked on.

As he made his way toward the river, he wondered how long this would continue and, more importantly for him, the repercussions should he get caught. In recent times, an air of suspicion and mistrust hung heavy over the Vatican. He felt it every time he walked along the marble and parquet corridors. Usually, a quiet and serene place of tranquillity and thought-fulness where the only sounds were that of respectful whispers; it seemed that the atmosphere had changed. Now, small groups of clerics huddled in corners, glancing warily at those who happened by, their fraught discussions abruptly ending whenever he strayed too close. They would nod reverently, pass on their blessings, and disperse quietly with bowed heads; their eyes fixed on the open prayer books resting on their palms. He wondered if he'd been reading too much into it; a consequence of heightened paranoia borne of what he had done in the past and what he continued to do.

The blast of a horn sounded, ripping him from his thoughts. His head jerked up, and he saw a large, US Army troop transport barrelling toward him. Instinctively, he leaped back onto the path, scrambling for a safe foothold. The truck glided past only inches from his nose in a blur of green and white decal, billowing a plume of grit into his face.

He froze, his eyes clamped shut.

Sweat oozed all over his body, his claustrophobic garments sticking, making him feel muggy and breathless. He squinted through an open eye to the sound of an evaporating 'Sorry Padré'. He looked to his right and watched the truck bounce on without having slowed down. It rounded a corner and was gone. He placed a hand on his forehead and let out a controlled sigh, before blessing himself; the prayer he'd offered a few moments ago perhaps saving him this time. An old man passing touched his elbow gently and asked if he was alright. Hernandez nodded with a grateful smile and thanked him before looking both ways and scurrying across the road.

He arrived at a busy five-way intersection with the 'Ponte Principe Amedeo Savoia Aosta' off to his left. He looked across the Tiber toward the meeting point on the eastern side of the city. A nearby church bell tolled which was echoed moments later by several others a little further afield – he had some time to spare. He spied a café nearby where a waiter gathered chairs from outside, tidying up after the day's trading. Hernandez slacked his tongue inside his parched mouth and slipped across the street to quench his thirst before the café closed for the night.

He sat on a rickety, wooden chair and watched the moisture droplets slide slowly down the side of a glass of iced water. He touched one and licked his fingers. Taking a sip, he sat back and listened as the Eternal City began to rest, closing its eyes for the night.

A young couple, in their late teens perhaps, argued a few tables away, their voices breaking the quiet in waves. He glanced across without trying to make it look obvious, trying to catch the tenet of their conversation. From what he could deduce, the young man was begging absolution for an indiscretion, the details of which, Hernandez couldn't quite make out. But, it sounded like there might have been another girl involved. At one point the man threw his arms in the air and looked around as though seeking vindication from anybody nearby who agreed with his point of view. He spotted Hernandez looking at them and slipped the cleric a sheepish glance before turning back to the girl and continuing a quieter plea for clemency.

Hernandez smiled to himself.

After all, the Italians had endured over the past few years under Mussolini's dictatorship and the subsequent German occupation, the struggles of only weeks ago appeared now to have been quickly forgotten and replaced by nuisances of far less importance. It never ceased to amaze him how his flock seemed to continually seek earthly torment when contentment through the divine was so easily attained, but then he wouldn't have much of a job if it were any other way.

His thoughts drifted to his troubles, and his face grew dark.

He had been caught. A Cardinal Sin, and an abomination against the Church – worthy of immediate defrocking. Although he had always known that on some basic, moral level what he'd been doing was wrong, such were his urges, he couldn't help himself. Sins of the flesh it seemed were not exclusive to those outside the Church. He had even heard of others performing similar acts with apparent impunity and so believed he was immune to persecution. Thinking back, maybe what it had been a mere rumor, innuendo perhaps, designed to flush out and cleanse the Church of sinners.

He had been a fool.

But, he had been given a second chance, an alternative to a public defrocking and that was why he found himself delivering the envelope which lay on his lap. His hand brushed across the top of it.

It was smooth to the touch and identical to the others he had delivered, although he knew, containing different versions of the same documents. He ran his tongue across his top lip and stroked his chin. Although a devout and obedient cleric and the possessor of many virtues, Hernandez struggled to control one in particular: curiosity. It had gotten the better of him on each of the clandestine trips that'd taken him beyond the confines of Vatican City. It teased and tortured, tempting him to sneak a peek into each of the unsealed envelopes he carried. What he discovered hadn't shocked him. In fact, he had half expected it. An assortment of official documents, providing new identities to those who needed them most and, more importantly, was willing to pay.

But this envelope was different. It had been sealed, which was a first, and not just by the slick flick of a tongue, but secured in place by a thick, burgundy-colored, wax blob stamped with an embossed seal. Hernandez gaped at it now, struggling to recall where he had seen it before which only served to heighten his intrigue.

Then it hit him.

He smiled and stifled a half-laugh. He looked at it again, rubbing a finger along the seal's circumference. It wasn't the most famous seal in all of Christendom and, if he were to guess, he would say that few inside even the Vatican would recognize it, let alone anybody unconnected with the institution.

Realizing the envelope couldn't be resealed once opened, he sighed, tossing it on the table. He stole a glance at the couple as they got up to walk away, the woman snatching her hand away as the man tried desperately to take hold of it. Hernandez shook his head, still wondering what could have them so worked up.

He lifted his glass to take another sip, his eyes dropping to the envelope and noticed the seal had inadvertently popped open. He stared at it for a moment, his heart beating a little faster. Hernandez wouldn't have classified it a miracle, but there it was: God had found a way to satiate his urge.

Unable to restrain himself, he reached forward and, glancing around, gingerly pulled the flap back. He peeked in. He slipped his hand in and withdrew two documents, leaving what he knew to be a falsified passport untouched at the bottom.

The first was a letter, which he hurriedly scanned. It hadn't come as a surprise, as all the other envelopes he had couriered had included a similar introductory document, referencing the unknown holder to be of excellent character and standing. He turned his attention to the second document; four pages stapled in the top left-hand corner. His eyes sifted through an itinerary, a dossier, and what appeared to be a detailed set of instructions to be executed as soon as the recipient arrived at his final destination.

Hernandez drew a sharp breath, his eyes wide. He raised a hand slowly to his open mouth, and glanced back at the letter, rereading the addressee's name even though he knew it to be an alias. His gaze darted to the signature at the bottom of the page. He whispered it with a gasp, his head shaking slightly. He had expected it to be that of the person whose family seal he had recognized; a man he had come to know very well, the man who had caught him all those months ago and then placed him in this dreadful position. But, the signatory was infinitely more eminent.

His pulse quickened, and he immediately understood why this particular envelope had been so tightly sealed. He quickly dropped the documents back into the pouch and pressed down, praying it would reseal. He waited a few seconds before lifting his hand. It held for a moment, but then popped back open. Hernandez grimaced, and a wave of panic began to fizz in the pit of his stomach.

He checked his watch – 10.07 p.m.

He only had a few minutes. Not knowing what else to do, he wetted the underside of the wax with his sweating fingertips and reapplied the pressure, hoping it would hold this time. With his hand still held firmly on the wax blob, he stood and looked around. He crossed the road and waited at the meeting point by the riverbank.

As Rome's magnificent architecture cast elongating shadows, the usually rampant city sounds had almost completely faded. Hernandez surveyed the length of the river. It had become the city's life-blood as it weaved its way from source to mouth. He peered into the rippling water that brushed against the bricked bank below.

The sound of an approaching vehicle followed by the screeching of brakes wrenched him out of his reverie. He turned and saw a U.S. Army truck nestle gently against the curb. The passenger door opened, and a soldier wearing a Military Police uniform hopped out. He walked around the front of the truck.

'You have something for me?' He glanced at the envelope in Hernandez's hand.

Hernandez nodded and, praying the seal would hold, handed it to the young man.

The soldier took it without speaking, completed an about-turn, and walked briskly back to his side of the truck. Hernandez expected to see the door open and the soldier hop back in, but instead, he watched nervously as the MP walked back around the front of the truck again.

'Is everything alright?' Hernandez asked, placing his hands as calmly as possible behind his back. His eyes darted down to the envelope and the loose flap that the MP was flicking with his thumb. In one swift movement, the MP unbuttoned his holster, withdrawing his sidearm. Without hesitation, he aimed and fired a single shot into Father Hernandez's chest. The priest staggered back against the low wall that guarded the river, his hand over the bullet hole, blood oozing through his fingers. The soldier walked up and, placing a hand on Hernandez's head, gave him a gentle push.

Father Hernandez's soul had already departed before his lifeless body hit the water some twenty feet below.

*

A Young Swiss-Guardsman stood to attention before the Vatican Guard Commandant, having delivered the message a few moments ago. He could feel his skin prickle and turn pale, and his mouth run dry. He watched Michael Valent's face redden, and his nostrils flare, and he prayed to be dismissed before his superior took his anger out on him.

Valent drove a clenched fist onto the surface of his teak desk with a force that made the office windows resonate.

The Guardsman's heart skipped a beat, his breathing quickening. He glanced down, expecting to see a crumpled hand such was the force of the impact, but instead saw only a few drops of blood, the glint of a ring, and the imprint of the same symbol that had sealed Father Hernandez's fate no more than thirty minutes ago.

CHAPTER 1

AN OVERWHELMING SENSE OF HELPLESSNESS swept over him. He was vaguely aware of his wilting head, and his closing eyes as tiredness overpowered him, and concentration was lost. Somewhere beyond the subconscious, a feeling of dread slowly emerged. A rumble, quiet and distant at first, accompanied by tremor, increased in intensity. He jerked upright, his eyes springing wide open, his brain trying anxiously to recognize familiarity out of the foreign. He regripped the steering wheel and pulled the car away from the grass verge and back to the relative safety of the road, poor as it was.

Daniel pressed his fingertips against his eyes and shook himself awake. How long had it been? Eight, maybe nine hours without a break? He wasn't sure. He'd lost track over the last couple of hundred miles. He leaned forward and rubbed his cuff across the fogged windscreen to better glimpse what little of the road he could see, the car's headlights failing miserably to penetrate the darkness and driving rain beyond more than twenty yards. He took his foot off the accelerator and slowed to a manageable thirty mph.

He glanced at his watch: 9.21 p.m.

His journey had begun in darkness over eighteen hours ago, and with only one pit-stop (to change cars and empty his bladder), daylight had first blossomed, peaked, and then withered. Over that time, he'd driven past miles of forests and meadows speckled by polka-dots of a tired, repressed, and isolated civilization. His eyes were heavy, his back stiff, and his brain numb, as darkness had fallen again; but he was nearing the end.

Traffic was virtually non-existent, and he struggled to remember when he had last seen any vehicle traveling in the opposite direction. But then, he was sure that anybody possessing even a modicum of intelligence would be heading the same way he was, to seek their fortune and salvation in the 'Land of the Free' or the next best place, which was probably everywhere west of the Iron Curtain.

Wherever 'the next best thing' was, it certainly wasn't here.

As he gobbled up the next couple of miles, he began to feel a grumble in the steering that eventually forced him to pull over once the shaking and accompanying noise became too much to bear. He'd counted on these cheap Soviet-made cars to be hardy little beasts, but there was little he could do if a wheel had snagged an unseen bush or hit a small animal.

The car came to a stop.

He turned off the engine and zipped up his coat. Putting his hand on the door handle, he braced himself for the inevitable blast of icy air and stinging rain, before climbing out. In response to the dreadful weather, his shoulders rose, and neck contracted automatically, the hair at the back of his head bristling against his upright collar. He turned to shield himself from the driving rain, backing up to check on the front wheels. Both were still inflated, maybe not entirely, but they seemed to be pointing in the right direction, which was good enough. He swiped at a tuft of grass that had lodged itself on a wheel arch, tossing it aside. He glanced at the road ahead. Just empty asphalt for twenty yards, the same view he'd had since the rain had begun.

He trotted around the car and inspected the rear, but silently cursing when he came to the passenger side. The tire wasn't completely flat, but it wouldn't get him the rest of the way. He looked around. Other than the sheets of rain and the wind sieving through the evergreens that lined the road, there was nothing. From a detailed reconnaissance he had undertaken before entering the Soviet Union, the nearest garage was a couple of miles away and, judging by the dilapidated tire, he knew he wouldn't make it that far either, even if the place were open. He scowled at the road behind and banged the car's roof with a clenched fist. Although he couldn't see it, he knew he was within spitting distance of the outskirts of East Berlin.

He snatched the keys from the ignition and quickly opened the boot, dragging out the spare wheel, a jack, and a tire iron. He threw them onto the grass, hunkered down and set to work.

Under the exertions of the tire change, it didn't take long for a steady stream of rain to seep down his back, which only served to make him more miserable. The only bright side, if there was one, was that he was now wide awake and unlikely to doze off during the last leg of his return trip.

He threw the punctured wheel behind him and blew on his stiffening fingers. He was about to slip the spare onto the axle when he spied a set of headlights coming up behind him. He watched the car come closer and, then annoyingly, slow down and pull over to the side of the road. His muscles tensed when he noticed the solitary unlit police light on the roof. He turned back and continued working on the wheel.

He heard the car door open and slammed shut, followed by slow and deliberate footsteps.

'*Punktion?*' The language was German, the voice croaky, as though its owner had smoked forty a day since the end of the war.

Daniel nodded, as he began tightening the bolts, another trickle of water running down his back, joining that which had pooled around his waist, soaking his shirt, and dampening the top of his trousers, along with his spirit.

'Need any help?'

Again, Daniel shook his head. He knew that, in this place, when somebody in authority spoke, even if they had nothing to hide, civilians kept their answers brief or didn't speak at all. He, on the other hand, had plenty to hide. He lowered the jack and wondered why the hell anybody, a policeman included, would get out of the warmth and dryness of his car to offer assistance. The thought didn't sit well with him.

He gave the bolts one last twist, before straightening up and tossing the jack and iron in the boot.

The policeman took a couple of steps closer. 'You're not from Germany.' It was a statement, not a question.

'No.' Daniel said in Russian, turning to face him and putting his hand up slowly to shield his eyes from the blinding headlights behind the policeman. He couldn't see the officer's features but was acutely aware that the man could see every blade on his unshaven chin. That wasn't a problem. But it could become one. The policeman might make it one.

'Where are you coming from?' The officer said in passable Russian.

Daniel could have picked anywhere along the road he had driven but had a rehearsed cover story that would suit most eventualities. It was time to roll it out.

'Moscow.'

'That is a long way.' The officer didn't sound the least bit surprised, which immediately alerted Daniel to the possibility that the encounter might not be all that accidental and so might not end all that amicably.

It was practically unheard of for people to drive half-way across the Eastern Bloc unless they had a damn good reason. Daniel had two, only one of which was genuine and would remain untold until he returned to Washington. In countries governed by a totalitarian regime, the number of long-distance travelers was few and generally restricted to those working for the regime itself. Daniel didn't, and he guessed the officer knew that to be the case. Did that mean the policeman suspected him of something? Daniel's Russian was flawless with an accent the same as those living in Moscow's Arbat neighborhood, though it was unlikely an East German policeman could tell the difference between one Russian accent and another.

'What are you doing this far from home?'

'I'm attending a funeral tomorrow,' Daniel said, the lie slipping off his tongue with ease. He still couldn't see the officer's eyes, but Daniel could feel them scour his face and study his body language for a sign, no matter how small, of an untruth. Sometimes, there didn't have to be a giveaway. Sometimes, people were arrested on some trumped-up charge and hauled away to some isolated part of the country. He wasn't prepared to let that happen tonight.

In the heavy rain and, with the wind whipping up around them, the two men faced each other. Daniel decided he couldn't simply hope the officer would give him the benefit of the doubt, and send him on his way. He'd have to nudge the German into taking that path. He leaned down, scooped up the deflated wheel, and tossed it into the boot next to the jack. He was taking a step toward the driver's door when the policeman spoke.

'Show me your papers.' It wasn't a request.

With his back to the policeman, Daniel closed his eyes and let out an inaudible sigh. He reached into his pocket and fished out his internal passport. The policeman continued to stare at him as Daniel handed it over. It looked authentic, and for all intents and purposes, it was, forged by some US government counterfeiter holed up somewhere in Washington. He wouldn't need it in a few hours, but even still, Daniel didn't want it exposed to the harsh elements for any prolonged period. Who knew how many times he'd end up having to show it to the authorities he was attempting to evade.

A genuine internal passport was a document issued by the Soviet Ministry of Internal Affairs and, as such, was the only valid personal identification a civilian could hold and furnish when requested. It had a photo of its owner which, in Daniel's case, and to ensure accuracy, was an old military mugshot taken seven years ago when he was twenty-five. His hair was a little longer now, his features subtly aged but then, being awake for so long had the same effect. Inside the passport was a stamped, but fake, Propiska which identified Daniel as an inner-city Muscovite.

'Who died?'

'My uncle.'

'Where is the funeral?'

'I'm not sure. I have to get to my aunt's home in Fredricksfelde.'

'Where does she live?'

Daniel tilted his head to one side and stared at the officer, dumbly. Hadn't he just answered that one?

'What street?'

'Oh.' Daniel smiled in polite contrition. 'Zornstrasse.' He slid a thumb across his watch, rubbing away the moisture that had accumulated. He had a schedule to keep and this interruption, coupled with the weather, was delaying him. It wouldn't be the end of the world if he missed it, but his flight was due to depart in a few hours, and he would just as soon be on it before the 'shit hit the fan'. He smiled dolefully at the quaint American expression he had picked up over the years, one which was appropriate for what was sure to happen back in Moscow very soon if it hadn't already.

'You are in a hurry?'

'Wet. I want to get into some dry clothes.' Daniel wondered if the policeman was feeling the same, but judging by his stoic stance, and the raindrops exploding off his saturated uniform, it didn't seem so.

A feeling of uneasiness, its origin obscure, began to fester in Daniel as the wailing wind gathered pace, spewing minute pieces of debris around them like an orgy of mosquitoes. Daniel had had enough; the inquisition, however brief, had dragged on for too long. In obedience, he had allowed the officer to demonstrate his authority and examine the passport. Now, they were both soaked through and, Daniel felt, the policeman was likely to be looking for any reason to get back indoors, change clothes and remain in the station, cupping a mug of hot coffee. Daniel couldn't afford to be this man's excuse to do just that.

'If you're not going to look at it, can I have it back?' Daniel held out his hand.

The policeman turned his head slightly and fired Daniel a look as though nobody had ever questioned him like that before. He didn't speak. Instead, he side-stepped Daniel and walked around the car, glancing side-long into the back seat before continuing. He leaned down and, wiping a film of rain from the window, stared across the front seats.

Even if Daniel had been careless enough to leave anything incriminating lying about, the policeman didn't get the opportunity to see it, as his head suddenly ricocheted off the window with a sickening thud, causing the glass to crack. He collapsed onto the waterlogged grass, rolling onto his back.

Daniel stood over him, the tire-iron hanging loosely by his side. He couldn't hear the man moan what with the howling wind, only see his body slowly contort in agony. Blood leaked from the back of his head like a broken faucet, briefly staining the grass before being washed away by the torrent of rain sliding off the road. If only the man had checked Daniel's papers, accepted his story, and gone about his business, then Daniel wouldn't have lost his patience and been forced to end their discussion.

Daniel moved closer and straddled the man.

He had grown accustomed to looking into the eyes of men who could smell the rotting cloak of death as it approached. Every one of them was different and yet, oddly, the same. Sometimes, when he was alone, a half-drunk glass of Hennessy in his hand, he tried to imagine what it was they felt, and thought, and saw. Did they know, or even realize, their end was near? Could they see things that he and those still living, hadn't yet seen, things that only those drawing their last shallow breaths were able or perhaps, entitled to see? Did their minds struggle for a way to prolong, or even escape, the inevitable? Daniel would sometimes force himself to remember the faces and eyes of the men whose lives he had taken. They may be windows to the soul, yet still, they revealed nothing, no way of determining a soul's final destination.

The storm around them appeared to be at its zenith when Daniel struck the second and fatal blow; the man hadn't even tried to stop him. Daniel walked calmly to the back of his car, wiped the iron on the wet grass, tossed it in the trunk, and slammed the hood. He returned to the body and, grabbing the dead policeman under the arms, dragged him away from the road and into the woods at the bottom of the slight incline. He dumped the body in a hollow about twenty yards inside the tree-line and straightened up to look around. Within the forest, nature, at its paradoxical best, provided a peaceful resting place for the recently deceased, while all around it roared as though wailing the loss of another life. Daniel walked back to the road without looking back.

After switching off the police car's lights, he turned the steering wheel and rolled the vehicle off the road. It would be some time before anybody discovered either and, by then, he hoped to be halfway across the Atlantic.

He slipped back into his car and pulled out onto the still empty road. His mission had been to kill one, but he was always aware the number might rise. He rubbed his sleeve across the windscreen as it started to fog up again.

The rain turned to hail and pelted his car like a hundred drum rolls as the dim lights of suburban Berlin came into view. Only the checkpoint remained between him and another completed mission.

CHAPTER 2

It had been more than six months since Daniel closed the door to his apartment. Now, he stepped across the threshold, dropped his bags on the floor, and leaned back against the door. He closed his eyes and allowed his mind to surrender to his other senses as they sought out and finally succumbed to the familiar. As the distance between himself and Moscow had grown, so too had the easily forgotten sensations of safety and comfort began to return and, for the first time, he relaxed. A fresh fragrance lingered in the air, and the distant growls of outside traffic drifted in through the partially open windows. Alona had been and gone.

He collapsed onto the sofa, an exhausted mass of aching cells that screamed for rest. His eyes were sore and bloodshot with bags beneath as big and black as the two he had left in the hall. He'd taken a cab from the airport and, judging by the mildly annoyed scowl received from the driver, Daniel presumed he didn't smell too good either. But, so long as he couldn't smell himself, then a wash could wait.

Despite the climbing March temperatures, Daniel shivered; a symptom of the fatigue that had infused his body, he thought. He dragged his overcoat tighter around him, trying to trap inside what little heat his body generated to keep the 'home fires' burning. As he tried to clear his mind and allow himself to drift into an unconsciousness that shimmered tantalizingly close, memories of his assignment flitted about like a train tearing through a brightly-lit station. Forcing his mind to go blank, he thought only of blackness and was reminded of the nights he had spent hiding beneath the unpainted ceilings of numerous Moscow safe-houses, all of which, were in varying stages of

16

decay. And, while most of those nights had been incessantly boring some, had been terrifying.

With his knees curled up to his chest and his arms wrapped around his legs, he huddled there for several minutes before finally conceding. Sleep would not come, no matter how tired he was. A shower might help soothe his body and dull his mind. Then he could flop into bed, pull the covers across, and block out the late evening bustle of downtown Washington.

Shortly after a war that had seen him tiptoe between warring armies in the profligate cauldron that had been Stalingrad, he'd departed his English homeland, and made the American capital his new home. Sent on a scavenging hunt for one of the Soviets Union's top research scientists, Daniel liked to think that the minuscule part he had played had some impact in making that battle a pivotal point in the demise of Hitler's Third Reich. Such was the level of secrecy that surrounded the assignment, he knew few would ever fully appreciate what he had done, or even know how close the world had come to a reality far removed from that which it now enjoyed.

He struggled to his feet and sloped off to the bathroom, discarding layers of clothing along the way. He looked at himself in the mirror and ran a hand across a jaw covered in several days' worth of stubble. He ran the shower to allow the temperature to rise while he searched for a razor. It was a ritual. Shaving while enveloped within plumes of hot steam. But, a swipe of his hand under the freezing spray put paid to that, abandoning all thoughts of self-grooming.

No steam, no blade, no shave.

But, he did need to shower, the icy water forcing him to hokey-pokey in and out until he was happy that he'd washed away most of the sweat and grime. As he toweled himself dry, a wave of fatigue and light-headedness swept over him. He reached for the sink and steadied himself. He closed his eyes, seeing pinpricks of light dance about his imagination. But, that too passed after a few moments. It had been more than fifteen hours since he'd eaten in Berlin, having not touched the onboard meal offered by the airline. Eating while flying was a throwback to when the air-force had flown him to hostile environments, and it had stuck.

He ran his hand through his hair and walked to the bedroom, discarding the damp towel in an empty basket along the way. He took a light blue Oxford shirt from his closet, slipped it on, and brushed a light layer of dust from the shoulders. Boxers, some navy, gabardine slacks, and matching socks were followed by a pair of ordinary, black shoes; size nine. He threw on a light jacket, looked around the apartment, and left.

Washington DC was not a city that had evolved over centuries of habitation, but rather one that had been planned by Pierre L'Enfant at the end of the 18th century at the request of George Washington. It comprised a grid of numbered and alphabetized streets, orientated north to south and east to west respectively with avenues slashed across the cityscape named after each of the forty-eight states. It made for an interesting and unique commuting experience as rarely could one predict with any amount of certainty the most efficient route from one place to another.

However, Daniel was on foot, so it took him little more than ten minutes before he found himself admiring the freshly painted sign of his favorite restaurant: The Blue Duck Tavern, just off New Hampshire Avenue. Even in his sleep, he would know how to get here. His stomach had grumbled since he'd stepped onto the footpath, and now his mouth watered in sympathy. He pushed through the door and went inside.

Washington restaurants were generally busy after 6 p.m. on Monday evenings, but at this hour The Blue Duck was less than half full. He took a table at the back near the kitchen, his seat facing the front door. He eyed the other diners who seemed more interested in their conversations and the food in front of them than in the single, unshaven man who had just walked in.

Frank Verdi, the restaurant owner, walked over, beaming a cheery smile.

'Nice to see you, Mr. Miller. You've been away for too long. Sales going well?' He spoke with a slight Italian accent that Daniel knew to be fake. The man was born and bred of Irish immigrants, a nation with a relatively meager culinary expertise, hence his transformation to one with a more palatable appeal.

Daniel rustled up a smile. 'Not as good as they could be, but it keeps the wolf from the door.'

Verdi placed a menu on the table which looked so old that the Founding Fathers might have cast their eyes over it before declaring some self-evident truths.

'Don't know why you keep giving me this. I always eat the same thing when I come in.'

Frank smiled, his brilliant, white teeth peeping out from beneath a well-trimmed mustache. 'Variety is, as they say, the spice of life and besides, someday you might change your mind.' He leaned in closer and whispered. 'A couple of new girls started while you were away. I'll have the prettiest serve you today.' He continued to beam a smile as wide as the Potomac. He stepped back to allow Daniel to view the two waitresses who were working today. Knowing Daniel was unmarried, Verdi often tried to tempt him when he came into the restaurant by offering one of the women from his battery only to be declined each time.

Daniel sat back. The Blue Duck seemed to go through waitresses quicker than a politician discarded a promise. He held up a hand. 'Not today, I'm tired. The flight took it out of me. Eat and sleep for me.'

Frank stood upright. 'You do look a little pale. You need more iron. I'll make sure chef puts an extra side of vegetables on your plate.' He shook his head. 'I can tell you're not taking care of yourself when you're away.' All that was missing was a 'tut'.

'Can you get me some water, too?' Daniel said with a half-hearted smile. He moved the menu to one side.

'Coming right up.'

Frank walked away, a confident grin etched on his face. He scribbled on his pad and stuck the note on a hook by the kitchen's hatch.

Daniel sat back and rubbed his fingers gently across his eyes. They felt tender as though tiny pieces of grit had nestled beneath his lids. As he'd taken his seat, he'd tried to avoid the numerous mirrors that adorned the restaurant walls which no doubt would have reflected a stark reminder of the toll he placed on his body: unkempt hair, scraggly beard, bloodshot eyes. No woman would go near him unless he threw her a few dollars, and Frank didn't hire that type of girl. He sighed. He rested into the seat, a sense of peace passing over him, the sounds around him becoming muffled and fading. His mind drifted between the events of the past few days. In truth, he was lucky to be alive. In Moscow, he had narrowly avoided capture and so evaded certain death. And on the road to Berlin, he had been forced to kill to ensure his escape. Upon reflection, his life had replayed the same recurring theme for the last ten years; approaching the brink of mortality, yet somehow finding a way to step back and survive another day. But, in searching his soul, he knew he couldn't keep getting away with it. It didn't matter how good he was. His luck would eventually run out. And, what did he have to show for it? A legacy of butchered bodies. And not just those he'd been contracted to kill. There were others. 'Innocents' he called them. Those who'd had the misfortune to cross his path, their corpses now rotting in his wake. It wasn't something for which he wanted to be remembered. Unlike others in his profession, he didn't kill for sport. He found no pleasure in it. And, although well paid, he didn't do it for personal wealth. He had turned down many lucrative contracts even though the 'marks' later died at the hands of another. In a business where it didn't pay to make too many enemies, he was aware that sometimes he frustrated, perhaps even angered his potential employers.

But, he was good at what he did. That's why they kept coming back, with yet more assignments. They paid, and he killed, everybody was a winner. Well, almost everybody.

The aroma of a warm dinner and the sound of a plate being placed before him clawed him back to reality. His opening eyes settled on a beautiful but young waitress. She wore the neat restaurant uniform of a tight, black skirt, its hem rising just above the knee, and a plain lilac blouse, the top buttons undone just enough to reveal a gentle, soft cleavage when she leaned over her customers. Her hair was light brown, tied up with a contraption that looked like it could be lethal in the hands of the right person. She placed a napkin on his lap, slipped him a flirtatious smile, and trotted away without a word. Behind her, Frank glanced across wide-eyed and grinned.

Daniel slipped him a reticent smile.

Over the years, Daniel had had the privilege of dining at many of the finest restaurants the world had to offer, but it had been his mother, Catherine, who (in his opinion) had made the best meals. Her family aside, cooking had been her true love. She had often taken buses to the towns near their village to trawl through the cookery books in their libraries in search of new dishes on which to experiment. During that time, she had amassed quite a collection of international recipes. But, despite her expertise, it was a local, everyday meal that remained Daniel's favorite. In the years since her death, Daniel had tried the dish in many places, but none ever came close to replicating her Shepherd's Pie, except perhaps, The Blue Duck Tavern.

He lifted his fork and prepared for the dig, but paused. Although hungry, a profound hollowness suddenly consumed him that he felt no amount of food would satisfy. A swell of anguish rose inside which was followed by wave after wave of misery. As tears coated his eyes, he struggled to recall ever feeling this way before.

He knew he had to leave.

He beckoned Frank over and set his fork down.

'I need to go. Can you pack this up for me?' He dried his eyes with the napkin.

Frank glanced worriedly from Daniel to the plate and back. 'Is everything alright?'

Daniel forced a smile. 'Yes, of course. It seems tiredness has beaten me today. I'll eat once I get a little rest.' He placed enough money on the table to more than cover the bill and put on his coat.

Frank called the young waitress over and told her to wrap the dinner in foil.

She returned a couple of minutes later and handed a box to Daniel. He thanked her and made his way to the door. Frank walked beside him.

'You know, you don't look all that well. Have you ever considered a different line of work?'

Daniel stopped at the door, his hand hovering over the handle.

'Something with less travel, something more local, perhaps?' Frank added.

Daniel nodded. 'Lately, I've been thinking the same thing, Frank. Maybe it's time to look after me for a change.' He wore an empty smile as he left.

CHAPTER 3

Daniel was hauled from a deep sleep by a dull hammering noise, and a sudden surge of adrenaline took hold. He looked around, his eyes searching, his mind balancing on the blurred boundary that lay between nightmare and reality, the subconscious and the conscious. The apartment was dark, save for a narrow, misty column of yellow that shone through a break in the living-room curtains. He laid his head back on the sofa, stared at the ceiling, and felt his breathing slow. The hammering came again, this time louder and longer. He sat, then stood, groaning as his exhausted body unfurled itself. He ached as he shuffled to the apartment door.

Alona Peers fired him a scowl as she breezed past, a couple of shopping bags in each hand that threatened to pull the arms right out of her sockets.

'You look like crap.'

She plonked them onto the kitchen counter and started to unpack, flinging cupboard doors open as she went. 'Bought you some things, seeing as you're incapable of looking after yourself.'

'Not the first time I've heard that.' Daniel touched the side of his head, feeling like he had gone eighteen rounds with Jersey Joe Walcott. He grimaced every time she banged another door shut.

'Thanks,' he said, appearing around the corner, and turning on the lights.

She stopped for a second and looked at him. 'You've been hitting the bottle again. Only back, and already got a hangover.'

Daniel tried to ignore her, like an errant child being scolded by his mother. He lumbered across the living room, poured himself another brandy, and slid back onto the sofa He watched as she put away the last of the groceries.

'Are you going to offer me one?' she said. 'And all I do for you.'

'You don't drink.'

'That's right, and you know why I don't drink?' She paused. 'Because one of us has to remain sober.'

Daniel swallowed half the glass and cupped it between his hands. Hearing Alona's rich Polish accent when she spoke always made him tingle inside. He couldn't quite put his finger on why but put it down to her uniqueness. Over the years, he had heard many non-native English speaking people charm their way through a sentence or two, but apart from another woman he'd met while on assignment in Yugoslavia, nobody had come close to evoking the same response. It was an accent he had tried to imitate but failed to get just right. Unlike the other languages he spoke fluently and attached an accent, hers was soft, musical, and rhythmic; if an accent could ever be described as all those things.

She lifted the tin foil off his uneaten meal. 'You went to The Blue Duck? Why go if you weren't hungry?'

He shrugged. 'I was when I left here, but not when I arrived.'

His eyes followed her as she set about brewing herself a cup of tea. She'd been on holiday last year to some part of eastern Asia that Daniel couldn't recall, and while there, she had become obsessed with herbal teas. She had since tried to encourage him to experiment by leaving an assortment of boxes scattered about his apartment. He wasn't even sure if some were legal, given the dubious origin and illegible markings on some of the boxes. She turned around and faced him, a gentle smile lingering, reminding him of the first time they had met.

It had been the spring of 1945, a warm evening, close to dusk. Daniel was part of a small, nine-man, force-orientated reconnaissance unit that had been dropped inside the crumbling Reich near the Czechoslovakian border. The unit's mission – to extract a German Colonel who had been passing information to the British since the invasion of Russia. The Colonel, along with his command unit, had managed to stay ahead of the advancing Russians, whose artillery could be heard pounding the collapsing frontline near Pilsen less than fifty miles to the east. Orders from Berlin to stand and fight to the last, long since disregarded. According to intelligence from a local militia group, the Colonel had hunkered down in the small town of Flossenburg. So, Daniel and the rest of the team had taken shelter within the woods that covered one of several low hills to the southwest of the town.

With the war nearing its inevitable conclusion and, rather than do something that might cost them their lives, Pearson, the unit captain, decided to lay low until the following day. They had gone over a plan of attack while eating. They expected the Germans to take the road that led to the larger sister town of Floss about ten miles to the west once day broke. If they made it that far, they could choose any number of directions to ensure their escape. With the road out of Flossenburg passing below the unit's position, no more than fifty yards at its closest point, it would be the perfect place for their ambush. The group would divide in two, with one half positioning itself on another small, tree-covered hill directly north of their current location. The first shots were to be fired on Pearson's command with care taken not to hit their VIP.

However, just before dawn the next morning, as the unit prepared to separate, they spotted a massive movement of personnel marching out of the town; the numbers not in keeping with that reported by the militia. At first, it looked like the remnants of whatever battalion the Colonel had commanded which stumped Daniel – the battalion's last known location was much further to the east. In the end, it turned out to be nothing like that.

Those who formed the procession didn't march in the strictest sense, their movement sluggish and lumbering, like coal miners returning from a double shift at the colliery. The uniforms they wore weren't regular Wehrmacht issue either. They were a dirty, dusty, and ragged grey, reminiscent of the sort of outfits 19th-century workhouse orphans might wear. German Soldiers secured the perimeter of the tired-looking column; their attention focused more on the ragtag group rather than the surrounding hills.

'What do you make of that?' Daniel said. He shifted slightly in his prone position, dropping a pair of binoculars on the ground beside him.

Pearson shook his head. 'Prisoners.' He nodded beyond the line, as it wound its way beneath them. 'A couple of half-tracks and a Kubelwagen bringing up the rear.'

'Is our man down there?'

Pearson grabbed the binos and scanned the vehicles' occupants. 'He's there, alright. Doesn't look too fuckin' happy, though.'

'He'll be a whole lot happier once we get him out of here,' Daniel said.

'He'll have to wait a little while,' Pearson said, 'We can't spring our surprise with the Krauts so spread out. Besides, we don't know who those others are. Might be friendlies and the like, and I'm not killing unarmed civilians or POWs only to have it on my conscience for the rest of my life.' He motioned for the unit to move away from the tree-line.

'Let's track them for a few miles and see where they go. By the looks of it, they won't be able to get too far before they have to stop for a break. We'll re-establish the ambush at that point, if possible.'

The unit nodded as one, accepting the risks if they attempted an attack now. Best to wait and see how the morning developed, just like Pearson said.

More than fifteen minutes had elapsed by the time the weary column and last of the German motorized vehicles passed. Daniel had been lying on his back, thoughts of home filling the blank cloudless sky. Pearson was right; it wouldn't be long before they were all safely back in England. He caught himself smiling. The weather was never as good as this in Yorkshire, and rarely a day when he could scan the breadth of the sky from one horizon to the other without happening upon the blemish of a cloud. He twisted around and looked at the road, now empty, a lingering layer of dust the only evidence that anything had been down there.

'Wonder where they're going?' He asked nobody in particular.

'Another prison camp?' one of the soldiers said.

'Why bother? War's almost over. Why not just let them go?'

'You know what these fuckers are like, fanatical to their dying breath. They'll do their duty for the Fatherland. Doesn't matter how lost the cause is.' Pearson said.

The nine-man unit fell silent and waited for the order to move out.

They had come from a variety of backgrounds, scattered across the length of Britain. And, when the call came, they had joined up to 'defend their island', each now eagerly looking forward to the day they would be reunited with their families and return to a humdrum civilian life; those were distant memories that they desperately wanted to rekindle.

Suddenly, as they lay in silence, the sound of machinegun fire filled the morning air. The team ducked below the crest of the ridge, clutching their weapons, each man looking to the next, wondering where it had come from and, more importantly, if it had been directed toward them. It was, however, distant, and dulled by the rolling hills and rebirth of vegetation following a bitter winter.

Daniel looked to Pearson and for the first time, saw uncertainty in the Captain's eyes. He watched the older man go through whatever decision-making process the army had instilled in its officer corps.

'We wait until the firing stops then proceed as planned,' Pearson said, eventually.

Daniel shook his head. 'That's German firepower we're hearing. What if they've ambushed another unit, have it pinned down? We need to do something.'

'I'm not risking our lives on a 'what if',' Pearson said. He had the look of a man who had never had his commands disobeyed. 'We don't know who, or what they're firing at. Might just be target practice for all we know. A little less than a company of them walked past, right under our noses. Do you seriously want me to engage them and risk our lives?'

Pearson leaned in close to whisper.

'I heard the stories about what you did, but you're the interpreter on this mission, that's all.' He looked at Daniel, his stare unwavering.

Daniel, tight-lipped, hung his head.

For more than five minutes, the sound of continuous gunfire filled the air and, with each passing second, a blanket of concern covered the unit. At times, it seemed that even Pearson looked to be second-guessing himself.

'That isn't normal,' Daniel said quietly, out of earshot of the other men.

Pearson's jaw tightened, but Daniel could now see hesitation were before there had been assuredness. The rest of the men hadn't budged since the shooting had started every one looking to their captain for his order. Almost as quickly as it had begun, the volley of gunfire stopped, replaced by echoes that faded across the hills.

It was another ten minutes before Pearson checked his watch and signaled wordlessly to two men to reconnoiter the road the Germans had taken.

They returned less than fifteen minutes later, their faces drawn and pasty, betraying some horror they had discovered. Daniel looked at Pearson, who now seemed entirely unsure of what the next move should be.

'Are they gone?' Daniel asked the two men.

Neither of them spoke, each looking to the other as though hoping he'd answer. Daniel looked to Pearson again, who nodded almost imperceptibly.

Silently, the unit left their position and retraced the footsteps of the two scouts. A gentle, but chilling breeze carried through the trees, as though the lost and despairing souls of the recently departed wandered about this corner of Czechoslovakia.

It didn't take them long before they came to the edge of a clearing that swept away below them. Shaded by the brush, they crouched and stared in dismay at the carnage before them. Two large pits, each the size of a tennis court, had been dug next to the road, and inside each what remained of the prisoners who had traipsed past them half an hour ago. A soldier to Daniel's left leaned away and puked his undigested breakfast onto the grass.

Pearson signaled to the unit's lone sniper, who began a scan of the surrounding hills through his scope. He shook his head after a couple of minutes. Pearson stood and, one by one, the unit emerged from the undergrowth, stepping like ghosts into the clearing. They approached the pits cautiously, each man glancing from left to right for the enemy, their gaze lingering longer during each sweep on the dead bodies before them. Their footsteps crunched a thick carpet of warm shell casings. They stopped a few feet from the edge of one of the pits and peered in. Hundreds of men and women, their emaciated bodies partly covered by shabby clothing, had been ripped apart by bullets, their limbs tossed about in a grotesque pose.

Another of the soldiers turned away in disgust.

Daniel and one of the men walked toward the second pit; the scene there identical. They stared at the dead and at the flies that had wasted no time settling in. Daniel had seen this before. On the banks of the Volga. The Germans had murdered Russian civilians in front of the Red Army that was moving into position on the other side of the river as it prepared for a crossing. It had both sickened and infuriated him; those feelings now returned.

It didn't make any sense.

Why go to the trouble of killing these people? Were the Germans trying to hide something? The answer had to be no, as they would have, at the very least, covered their crime to prevent anybody who happened by from discovering it.

The other soldier broke out a pack of cigarettes and offered one. Daniel barely noticed as he surveyed the horror before him. He swiped absently at a passing fly as something, in the corner of his eye, caught his attention. He turned and stared into the pit but saw only stillness and death. He was about to turn when he saw a movement from under the bed of corpses. A shiver crackled along his spine.

He took a step nearer, his brain straining to make sense of what his eyes were seeing.

A bony hand stretched up from beneath the dead, clawing at a torso, pushing at a lifeless arm, trying to resist the suffocating pull of the other corpses. It reached out, seeking salvation, clinging to life.

Daniel flicked his hand to the soldier nearest him. 'Somebody's alive in there.'

He scampered to the edge of the pit, got down on his belly, and leaned in. He couldn't reach. He looked desperately at the soldier. 'For fuck's sake. Help me.'

The soldier threw away his cigarette, hurried across, and dropped to his knees beside Daniel. They looked across the sea of bodies; it's surface a couple of feet below. Even stretching, the grasping hand was still more than eight feet away as a muffled plea in a language neither of them understood, tried to cry out.

Daniel sat on the edge of the pit and was about to step in when the soldier grabbed his arm.

'You might sink into that mess then we'll have to get you out, too. Here.' He took his back-pack off and rummaged through it, pulling out his blanket.

Daniel nodded, acknowledging what he had in mind. He removed his blanket also and, leaning in, draped it across several bodies. He crawled into the pit carefully and, sliding along the sheet, put the second ahead of the first. The bodies beneath were still warm with patches of blood oozing from gaping wounds. But, more than that, it was the accompanying stink that threatened to overpower him. Daniel felt a wave of nausea wash over him, forcing him to breathe through his mouth so he wouldn't vomit. He slithered further into the pit, gasping for mouthfuls of fresh air where he could, and to within touching distance of the flailing hand. He stretched across, flapped aimlessly before eventually grabbing hold of the hand. He pulled, gently at first, then as hard as he could, but he still couldn't dislodge the person beneath.

After more than a minute of trying and failing, he rolled onto his back, breathless, and called out to the rest of the unit. Before long, more blankets were flung near him, and two more soldiers joined him on top of the dead. Between them, they managed to circle the person they were trying to free and, working together by pulling and pushing dead limbs out of the way, burrowed a small trench, large enough so they could see the head and torso of the living. It was difficult to tell at first, but it looked like a young woman. She had maybe a month's growth on top of what had once been a shaved head. Where the rags she wore had rotted away from her body, they could see only pale, translucent skin covered with bruises and infected sores, beneath which, streaked her veins.

Daniel looked into the woman's eyes and saw a range of emotions that he would later find both difficult and heart-breaking to describe.

The end of a rope landed next to them, which they wrapped around the partially embedded woman's waist. The two soldiers who had joined Daniel crept back and climbed out of the pit. With Daniel tugging on the woman's hands, the other four men pulled on the rope. The woman let out a soft cry of pain, her face contorted in a new agony, as the line dug into her bones. Bit by bit, she was inched out until she lay on one of the blankets next to Daniel, both of them panting and sweating from their exertions.

It took several more minutes of stop-start pushing and dragging before she lay on the ground near the edge of the pit. The unit medic examined her, applying antiseptic ointment where needed and bandaging up any open sores where he could. He dressed the single wound just beneath her right collar bone, the bullet having passed straight through. She had been lucky if one could call her that. The bullet hadn't punctured any internal organs or sliced an artery. He gave her only a few small mouthfuls of rations and allowed her to drink a few sips from a canteen. He wasn't about to let her die from over-feeding if she didn't succumb to sepsis first.

Daniel stayed by her side, holding her hand while the rest of the unit walked between the two pits, calling out for other survivors.

They didn't hear any replies.

Even if there were others alive, they might be so deeply buried or perhaps so weak they would never be heard. Pearson walked over to Daniel, a pensive expression on his face.

'The mission is over. We'll make for the extraction point.'

'What about the Colonel?'

Pearson nodded towards the other pit. 'He's in there. They must've found out what he'd been doing.' He looked at the woman. 'Will she be OK to travel that far?'

Daniel nodded. 'I'll carry her if she can't walk herself.'

'At least some good will come of this.' He turned away and called the rest of the unit to him, leaving Daniel and the woman alone.

'You're doing it again.'

'Am I?' Daniel's response was automatic. He looked at Alona, a steaming cup of some god-awful concoction in her hand. She took the chair opposite, a small coffee table between them.

'What time is it?'

'After ten.' She lifted the cup and inhaled, the corners of her mouth creasing into another smile. More than anything else, it was that which Daniel liked most about her. Despite the atrocities she had experienced and suffered throughout her short life, she had still managed to maintain an inner harmony which manifested itself as one of the most dazzling smiles he had ever seen.

'You gonna tease it or drink it?'

'Savoring it.' Her eyes opened, and she looked across, her smile gone, an odd look on her face. 'I heard about the policeman.'

He detected a tone of acceptance but knew she understood the necessity of what he had done. For almost eight years, his job had taken him all over the world. During that time, he had encountered many people and had had to kill some who got in his way. However immoral, those lethal actions had been unavoidable as they allowed him to dispatch a higher moral justice, something Daniel ultimately viewed as a balancing act – the taking of 'an innocent' life while serving a greater good. At first, it troubled him before understanding and acknowledging it to be a necessary evil. Unlike others in his profession, he never sought forgiveness in a confessional or, for that matter, solace at the bottom of a bottle. Instead, he would purge his sins by quiet meditation, spending days, sometimes weeks hibernating from the world, only to emerge a little more tainted and slightly less pure. It was through Alona however that the purification process was sped up. Over the years, she had become both his confidante and confessor.

He turned away, the distant sound of random, late-evening traffic the only disturbance. He thought about what had happened on the road to Berlin and could feel the adrenaline race through his body, his heart speeding, his palms growing clammy. He finished off the brandy and sat, swirling the empty glass in his hand.

'Do you want to talk about it?'

He shook his head, not looking at her even though he could feel her eyes on him.

Her tea had gone cold by the time he next spoke.

'I'm not getting any younger,' he said.

'None of us are.'

'I'd like to grow old.'

'We'd all like that.'

'Peacefully.'

She paused a beat before she spoke, but they were both aware of it. 'Without your demons?'

'If that were possible.'

The room fell silent once more until Alona spoke again.

'Have you had enough?'

It was a question that had plagued him for some time, perhaps a year before he had embarked on the Moscow assignment. He had attempted to push it to the back of his mind only to have it resurface without warning, forcing him to reflect on what had become of his life. It seemed an age, a different time, a different life since he had played with his friends in the undulating Yorkshire Dales. So much had happened since then. The world had changed; his life had changed. And, even after profound reflection, he felt he was still no closer to a satisfactory answer. It wasn't that he feared death, although his mortality had crossed his mind. It wasn't the excitement of a fresh kill, although it sometimes brought some satisfaction. He wasn't a psychopath, tearing around the globe, destroying all in his path without giving it a second thought. He dreamed of a life without killing, without blood on his hands. Of course, he knew he couldn't eradicate the sins already committed but did he have to continue to ratchet up the body count? He had amassed enough personal wealth to live a comfortable life several times over without ever having to do another day's work. So why not just give it all up.

Start over.

Alona went across and fixed him another drink, replacing the empty glass in his hand with a full one.

'You trying to get me drunk?'

'So I can take advantage of you?' There was that smile again. Daniel looked into the glass and set it on the table.

'Do you think I should stop?'

'That's not for me to say.' It was a hurried response, and Daniel knew she had thought about it.

He locked his fingers together and raised them behind his head. His body was straight, legs crossed at the ankles, his eyes staring at the ceiling, unfocused.

'We've had this conversation before,' Alona said.

'Many times.' He paused. 'It feels different now.'

'What makes it different?'

Daniel shrugged. 'Time, age, tiredness, the need to do something more with my life. Any, or all of those, I guess. It's not like I ever wanted to do what I do. I don't enjoy it.'

'So, why do you do it?'

His response was immediate. 'It seemed the natural path to take after the war. I never put much thought into what else I could do.'

'Plenty of soldiers returned to civilian life after the war,' Alona said. 'Don't you think yours was a more unnatural path to take?'

He half-smiled at the eloquence of her turn of phrase. 'When you put it like that.' He shrugged.

'Besides, don't you believe you're doing some good? Providing a service that few can offer?'

'I don't know if I still believe in it, anymore.' He sipped his drink. 'Nature abhors a vacuum. I kill one bad guy, and another takes his place.

The status quo is maintained, balance restored, and the tug-of-war between good and evil continues with more bad guys to kill.'

'And if you quit?'

'Then somebody takes my place, and somebody fills the void.'

'So, it doesn't matter if you stop, the killing will continue.'

He nodded. 'But, it wouldn't be at my hands.'

'And your conscience would be clear.'

'I don't think it can ever be clear.'

They stayed quiet for a short time, the only break in silence that of a sleepy Washington settling for the night. Alona looked at him.

'Whoever replaces you might not be as careful.'

Daniel looked up, clearly not understanding.

'The next guy might kill lots of innocents and think nothing of it. Isn't that what this is all about? Regret for having killed others along the way?'

Daniel turned away. He did feel overwhelming remorse for those he'd killed in the execution of his duty, accepting the deaths as necessary to ensure he kept doing what he did. But, it was the loss of his internal moral compass that preyed on his mind most, and the worry that the equilibrium between the good he bestowed in killing might eventually be outweighed by the bad. If the scales became so tipped, he knew he'd have to stop, but equally, he feared he might not be able to recognize when the time came.

CHAPTER 4

ALONA'S MEANDERING THOUGHTS WERE DISTURBED by the sudden shrill of the doorbell. She stopped stirring the stew and placed the wooden spoon next to the stove. She checked the clock and smiled. The hours had dragged along, but now, her little man was home. She wiped her hands on her apron; a Christmas present from her neighbor, Peggy Walsh. She skipped to the front door and opened it, bearing a beaming smile that was mirrored by Anthony on the other side. She leaned down, and he leaped into her outstretched arms, the two embracing as though they hadn't seen each other in weeks.

'Come in for a tea.' Alona beckoned Peggy with a nod.

'Nah, you're grand,' Peggy said. 'I can smell your dinner, so won't interrupt.' She turned away and headed down the hallway.

'Come by later?' Alona said.

'Sure, after Jack Benny,' Peggy said, without turning around. She gave a small wave and disappeared into the apartment next door.

Alona dropped Anthony gently to the floor and took his school satchel off his back.

'How was your day?'

'Great,' he said, scampering off to the living room and leaving Alona standing by the door.

It was the same ritual every day, and one she would never change. Rarely did her son come home from school without a smile and a seemingly boundless amount of youthful energy, before tearing into the living room to do all the fun things a six-year-old boy did to pass the time. A relaxed and cozy sensation grew inside, and her smile broadened. She didn't know for sure if his smile was meant for her, but it didn't matter. He was her little prince, her little miracle.

Anthony had been born a month prematurely on November 1946, just a couple of days before Hanukah. It had been a difficult if not potentially fatal birth with him popping into the 'new world' with what the midwife had said was a nuchal cord. To everybody else, that meant the umbilical cord had become wrapped around his neck. Feelings of dread usually filled an expectant mother if ever she heard such a thing, but Alona had later discovered that it was quite a common occurrence and rarely, if ever, did it result in the death of a newborn. Still, she knew that mothers would be forever fretful and protective of their offspring and no amount of comforting persuasion to the contrary could ever allay their fears.

She went back into the kitchen and stirred the stew again.

'Dinner will be ready soon,' she called.

There was no response. Alona wouldn't get another word out of her son until they were seated at the table. She sat and resumed reading Steinbeck's *East of Eden* which had been a Christmas present, this time from her son, although she knew that Daniel had bought it for him to give to her. After all, how could a six-year-old afford to buy any Christmas gifts?

But, she found it difficult to concentrate on the narrative today.

She had been reacquainted when Daniel had found her recuperating in a convalescent hospital in Cheltenham in September 1945. The fact that he'd been able to locate her at all said a lot about the man and his resourcefulness.

The nature of modern warfare hadn't discriminated between civilian and military populations. Millions had died or were wounded, and millions more displaced or become homeless. Those remaining had to rebuild their lives and their homes while the victorious nations drew new borders and rebuilt their countries under the Marshal Plan. Life on the continent was fluid, and the various governments found it incredibly demanding if not impossible, to maintain any semblance of control.

But, found her he had, even though she'd moved from the field hospital in Leonberg where he'd left her (situated to the west of Stuttgart), to the 15th General Hospital in Brussels, before eventually completing her medical merry-go-round in England. By then, she'd been well enough to leave the hospital for short periods at a time. He'd stopped by every day for a fortnight and took her into town where they strolled through flora-rich parks and browsed an assortment of shops and their wares. Conversation was awkward and disjointed at first and not because of any language barrier. She had been amazed at how good his Polish had become, considering he hadn't a word of it when he'd rescued her from the pit. It was undoubtedly better than her English which was limited to 'yes' and 'no', without ever having any real understanding of the questions she'd been answering.

During those formative weeks, she'd discovered they'd come from diverse backgrounds, cultures, and beliefs. She likened those initial few days to that of a newly formed couple unsteadily finding their collective feet. At the time, she hadn't understood why he kept coming back day after day, and although she grew fond of him and enjoyed his company, she felt no measure of sexual attraction toward him. It was only years after that she realized her rescue had been one of a few fragments of decency he'd witnessed or, for that matter, achieved, whether by him or others, during the war. And so, she believed that perhaps, he needed to maintain a connection or face the prospect of becoming both spiritually and emotionally lost. In that respect, she liked to think that she rescued him from a descent into hopelessness from which, given his current frame of mind, he may never have recovered. Maybe, their time together had enabled a mutual rehabilitation that had saved them both.

As a seventeen-year-old, in the spring of 1946, she had followed Daniel to Washington. Although daunted by the prospect of beginning a new life in such a vast, multicultural land that she knew nothing about, she had decided to embrace the many aspects of American life. This was in stark contrast to many other European refugees who seemed to have taken isolationism in the 'land of the free' to a new level. As a young Jewish woman with limited but improving English, she knew that others of her faith frowned upon what they deemed the erosion of her religious identity by openly accepting other religious feasts and festivals – she even bought and decorated a small Christmas tree each year.

However, her new life had become even more complicated after she'd become pregnant a few weeks after stepping onto the tarmac at Baltimore Airport. It had followed a weekend fling with a handsome Hispanic man who had subsequently headed west to seek his fortune. Consequently, he never knew that Alona had become pregnant. And so, as a prospective single mother, facing the possibility of vilification and ostracism from not only the Jewish community but others, she'd felt compelled to hide her pregnancy as best she could. Luckily, she hadn't started to show until her third trimester by which time the weather had begun to turn for the worst, allowing her to conceal better her growing bump.

She had moved to a spacious apartment on Randolph Street in Bloomingdale and had been lucky to have befriended a compassionate neighbor in Ms. Walsh. Peggy was a sixty-something retiree, first-generation American, her parents having crossed the pond from Ireland in the latter part of the nineteenth century. As it turned out, Peggy was an atypical senior citizen. She possessed a zest for life with grand notions of female liberation that the younger generation had only begun to adopt. Although generally reserved, Alona had (on several occasions) witnessed Peggy scythe into those who, she believed, had overstepped the mark.

Over the years, she had become something of a mother-figure to Alona, supporting her every step of the way despite both the age and religious divide. She and Mr. Walsh hadn't borne children and never spoke of it. There had been times when Alona had caught Peggy looking upon Anthony with profound sadness. Even though she was curious, it hadn't been a topic Alona wished to discuss – some things were better left unsaid.

She put the book down.

She was worried about Daniel. She was always worried about him, especially when he went away. In the years they'd worked together she'd come to understand him probably better than he did himself. His likes and dislikes, moods, mannerisms, what drove him. She'd come to accept as normal, his behavior upon returning from an assignment as a period of reflection that at times seemed to smother him. However, his brooding rarely lasted more than a day, two at a stretch. It was his way of dealing with the pressure and demands that came with a job that few in the world would ever really comprehend or fully appreciate. He rarely spoke of what happened while away, choosing instead to internalize his thoughts and emotions.

But, this time, it had been almost two weeks, and he still hadn't surfaced.

From what she'd been able to determine, he only left his apartment to walk as far as Penelope's, a small coffee shop that was less than a hundred yards from his door, to have a 'half 'n half', as he liked to call a cappuccino.

Thankfully, he hadn't taken to the bottle, although she knew he downed the occasional brandy whenever the mood took him. Most of the conversations they'd had over the past fortnight revolved around the same subject: him wanting to do something else.

She wiped a tear from her cheek that seemed to have appeared from nowhere. She went to the stove and gave the stew another stir before setting the table for two.

As promised, Peggy came by once Jack Benny had run his course. By then, Anthony was in bed, whether he was asleep was another matter. Alona had already placed two small glasses on the living room table with an open bottle of port between them.

The two women sat side by side on the sofa, looking at the TV, but only Peggy was concentrating on the program. She glanced at Alona a few times before setting her glass aside.

'I've been here for nearly twenty minutes, and you haven't said a single word. Is everything all right dear?' She placed a hand on Alona's knee.

Her young friend turned to face her but didn't reply.

'Is everything alright with Anthony? He's getting on OK at school, isn't he?' She leaned in and said quietly. 'Is there something the matter with you? You're not sick, are you?'

Alona shook her head and smiled, but Peggy could see the torment in her friend's face.

'You don't have to tell me anything. If you're not ready, then that's fine.' She turned back to the TV.

'It's a friend of mine,' Alona said a few moments later. 'I'm worried about him.'

Peggy remained silent.

'He's been despondent for the past while and I don't know how to help him.'

'Is he middle-aged? Maybe it's a mid-life crisis? I've heard people sometimes get that when they reach a certain age.'

Alona half-laughed and wiped a few tears from her face. 'He isn't that old.'

'Maybe an early-life crisis then?' Peggy smiled.

'Maybe.'

'Do you know what's brought it on?'

'Work. He travels out of town a lot.'

Peggy sat back and thought. 'Is it that English gentleman I see stop by from time to time?'

Alona nodded again.

'He's a fine-looking man. Would make a great catch for the right lady.'

'Oh, it isn't like that between us, we're just close friends.' She paused. 'I owe him my life.' She whispered it so quietly that Peggy could hardly make out what she'd said.

'And you want to help him in return?'

Alona nodded. 'But I don't know how.' She looked miserable.

Peggy refilled both their glasses and snuggled back into the couch. She knew that difficulties like these were exactly that – difficult to resolve. Any number of reasons could cause a person to fall into depression if that was indeed from what Alona's friend suffered. Daniel. That was it. The name came to her at last. From what she could remember, he would have been prime fighting age ten years ago, and so she too began to worry. From time to time, her husband spoke of some of the men from the bowling club, men who crossed the county line to visit the Veterans Administration center in Alexandria. Some went further afield to Perry Point up near Baltimore although he didn't know why, 'maybe the meals were better up there' he'd mused, although she didn't think that was the case at all. He'd passed on to her in confidence snippets of what they'd told him over a couple of beers. They'd harbored feelings of guilt, depression, anxiety, even experienced 'flashbacks' after unexpected loud noises. He'd heard tales of others who were, even more, worse off, permanently hospitalized with little chance of recovery; nobody spoke about those men.

'Maybe he could go to one of the VA Centers?' Peggy said, taking a leap of faith.

Alona looked sidelong at her. 'Oh, it's nothing like that.'

Peggy suddenly felt very silly for having mentioned it.

'He's trying to figure out what to do with the rest of his life, that's all.'

'Plenty of jobs out there for a man willing to work.' Peggy set herself firmly against the sofa, a feeling of irritation suddenly coming over her.

'You're right, of course, but it has to be the right thing for him. I have one idea, though. I'm just not sure he'll like it. I'll make a phone call in the morning.'

Peggy looked sidelong in return. 'He's a lucky man to have such a friend.'

'I'm the lucky one,' Alona said, her voice barely more than a whisper.

CHAPTER 5

Away from the glare of a city's lights, a clear, moonless sky has much to behold. But the wonders aside, it also provides some measure of illumination for a weary traveler as he makes his way home. Jed Harris drove his truck across the desert towards a single-story shack that his father William had built after the turn of the century when he'd worked for the railroad company that had been constructing a line that swept across the Nevada desert and into Western California. It was a trip Jed made most nights and almost always shrouded in a cloud of drunkenness. Truth be told, he could probably have driven home blindfolded and still arrived safely.

Tonight, as he sat behind the wheel, his mind wandered, his eyes drifting across the flat terrain. He sometimes thought about how his life had taken a turn for the worse and what he could have done differently to prevent what had happened to him nearly twenty years ago. A fall from height when constructing the Hoover Dam prematurely ending his career and permanently placing him on the paltry disability pension that his former employers reluctantly forked out.

A flash of light away to his left pulled him back into a groggy reality. He looked across the sand, slowing the truck to a crawl. It was followed a moment later by a second flash.

He hit the brakes hard.

He rubbed his eyes and squinted into the darkness, but could see little beyond a few feet. He considered driving on, putting what he thought he had seen down to a drunken mirage. But instead, he cut the engine and rolled down the window. The cold, spring, desert air washed across his face, tearing up his eyes. He wiped a dirty sleeve across his face, stared into the blackness, sat still, and listened.

He heard nothing.

Then, a few moments later, carried on the wind, the sound of an engine coughing to life. Jed had lived in the Nevada wilderness all his life and knew that nobody strayed off the roadways unless they had a damn good reason, and those reasons weren't usually anything they wanted anybody else to know about. A trickle of panic began to flow through his body. He slowly reached forward and turned off his lights, hoping, as unlikely as it seemed that whoever was out there hadn't noticed his approach. Tight-lipped, he caught his breath, trying to make out if the other vehicle was approaching or departing. He let out a deliberate sigh when the stillness he was used to, returned. He sat quietly for a couple of minutes before starting up his truck to resume his drive home.

He hadn't traveled more than twenty yards before he swerved off the track and across the sand to where he thought he had seen the flashes. He leaned forward, peering through the dust-covered windscreen, his eyes scanning the illuminated beige sand and brown scrub brush that mottled the landscape. He tipped the brakes, slowing the truck to a crawl. He craned his neck forward and strained his eyes. A few yards ahead lay a mound of flesh and blood. He came to an abrupt stop, immediately recognizing what he had stumbled upon.

He rammed the gears into reverse and, hitting the accelerator, turned the truck to face the way he had come. He ground the engine through the gears; fear had grabbed hold, a sticky sweat coated his body, his drunkenness temporarily dissipated.

*

Through a haze of exhaled smoke, Gabe Collins looked across the wasteland at the myriad twinkling lights. Whenever time allowed, he liked to get away from the city with its seemingly uncontrollable evolution and disappear into the wilderness. It wasn't the rapidly expanding urban environment he disliked, but rather the swelling ranks of sinners who had, over the past forty years, infested the small city. Although kept busy by their immoral transgressions, he would have preferred a far more tranquil existence.

Unfortunately, this wasn't one of those times.

'Whatcha' think?' Kilchii shone a torch over the body lying in a crumpled heap on the sand. He scribbled onto a notepad.

With his back to the deputy, Collins ignored the question. He sucked on a cigar, burning it to the butt before tossing it away, the tip flaring as it traveled through the air before dying on the sand.

'Gamblin' debts?' Kilchii said. 'Robbery gone bad? Take your pick, I guess.'

Kilchii hunkered down and placed the torch and pad on the ground. 'This fella here pissed his pants, shit himself too. Smells like a damn sewer.' He turned his head away in disgust. He reached for the pile of clothes that had been neatly folded and stacked beside the body and began a search through the pockets. He stood a moment later, his hands full of treasures. He let out a soft whistle as he leafed through a wad of $50 bills.

'Hey, Gabriel. Get a load of this.'

Collins turned and let out a tired sigh. He hated it when people used his full name, preferring instead, the abbreviated version. He was sure the young officer did it just to piss him off.

Kilchii shone the torch on another of his finds, an eight-year-old passport.

'Name's… Jesus, I can't pronounce this… Andreas Lenz. Somethin' like that anyhow. Sounds foreign.' He stared at the photo and looked back at the body. 'Might be him. Can't tell with half his face missin'.'

The product of a one-night liaison between a woman, who subsequently became Gabe's ex-wife, and some out-of-towner she had screwed, Kilchii was so young that Gabe felt sure he had stopped feeding on his mother's tit only a few years ago. Zits the size of strawberries, polka-dotted a face that not even his mother loved. An ill-fitting uniform draped loosely around his scrawny body, a standard-issue pistol hung limply by his side, Roy Rogers' style. In any other law enforcement jurisdiction, he would have been a laughing stock, but it was still the Wild West out here, so he looked like he fit right in.

'It's German,' Gabe said. 'Maybe Austrian.' He walked toward his deputy and held out his hand. Kilchii offered him the passport; Gabe shook his head and pointed at the torch.

He moved closer to the body, shining the light on the surrounding ground.

'Plenty of activity here. You?' His tone was semi-accusatorial.

His deputy's below-average intelligence notwithstanding, he had trained the kid as best he could; approach from one side only, careful not to contaminate the crime scene, don't touch anything before photos were taken. They weren't strict rules, but they helped him do the job. He moved the beam a few feet away from what remained of the victim's head.

'Shot out here anyway.' Gabe pointed. 'See, blood spatter? Brain tissue, too. A wonder it hasn't been eaten by the critters.'

A few more paces took the sheriff past the victim's feet.

'We're a ways from the city, and old Jed said he heard an engine. If we haven't already run 'em over, you should check for tire threads.' He nodded beyond the patrol car. 'Go get another torch… try not to stand on anything that looks like it might be evidence.'

He watched his stepson dither momentarily before heading off in search of illumination which, Gabe knew, would never be of the conscious enlightenment variety.

He had been pushed into hiring the boy in return for reduced alimony payments, an arrangement that worked well for the most part so long as the kid was hidden away from the public. Performing mainly desk duties, he was usually removed from what Gabe considered 'real police work'. Unfortunately, the city's inhabitants had a voracious criminal appetite, and they had exceeded their personal best tonight. Gabe's co-workers were scattered the length and breadth of the jurisdiction, hot on the trail of a litany of alleged lawbreakers while, back at the station, a shivering officer with a temperature of 103° did his best to triage the influx of call-outs. As a result, Gabe had drawn the short straw and found himself working the graveyard shift with his dim-witted stepson.

Gabe examined the body again. Two gunshot wounds to the head which he thought was overkill as the first shot had probably been enough to do the job. The caliber of bullet was unknown and, given the damage, he'd have to wait until it was light before searching the area for it.

Sand scuffs aside, the victim's clothes appeared expensive: a dark-brown, single-breasted suit, vest, boxers, black socks, and matching black shoes. He slipped a finger under the jacket to reveal a waistcoat, shirt, and trousers beneath. Other than some desert sand that had blown over it, there were no other marks. If he were a betting man, Gabe would have guessed it had been worn for the first time tonight. He checked the inside and read the label, 'Henry Poole'. That didn't mean anything to him, it might as well have been the name of any number of cheap high street stores, but he made a note to check it out, nonetheless.

Without a face, it was, as Kilchii had said, nearly impossible to determine if the man was the same as the one in the passport. The hair was a couple of shades of brown lighter than the suit and fashionably cropped interspersed with a handful of grey streaks. Gabe lifted a hand, gently bending the arm at the elbow. Rigor hadn't set in. That made it a recent killing, all in line with what Jed had told him less than an hour before. He examined the hand, which was unmarked. The skin was smooth, and the fingernails recently trimmed; the victim took care of himself. Gabe leaned across the body to check the other hand. Except for a gold wedding band wrapped around a finger, the hand was a mirror image of the first.

Gabe stood and, staring at the body, pursed his lips. No wallet, no driving license, no signs of struggle, only a wad of cash, and a passport. Maybe the guy was a tourist passing through who had bumped into the wrong person. He had seen this sort of thing before: horny guy meets willing woman. They hit it off, and he tries to get it off. But, she turns out to be somebody's husband, sister, or worse, she's connected. Usually, the punishment was a couple of punches and a kick in the nuts. Rarely did it end up with a couple of bullets to the back of the head.

He leaned down again, moved in closer to the victim's neck and sniffed. Apart from the pungent stench of defecation that Kilchii had already commented upon, there was an underwhelming odor of cigarette smoke and expensive cologne that Gabe didn't recognize. He looked back at the victim's hands again. There were no tobacco stains on the fingers. He rummaged through the pockets to see if Kilchii had missed anything, but came up empty-handed.

He stood, and tilted his Stetson to the back of his head, prowling cautiously around the body, staring at it. Something was way off, and it bothered him. He had been in the police business since the city had set up the department and, during his time, had seen all manner of criminal behavior. This was a homicide pure and simple, but the victim had been forced to undress and stack his clothes in a neat pile beside him. It was only the start of the investigation, but he had a growing sense he'd struggle to close it out, adding it instead to a small, but growing box of cold cases.

He turned back to the car.

'Kilchii? Get your ass over here.'

The kid stumbled out of the darkness a few seconds later, his flashlight bobbing as he drew closer. He looked expectantly at Gabe.

'Radio in the coroner, tell him what we've found.' He had deliberately held off making the call just in case they were being led on a wild-goose chase.

Kilchii was half-turned when Gabe added, 'Find anythin' out there?'

The deputy shook his head. 'Can't see nothin' in the dark.'

Gabe nodded. 'You can check again at first light.' He could see the boy's shoulders slump. It meant staying out here for the next few hours, and the youngster wasn't exactly the outdoors type which was bizarre given his ethnicity.

As Kilchii ducked inside the patrol car to make the call, Gabe moved away from the body. He retrieved a pack of cigarettes from his pocket and lit up.

No more than three miles away the city glistened unaware of the killing on its outskirts. It shimmered like a miraging oasis, beckoning those who strayed near to come closer, casting a spell of paradise on earth, where a fortune could be won but was inevitably lost. The illusion promised all that and more until the surface was scratched and the golden luster dimmed as grey.

Gabe puffed silently and thought.

He would have to crack some heads to get answers yet somehow, guessed none would be forthcoming. Deep down, he knew the perpetrator of this murder was long gone, having slipped away as easily as he had snuck in. He stroked a thumb across his chin, the sound of bristling drowning out Kilchii's report behind him. He would have to make a call of his own as soon as he got back to the office. It just didn't feel like any other run-of-the-mill murder and, as much as he despised the idea, reinforcements would have to be flown in.

The temptation to grab a shovel from the trunk and do himself a favor spiked for an instant. A light smirk briefly appeared. Las Vegas would like that; would like that her seedy underbelly had become victorious in her battle after years of gnawing at his soul.

CHAPTER 6

Nathan Simmonds blew warm air onto his crippled fingers and grimaced. Perhaps, it was his slowing circulation, a symptom of a life well-lived, but he couldn't remember a colder March in Washington. He felt sure the lousy weather was close to turning, maybe no more than a couple of weeks away. He walked to the window and looked at the pedestrians strolling through Lafayette Square below.

Most of the men wore suits, yet only a handful was dressed in over-coats, surely a democratic indication of the approaching fair weather. The women, however, still preferred heavy, knee-length coats with matching gloves that he presumed were the latest fashions the European catwalks had to offer.

He couldn't tell and didn't care that much either.

Cosmetics in all its form held no interest for him, but he took some solace from the fact that he wasn't the only one feeling the effects of a chill wind sweeping in from the east across the Potomac. Why, as recent as yesterday, he had overheard others within his organization, most of them younger than he, complain about the 'never-ending winter'. Nature though had shown her hand early and begun to replace the tulips that had blossomed over a month ago by an altogether more diverse and colorful fauna. Spring was in full bloom, and the unexpectedly low temperatures would do nothing to stunt its progression.

As he surveyed the park, his eyes were drawn to a tall, slim man dressed in a plain, dark-gray suit and matching Homburg like that worn by Eisenhower on The Capitol steps back in January. The man stopped next to the giant statue of Andrew Jackson that dominated the center of the square. He looked up at the hotel. Although Simmonds knew he couldn't be seen against the sky's reflection off the 6th story windows, he took a step back. It was an automatic response to years adopting an almost reclusive and evasive lifestyle. The man dragged on the last of a cigarette and stood on the butt before striding toward the entrance of the Hay Adams Hotel.

Simmonds looked beyond Jackson's statue to the ornate building facing him.

Eisenhower had taken up residence there less than three months ago, following a landslide victory over Democratic nominee Adlai Stevenson in the election the previous year. In carrying 39 states, he had amassed 442 Electoral College votes against Stevenson's paltry 89, those coming from 9 of the 'Solid South' states. His manifesto had promised two things: increase pressure on the Soviets thereby refrigerating further the already frosty relationship between the two superpowers, and reducing the federal deficit, which would be a neat trick, as Simmonds couldn't recall any Republican doing anything other than increasing it. And while 'Ike' liked to remind Simmonds of the former at every opportunity, it was the latter which Simmonds would strive to ensure would remain intact. After all, federal oversight required ever-increasing budgets to ensure the nation's security was maintained if not enhanced.

A knock sounded at the door.

'Enter.'

A waitress, her trolly laden with refreshments of sandwiches and cakes, and a pot each of tea and coffee pushed the door open. She brought the cart to a stop next to a rectangular table and went about shifting the brunch from one to the other. Simmonds felt her anxious gaze wash over him.

'That'll be all,' he said without turning around.

Her trolley empty, she departed without waiting for a tip.

He waited a few moments before moving to pour two cups: tea for him, coffee for his guest who by now would be stepping off the elevator and making his way to the room. In the past, he had toyed with the idea of ordering only tea as a means of annoying the other man, but ultimately he felt it a childish act, something he knew his guest would perpetrate had their roles been reversed.

Another knock sounded, this one sharp and staccato, and the door swung open, the guest not waiting to be beckoned inside.

Simmonds took a chair at one end of the table and pulled his saucer close to him, a triangular sandwich balanced precariously on one side, a spoon on the other. Without a warm smile or friendly greeting, he eyed Leon Knox, as the younger man dropped a handful of sugar cubes into his cup and plonked himself on the other side of the table to face him.

'What are you doing about our problem?' Simmonds said. He lifted his cup and held it with both hands, the heat soaking painfully through his thin skin and into his stiffened bones.

'What, no small talk? No foreplay?' Knox said. He removed his hat and placed it on a sideboard that wouldn't have looked out of place at Buckingham Palace.

'No time for that.' Simmonds said.

'But time enough for tea and scones.'

Simmonds' face remained impassive. He wouldn't be goaded by the arrogant pup the CIA sent him each week, especially when the topic of conversation was this important. Their meetings could generally be best described as humdrum, and yet, although tiresome to the point of catatonia, they were necessary if both the FBI and CIA were to influence how the new President would view each organization's future place in America. That said, in Eisenhower, they had a man who thrived on information. After all, he had managed to win a war with it, and so his patronage was considered a given; it was its extent that remained in doubt. If there was a downside, it was in trying to manipulate a man who had accumulated a wealth of experience in dealing with the intelligence community. A flexible approach where the security agencies worked together, regardless of their mutual mistrust, was therefore required.

Simmonds waited for Knox to get to the matter at hand, listening to the slow second hand of a large ornamental clock that rested on the mantelpiece, tick by.

'We're making some headway,' Knox said at length.

'How much progress?'

'The investigation is ongoing.'

Simmonds could feel his temperature rise. Whatever about the caliber of man the CIA sent to meet with him; he hadn't time for the games it played. Knox must have noticed Simmonds' increasing agitation because he continued.

'We're looking at employees and compatriots who might have had reason to kill the three men. Nothing has turned up yet.'

'That's it?'

'What else is there?'

Simmonds slammed the table with an open palm that made Knox jump. The veins that crisscrossed the older man's balding scalp had begun to pulse.

'You put somebody onto it. You investigate the murders. You hypothesize. You draw conclusions…' Simmonds held his breath. 'Have you determined a motive? What about the murder weapon? Other than what we already know, what had the three victims got in common? Why were they targeted? Have you drawn up a list of suspects? You undertake an appropriate investigation. You don't show up here with 'the investigation is ongoing' and think that's a sufficient report. If I didn't know better, I'd say you weren't taking this very seriously.' He leaned forward, his eyes bulging in anger.

'The CIA doesn't investigate murders. That's a job for local law enforcement and the FBI when required.' Knox chewed silently on a sandwich and brushed a crumb off his tie. If anything, he appeared even more relaxed than when he stepped into the suite. 'Let's not get ahead of ourselves, Nathan. We don't know that these killings are anything other than somebody taking issue with the victims'… questionable proclivities.' Knox smiled suggestively.

'That may be true of Lenz and Otte,' Simmonds said, acknowledging the two men's illegal activities. 'But the same cannot be said of Hasse.'

'Hasse's death was nothing more than an unfortunate hunting accident, completely unconnected to the other pair. Let's not make more of this than it is.'

'Which is what exactly?'

'A run of bad luck.'

Simmonds held his breath, wondering if the young man was so naïve as to be blind to what was right in front of him, or if he was playing some game. If it were the former, then he would be forced to take matters into his own hands. If it were the latter, then Knox would eventually come to learn that an Assistant Director of the FBI wasn't to be trifled with. He found the nonchalance with which Knox viewed the recent events both incredible and, at the same time, quite unsettling; the utter recklessness he displayed on behalf of his agency, and the peril that might befall it. Surely, he must be aware that the best-laid plans of more than a decade ago were unraveling before their eyes for the entire world to see. Of course, composure and clarity of thought were essential to ensure that secrets of yesteryear remained so, but action had to be decisive and swift to minimize exposition of their ill-gotten intellectual property.

'What if they are connected?' Simmonds said. 'What if Hasse was also murdered? That's too much of a coincidence to believe there isn't a commonality. That means somebody is aware of the program, what we've done, and what we're continuing to do.'

'Do you think I haven't thought about that,' Knox said, 'That some-body may be hunting these guys?' Knox smiled again, which was starting to irritate the older man. 'The very idea of it is far-fetched.'

'Truth is sometimes stranger than fiction,' Simmonds said, his voice rising. 'All possibilities need to be thoroughly investigated and eliminated until we find the person responsible for at least the last two murders. I'd be a whole lot happier if we discovered that Hasse's death was an accident, but if it wasn't and it is connected then at least, we'll have plugged a leak, so to speak.'

Knox adjusted his tie. 'Look, Nathan, these guys didn't just jump off the boat at Baltimore harbor and begin a new life in America. Both our agencies had a hand in bringing them here.'

'I'm well aware of our past endeavors,' Simmonds said. 'That's the only reason I'm speaking to you about this today. It's also the reason I believe there's something more to this than what we're seeing and why I believe we require a more rigorous and thorough investigation.'

'And I thought you enjoyed my company.'

Simmonds let that remark slide. He knew he wasn't getting anywhere with the man. If anything, it heightened his suspicions of both Knox and the agency for which he worked, an agency that appeared to go about its business without any degree of congressional supervision, responsible for nothing, answerable to nobody, and yet continually exceeding both its brief and budget with impunity.

Knox tilted his head and looked at Simmonds. 'Perhaps, there is something more we can do. Let me discuss it with Mr. Millman this afternoon and see if we can agree on a way forward.'

To Simmonds, Knox sounded almost friendly and sincere and, had it not been for the predicament in which he found himself, would have said as much. But, he had to give the younger man a chance to come to terms with the gravity of the situation and then consider and propose a solution.

'This meeting is over,' Simmonds said, eventually. 'Toddle off to your superior, and I'll see you back here at 10 a.m. tomorrow.'

Leon Knox stood and was at the door before Simmonds could draw breath.

'Don't think for a moment that your place at the Agency is secure. Millman of all people is constantly looking to recruit the best, brightest, and most ruthless of individuals. If you're not up to the job, he'll replace you with somebody who is. You had better come more prepared than you did today.'

Knox glanced back with that same coy smile he'd worn when he'd entered and disappeared out the door.

Simmonds sat alone for the next few minutes, lost in thought. The apparent inaction of the CIA was deeply troublesome. Either they were genuinely sure that the three deaths were nothing more than a series of unrelated incidents and unworthy of a thorough investigation, or they were working the case properly but keeping their findings to themselves. His thoughts lingered briefly on the possibility that the CIA might want to cover up whatever they had discovered to prevent exposing somebody from within its ranks who might have had a hand, no matter how minor, in the killings. But, he dismissed the notion almost as soon as it crossed his mind. Even the CIA knew that the truth eventually came out, regardless of effort employed to conceal it. Either way, he couldn't risk either their incompetence or worse, the likelihood they wanted to keep the FBI in the dark.

He stood and padded across to a door that led to the neighboring suite. He entered without knocking.

'You catch all that?' he said to the man in the other room.

Bradley Witten removed his headset and flicked a switch on the recording device he had been monitoring. 'Every word.'

Simmonds nodded. 'I don't trust Knox. We need to run a parallel investigation. Put a small team together. Only people we can trust. Examine every living soul who knew the three dead men, their compatriots, and how they came to be in this country in the first place. Then draw up a list of anybody or any organization that stands to benefit from these murders.'

'That list is sure to be quite large.'

'That's irrelevant. Use all available tools and personnel at your disposal, requisition more if you need to.' He checked his watch. 'I want an update at 8 a.m. and 8 p.m. every day until we get to the bottom of this.'

Simmonds retraced his steps into the other room and left Witten to gather his equipment. He'd been too long in the game and wasn't about to let the CIA hang him out to dry.

CHAPTER 7

THE LAST THREE HOURS HAD been slow but not tedious, creeping through the dense and damp undergrowth of the Pocomoke River State Forest. After a winter that had seen temperatures dip as low and -7 and soar as high as 21 Celsius, the forest's annual rebirth was beginning to take hold and, what would have been bare branches a month ago, now displayed a bright and colorful flora. Along with the rejuvenated forest came a burgeoning animal population and the reason for Alona's trip into the wilds.

She was covered in a veneer of sweat, and her muscles ached from being in the same statuesque position for longer than was good for her. Despite having eaten a large breakfast before she'd left home earlier that morning, her stomach grumbled, and the pressure on her bladder had become mildly annoying. But, she forced the pain to the back of her mind. She picked a probing mosquito off her neck, making sure to keep her movements to a minimum. She scowled and muttered the old Yiddish swear 'shtup', hoping she hadn't given her position away. She stared directly ahead through a Rangefinder. Today's quarry sat no more than fifteen yards away.

The Red-Cockaded Woodpecker enjoyed the habitat offered it by both the Loblolly and Longleaf Pine tree, forests of which were scattered throughout the wilds of North America from Maryland to Texas. However, the wilderness was shrinking, and the species population was in decline as it clung unknowingly to the precipice of extinction, a process exacerbated mostly by an emergent America Incorporated. Progress, it seemed, waited for nothing, whether beast or man.

She crept so as not to disturb the bird as it gorged on a hapless wood beetle. It stopped as the sharp sound of her camera's shutter broke the silence, its head darting from side to side, seeking out a threat. It resumed its feast after a few moments, its fears seemingly allayed.

Alona steadied herself and took three more photos in quick succession, the noise of which was enough to startle the woodpecker to flight and vanish into the blossoming canopy overhead. She got onto her knees, the merest hint of a smile brightening her face. She scanned the forest as she wound the roll to the end, removing it and dropping it in a bag where it nestled next to several other undeveloped reels. It had been a long, tiring day that'd delivered more than she'd hoped when she'd set out.

As a pre-teenager, she had been quiet, preferring, like other children her age, to merely exist in the shadows of others. When required, she had helped in the family tailoring business in Rosenheim (to the southeast of Munich) where she stacked shelves whenever the latest deliveries arrived. Having sensed the growing unease and witnessed an increasing hostility toward Jews, her parents had decided to relocate west. That'd been the summer of 1938; they later learned the shop and their home above had been ransacked and razed to the ground only a few days after their departure. Several more moves followed before they eventually settled in a small village in the Bordeaux region of France. Her family was offered employment by Nikolas Millot, a famous vineyard owner from the area, where they spent the next couple of years tending his winery.

That had been before the Germans came.

They, along with thousands of others, mostly Jews, were rounded up and dispatched to the east for 'resettlement', and so had begun almost five years of indescribable horror. After so many of her kinsfolk had been slaughtered, she had been given a second chance and so had made a conscious decision to embrace all that life had to offer. She had taken up a couple of hobbies that had previously passed her by or that had been taken for granted. Her younger brother, Orel, had been a piano-playing protégé before his life had been cut short at the age of nine. Although she had never been musically inclined, she believed she could honor his memory by taking up the instrument. She practiced hard through bouts of crippling back-pain and calloused fingers, sometimes for up to five hours a day, but still found it challenging to master. She wondered if it could only be learned at an early age when both the brain and body were malleable and entirely open for new experiences. At times, she despaired, believing she was doing Orel more of a disservice. They were, after all, siblings and comprised of the same genetic material, so she never gave up hope that a musical breakthrough was just around the corner; she had recently read an article on the latest scientific discovery about genes. In the end, she could play from memory a moderate number of intermediate pieces by, among others, Mozart, Chopin, and Schubert.

But, it had been ornithology that had captured her imagination and passion. After years of crawling across forest floors for hours at a time in search of rare species of birds from right across North America, she had amassed a collection of thousands of photographs. She had researched and meticulously cataloged her findings and, from time to time, written articles that were later published in some of the more discerning, specialist periodicals.

She ate a tuna sandwich as she drove across the recently opened Bay Bridge which spanned the Chesapeake, enjoying the time it saved by not having to stand on the deck of the now-defunct Claiborne-Annapolis ferry which had ceased operations as soon as the first commuter had driven from shore to shore. Between bites, she fiddled with the car radio, trying to tune in a static-pocked number by either Dean Martin or Perry Como, she wasn't sure who. Eventually, she switched it off and allowed her mind to wander.

She had dropped across to Daniel yesterday, not to bring him another assignment, but to chat and check on him. She was disheartened at seeing his mood unchanged. From what she'd seen, his remorse hadn't subsided, so she'd finally decided to call in a favor. She checked her watch and pressed the pedal a little harder. She couldn't be late for this particular meeting.

It was a straightforward drive into Washington on a highway that toggled between Route 50 and the 595 which eventually became New

York Avenue. She took a right turn at Florida Avenue and drove towards Bloomingdale, pulling into a parking lot adjacent to a small row of shops that serviced part of the affluent residential area. She slipped into 'The Friendly Bean', a quaint coffee shop and the venue chosen by the man who'd contacted her earlier that day.

She took a seat by the window and ordered a coffee with cream, and a double chocolate muffin. She was no expert and as far as she could tell the coffee at 'The Bean' was the same as everywhere else, bitter, black and a little on the lukewarm side for her taste, but the range of homemade confectionary they sold was to die for.

She looked out the window as pedestrians passed without really noticing any of them. Somebody sat on the seat next to her, a man she guessed, judging by the aftershave; neither overpowering nor underwhelming. He opened a newspaper, but she didn't pay him any mind.

The waitress placed a coffee and cake in front of her a few minutes later and asked the man if he would like to order.

'I'll have what she's having.'

Alona smiled. 'Are you following me?' She turned towards Thomas Mitchell.

'All the guys rave about this place, thought I'd give it a go.'

'What a coincidence.'

'Isn't it.'

She glanced at the paper he had folded to the sports section. 'You think the Senators will make a run for it this season?'

He shook his head. 'Haven't the bullpen.'

'Or the hitters I'm told.'

'I'd give anything to have some of those Yankees on our team this year. They'd four All-Stars last year, probably be even more this time around.' His voice trailed away as he looked at a passing car that'd slowed then sped up again.

They didn't speak again until after the waitress had delivered his order and was out of earshot.

'Did you think about what I said?' Alona asked.

'Of course.'

She looked expectantly. 'Well, don't keep me waiting.'

'I've something that might be of interest.'

Alona paused a beat before speaking. 'It can't be like the others.' She tilted her head gently to one side and gave him a soft smile.

She and Thomas Mitchell had a unique relationship, cultivated over the past six years by trusting each other completely which, in the business of espionage and covert contracts, was difficult, if not impossible, to acquire in the first instance, and maintain in the second. During that time, the initial meeting for any assignment had always been instigated by a simple request sent to a PO Box that was rented and checked by Alona each day. She had checked it today on her way to Pocomoke and found in it a note stating a time and the name of the establishment in which they now sat. While she was the business face for Daniel, Mitchell was her opposite number and point man, for whatever agency sought Daniel's services. When they negotiated terms, they always used the first person; it was just easier that way. It meant that both assignor and assignee never had to meet and could deny any wrong-doing if a particular assignment didn't work out as well as they all would have hoped. While Mitchell was her only client, she suspected he had many contractors; it was, after all, a big, bad world, littered with opportunity, and limited only by man's capacity for manipulation and deceit.

She regarded him as he nibbled his muffin. He wasn't much to look at and certainly not what any trophy-seeking woman would look for in a potential mate. His face was redder than a field of poppies in summer, and his hair had thinned over the years to the point where she almost suggested he take a razor to what remained. At least that would have had the added benefit of hiding the stray grays. He had once told her he was born on the first day of the century, which meant she or anybody else for that matter, didn't have to perform any mathematical gymnastics in figuring out his age. He walked with a limp; an injury acquired, he had said, in the trenches of the First World War that subsequently kept him off the frontlines of the Second. For a fifty-three-year-old, he had a keen sense of fashion that wasn't in keeping with others of similar vintage, instead choosing the more casual look as worn by the younger American generation. He had told her his parents had named him so by attempting to continue a long line of Thomas Mitchells, one he said he could trace back as far as the middle-ages in the 'Old Country' (wherever that was) long before Columbus had even considered setting sail for the New World.

As much as she liked him, she believed none of what he ever told her of his personal life. She had learned over the years that trust on a personal and professional level in this business rarely aligned.

He sipped his coffee and sat back with a contented sigh.

'You approve?' she said.

'Very much.' He looked sidelong at her but didn't say anything. Her curiosity eventually got the better of her.

'I suppose you can tell me about it before I reject it?' she said.

He turned awkwardly in his seat to face her the way a large ape might if it had to turnabout on a branch that might not bear its weight. He leaned in to whisper.

'Three scientists have been killed over the past week. The assignment is to find out who is doing it and stop them adding to the body count.'

Alona raised her eyebrows in anticipation of further information. None was forthcoming, forcing her to ask the obvious. 'Where?'

'Right here.'

'Washington?'

Mitchell shook his head. 'One in Washington State… two in Vegas.'

Alona leaned back. 'Seriously?'

He ate a chunk of muffin and washed it down with more coffee.

'Isn't that something the local police departments should be investigating or the Feds if they're connected?' She paused. 'What makes you think they're connected anyway?'

'I don't know they are for sure. Local Police Departments are doing what they can within their jurisdictions, but they only see part of the picture. As for the Feds well, that's why I'm here.'

She stared into his eyes, searching for something else, but there was nothing. 'What aren't you telling me?'

'Lots.'

'That's an overstatement.'

Mitchell giggled a gentle sound that belied his size and gender. 'What is there to tell? It's a couple of days hiking in the Rockies, then some more sunning yourself in the desert with a little investigative work thrown in.'

Alona sat back, wrapping her hands around the coffee mug. She stared outside. 'Not really what I'm used to.'

'No, it isn't.'

'Working with the FBI?'

'Yes.'

She could immediately see the upside. If it went well there might be a more permanent arrangement put in place and Daniel would have the change in career he craved, but if it didn't…

'And the FBI came to you with this?'

'In a manner of speaking.' Mitchell glanced at her, a smirk appearing at the corner of his mouth. 'I might have volunteered your services.'

Alona scrunched her face for a time.

'Why me?' she said, at length. 'This isn't the best use of my skills.' She made it sound like Daniel worked for the US State Department or the UK Foreign Office, but if she gave it much thought, she would have concluded that some of the assignments he had completed were probably on behalf of those two branches of government anyway. 'I've never done anything like this before. Wouldn't it be better to hire a private detective, somebody who has experience in this area?'

'It's all I have at the moment. Perhaps you can add a string to your bow? Learn something new while on the job?' Mitchell said. There was a mischievous glint in his eye which made her wonder.

STEPHEN FRANCIS

'Unless there's an international element to it?' She was fishing for more information, but as with their other conversations, she knew he wouldn't take the bait. Not here, anyway. She turned back to the street, staring at nothing in particular.

By the time she spoke again, her coffee had gone cold, and she had lost her appetite for what remained of the half-eaten muffin.

'Leave the details in the usual place, and I'll consider it,' she said.

Mitchell nodded his approval. 'Mind if I?' He pointed at her cake.

Alona waved her hand. He tossed it into his mouth and threw a handful of crumpled dollars onto the table to cover the bill. A moment later, he was gone.

She reached across the table and picked up the paper he had left behind. She flicked through the pages, noting the numbers 5-8-0-2-4 that were underlined in pencil on different lines of the third page. She checked her watch and made a quick calculation. If she hurried, she would be able to get to the Post Office over on F-Street in Penn Quarter, collect the package that Thomas had left in the PO Box, and still get back in time to start dinner before Anthony got back from school.

CHAPTER 8

DANIEL STARED AT THE CEILING. He'd been doing it since he'd woken to use the bathroom around 4 a.m. and had watched as the room brightened from a dim, street-lamp luminescence through to sunrise, with shadows from the buildings on the other side of the street melt slowly down the wall. He rolled onto his side and closed his eyes, trying to clear his mind, but knew it was a wasted exercise as he'd been trying the same thing for the past two weeks. Once they reached the floor, he decided enough was enough.

He swung his legs out of bed, went to the bathroom, and looked in the mirror. His eyes were pink, circled by a blackness that seemed to be fading, which he took to be a good sign. He threw warm water on his face and ran a hand across his jaw, deciding to forgo a shave for today. Keeping the teeth clean, though, was a must.

He walked across to his window and looked out at the street in various stages of awakening. His eyes were drawn to a young woman, leaving a house opposite. He'd bumped into her once, last October he recalled.

The day had begun pleasantly, warm with sunshine and a sky interspersed with cloud, but had turned nasty as the day wore on. Storm force winds swept in from the Carolinas through Virginia, bringing with them raindrops the size of walnuts that threatened to burrow through anything in their path. He'd been out for a run and spotted her getting out of a cab with armfuls of shopping bags that disintegrated before she'd managed to take more than a few steps, shedding her groceries all over the sapping ground. He slowed down and helped gather her goods then helped her up the steps and inside her house.

'Just throw them anywhere,' she said, nodding to the kitchen counter-top. 'That was awfully nice of you.'

'I was wet anyway,' Daniel said.

She turned to him, wiping a dishcloth over her face. She stuck out her hand. 'I'm Gail.'

'That's apt.'

She looked puzzled before smiling. 'Oh, the weather?'

They shook. She had light-brown, shoulder-length hair and a beautiful bright smile, framed by a thin pair of pink lipstick-free lips. She glanced down at a pool of water that'd formed about Daniel's feet.

He took a step back and looked around awkwardly for something to dry the floor.

'Don't worry. I'll get that.' She grabbed a kitchen towel from the counter and wiped up what she could, but each time Daniel took a step back, he left another pool where he'd stood.

'I'll get out of your way,' he said, making his way to the front door.

'You live across the road, don't you?'

'Yeah.'

'Would you like to stay for coffee?' Her face turned red, perhaps at the boldness of the question.

He stopped and faced her. It hadn't sounded like anything other than a stranger offering a thank you by way of a warm brew. If anything, she seemed lonely. He could understand that.

'Another time, perhaps?' He returned her smile before closing the door.

'Another time' had never materialized. He'd been busy sorting out the logistics for Moscow, and she'd never followed up on the invitation. Looking at her now, a cherry-red beret fixed firmly to her head as she walked south on 17th Street, heading towards Massachusetts Avenue, he thought it might have been the chance of a new friendship missed. But, as can sometimes be the case, circumstances had dictated the path chosen, and maybe that's just the way it was meant to be.

He turned away and looked around the room. A rumpled bed, some clothes scattered about the floor – he'd let himself go.

He slipped into a tracksuit that'd been thrown on a chair and a pair of sneakers that'd been tossed underneath and took another look in the mirror. He'd worn the same outfit every day since his return and was starting to look shabby. A couple of years ago, he'd signed up for a part-time course in Philosophy at GW and had joined the campus running team to help meditate on the core topics of 'existentialism and metaphysics'. He'd bought two identical tracksuits which sported the university's name and logo. He wondered now if a part of his divine soul had not already begun to dismay upon his worldly occupation and in doing so, had started to weave doubts in his mind about the direction his life was taking.

He left the apartment and walked the hundred or so yards north up 17th Street to a little place he liked on the corner of Q-Street, buying a copy of the Washington Post from 'Lenny' along the way. He went in and found a table with an unrestricted view out the front window.

'Penelope's Diner' was owned and run by Deborah Anderson, the daughter of a Danish immigrant who'd made the journey west sometime after the turn of the century but before the Great War. She'd lived all her life in this neighborhood with the family home situated on Corcoran Street a couple of blocks away. If there was anybody else in the world that epitomized the ying-yang of life more than she, Daniel had yet to meet them. Her father had opened the diner only months after landing in America but had found it difficult to make the business work as well as was needed to keep his family fed. The US entered the Great European War around the same time he was thinking of selling up and moving into another area that might better suit his talents, but instead, he joined up, believing the extra income from soldering might be enough to keep it afloat. He'd been with a unit of the 79th Division that'd set out to capture Montfaucon during the Meuse-Argonne offensive in late September 1918 but died of wounds received by sniper fire in early-November of that year.

The money he'd sent the family while in service, along with the 'gratuity' they'd received from the Department of War after his death, had been enough to ensure the business would run for another few months. But, the diner was already in good hands. Deborah's mother, Julie, had an excellent business brain and had transformed and revitalized the restaurant rather than allowing it to deteriorate to the point where a sale was unavoidable. As a consequence, the place had prospered under her guidance. She died of sepsis in 1936 and left the diner to Deborah and her husband, Sebastian. Sebastian had taken it upon himself to carry out the day to day running of the business, leaving Deborah to helplessly watch as he drove it into the ground much as her father had twenty years before. Only when Sebastian died at the Battle of Casablanca in November 1942, was she able to resurrect the business for a second time. Eleven years on, and the place thrived under Deborah's firm but guiding hand. And so, it was confirmed. The men didn't know diddly about running a diner while the women, although saddened, were somewhat grateful for their husband's wartime deaths.

It was Deborah who greeted him today, as she had done every other day.

'You're getting earlier each day.' She held a notepad and a pen at the ready.

'I wake with the sun.' Daniel smiled.

'Well, after April you'll have to find somewhere else to go. We don't open before 6.30 a.m.'

'Even at the weekend?'

'Especially at the weekend.'

'I can probably wait around until then.'

'Usual for you today? Cappuccino?'

Daniel sat back and looked at a pair of chatting cyclists pass by. 'No, Deborah. I think I'll have tea with a ham and cheese bagel.'

'Glad to hear it, Honey. The thoughts of you wasting away are too much for me to bear.' She regarded him for a moment. 'You getting much sleep these days?'

'Enough,' Daniel said. 'Some job difficulties I have to work through, you know how it is.'

'I surely do. You want fries with the bagel?'

He shook his head.

'I'll bring a pot of tea right over so you can start while you read your paper.'

Daniel smiled as she hurried away and glanced at the front page of the Post, where the leading article was the impending death of Alfred Thiel.

Thiel was a black taxi-driver who'd been tried and convicted of the double homicide of two white brothers, Mike and Irving Holt. They'd had the misfortune to get into his car armed only with a pair of knives and bad intentions. They'd attempted to steal Alfred's meager nightly takings and, being a proud black man, he had defended himself as one sometimes does in those circumstances. But, as the saying goes, you shouldn't bring a knife to a gunfight, which is what the two white men had unknowingly done. That'd been their last mistake, as Thiel had at first disabled them by firing into their bodies from the front of his cab, before calmly getting out and firing multiple rounds into each of their heads from close range. On the surface, it'd been a simple case of self-defense versus second-degree murder, but there were undercurrents of race fury from the white demographic in DC and surrounding states. In the end, the state won its case, Judge Thomas Hamilton citing an 'over-zealousness' on behalf of the unfortunate Mr. Thiel. But, it was hard to see which was more unfortunate, the white brothers, or the black cabbie, not that it mattered because, by midday tomorrow, all three would be dead.

And this was why Daniel promised himself every day never to read the newspaper. It was filled only with bad news. He tightened his jaw as Deborah set a mug and teapot next to him. He pulled the sugar and milk closer and poured himself a cup.

'Awful business that,' she said, motioning to the paper's headline article. 'Poor man just going about his job, was in the wrong place at the wrong time and now he's gonna pay for it.'

Daniel nodded absently, his mind having wandered back to his escape from Moscow. Even now, he wondered if there was anything different he might have done so he might have spared the policeman's life. But, it didn't matter how often he challenged himself; the same scenario always came to pass. The guy was just in the wrong place.

CHAPTER 9

HE WAS RUMMAGING THROUGH A fistful of dollar bills, as the cab fishtailed to the curb. He gave the driver more than enough to cover the short trip from McCarran Field and reached across the seat next to him, grabbing his holdall and stepping onto the pavement. The cab pulled away, coating Daniel in a cloud of Nevada dust.

He dropped his bag, breathing a high-pitched sigh as he stretched his back, the cramped plane ride from Washington, which had been exacerbated by the maniacal cabbie, still ingrained in his muscles. He looked away to his right and saw several large buildings a short distance away. Alona had booked a room in one of the city's multi-storied hotels, courtesy of the federal government, while he worked on their dime. The city's reputation for all manner of entertainment was well-known and he wondered if the same courtesies might be extended to him; a few hours hovering over a blackjack table, as he drank himself silly on the free liquor.

Before any of that, though, he had work to do.

He turned back and sized-up the building before him; a square, one-story, sandstone edifice with rectangular windows (coated in a fine film of dust) on either side of a pair of glass doors. Gold writing on one of the windows, in a 'Wild West' kind of font, proclaimed it to be the Sheriff's Office. Judging by the outside, there appeared to be little going on inside and Daniel wondered if maybe the place was closed, perhaps even relocated to bigger premises closer to the center of town and, consequently, the center of trouble.

He tried the door. It swung noiselessly inwards.

An acrid blend of sweat and gunpowder assaulted Daniel's senses as soon as he stepped through the door, the stale air being smoothly whisked by a single fan on a cabinet away in a corner. The station was spacious with three desks lining the walls on both sides, each accompanied by pairs of wooden chairs sitting at odd angles to each other. The walls were made of bleak, unpainted concrete blocks (which Daniel assumed was an attempt to dissuade any would-be recidivist from ever showing up again) adorned with a range of scattered posters declaring 'America's Most Wanted'. Daniel didn't examine them; they may have been mugshots of local crime bosses or casino owners; if there was a difference between the two. The only dash of color in the place was the sparkling red hair of the deputy sitting at the muster desk facing the main door. He was a young man, probably in his mid-twenties. He sat hunched over a newspaper, his finger tracing a line across the page, his lips moving in concert.

Daniel walked toward him and placed his bag on the floor.

'Help you?' the deputy said, without looking up.

'Is Sheriff Collins around?'

'Nope. You wanna leave a message?'

Daniel looked at the deputy's name tag, then past him to the small, empty office behind. 'You know when he'll be back?'

The deputy shrugged.

'Anywhere I can grab a coffee?' Daniel asked.

'Other side of the road, a couple of blocks down a ways.' He flicked a hand away to his left.

'OK. Will you let the Sheriff know Daniel Miller was looking for him?'

'Sure.' The deputy nodded and turned over a page of the paper. Daniel waited a few seconds, taking the deputy's nonchalant acknowledgment that the message was safe in his hands as his queue to leave.

He stepped out of the station and raised an arm to his forehead, shielding his eyes from the dazzling sunlight. Once they had adjusted sufficiently to the glare, he spotted a diner not too far away in the direction the deputy had indicated. It lay on the other side of the road which appeared broader than the narrowest part of Grand Canyon and, with the volume of vehicles racing past, was likely to be just as treacherous to cross. A look to his left and right told him he'd have to take his chances if he was to quench the thirst and hunger that had set in since he stepped off the plane.

It took him a couple of minutes and several false starts before he managed to dance across to the other side, wondering as he did if jaywalking laws were strictly observed in the state. A warm and sticky film of sweat covered his body once he got across safely. With his bag slung over one shoulder, he walked the hundred or so yards down the path and stopped outside the diner's entrance.

Like the police station, it didn't look much from the outside. Painted a gaudy yellow, it epitomized everything for which Las Vegas had become known: harsh, brash, and headache-inducing. A large, dust-coated window that looked as though it hadn't been splashed by water since the previous decade sat next to a door with a crooked sign declaring the place 'Open for Business'. Daniel resolved to find somewhere else to eat if the inside was as decadent.

He was pleasantly surprised when he walked in.

The place was large, airy, and bright. High, brown-leather stools nestled beneath a countertop that ran most of the diner's length on the left, while a row of booths that could comfortably seat four ran along the wall to the right. A couple of ceramic plates filled with food orders sat neatly on an aluminum shelf that bisected a kitchen area where on one side a rotund, middle-aged waitress poured coffee for an older man while a short, skinny chef tossed something that might have been fried chicken on the other. Barely audible above the circling casual banter, a radio played a tune by the Percy Faith Orchestra.

Daniel moved to the back, nodding to the waitress as he passed and sidled into an empty booth. He scanned the small menu, settling for the Chef's Special Sandwich and a pot of tea. He sat back and stared blankly through the translucent window at the passing traffic, recalling the events that had led him here.

It had started two days ago on the afternoon of March 16th, with a phone call from Alona, asking him to meet her on the corner of New

Hampshire and 24th Street at 4 p.m. She hadn't divulged any other details, which was standard operating procedure: discussing an assignment over the phone was strictly prohibited. Of course, he didn't know what lay ahead, either. She might as well have been asking him to view a new car.

He showed up at the appointed time, the heart of Foggy Bottom, the business area of Washington, DC. She escorted him to a nondescript, rectangular office building on I-Street.

Once inside, they took the elevator to the 4th floor which opened out into a small foyer, where an unattended reception desk faced them. They stepped out and turned left through a set of glass doors and into a sizable, open-plan office space that had window views on three sides, the fourth comprising glass-fronted offices, and meeting rooms; *all ultra-modern*, Daniel thought to himself. A grid of cubicles stretched from one side of the building to the other with only the head and shoulders of the scattered male occupants visible. It wasn't what he would call a bee-hive of activity.

He didn't know what type of work was carried out here, but he was picking up clues as he went, which only served to heighten his intrigue.

She turned left, glancing through the doors of the open meeting rooms as she went, before stopping outside one of them. She turned to Daniel with a lob-sided grin and gestured for him to enter. He looked in and saw a young man, sitting at a table with an assortment of files piled on one side and a single glass of water on the other.

'I'll be right over there,' Alona said, pointing to a row of four chairs propped next to a cubicle wall.

Daniel looked after her as she walked away before turning back and entering the room. The man stood and held out a hand, introducing himself as Bradley Witten, Special Agent of the FBI. That confirmed Daniel's guess as to where Alona had taken him (he'd found it unusual that the agency hadn't yet managed to advertise themselves on one of the walls on the way in).

'Sorry for the secrecy, I understand Ms. Peers hasn't told you much about this and why we've asked you here. Would you mind getting the door?' He sat back down.

Witten was a few years younger than Daniel and looked as though he had never had to endure the trials of war. He wore a dark navy, off-the-rack, three-piece suit, white shirt, and a dark green tie. His hair was short and brown, parted on the left and set in place with a lotion that Daniel had smelled as soon he'd stepped into the office; although it might also have been the man's cologne.

Very dapper.

By contrast, Daniel looked like the man's delinquent older brother.

Pleasantries were exchanged, and Witten pointed to a chair. 'Please take a seat. Can I offer you something? Coffee?'

Daniel declined, sat opposite, and watched Special Agent Witten prepare himself. He looked apprehensive, as though unsure of where he should start. He took a breath and began.

'In the spring of 1945, MI6 happened upon a list of more than 1,500 German scientists, mathematicians, mechanics, and engineers, all of whom had worked on the Reich's research programs. Soon after, the list was copied and given to US Intelligence and so began a move to round up many of Germany's intellectuals. Initially, we only wanted to interview the scientists and learn what they knew, but we later thought it'd be more beneficial if they started working for us rather than have them falling into Soviet hands.'

He stopped to be sure Daniel was keeping up. Daniel remained silent.

'The US Joint Intelligence Objectives Agency, JIOA for short, began evacuating and relocating to the US, all the scientists, and technicians we could find, along with almost 4,000 members of their families.' He took a sip from a glass of water. 'However, it wasn't without its political difficulties.'

'Like them being Nazis?'

'Yes.' Witten shifted uneasily in his seat. 'President Truman hadn't wanted former Nazi Party members to be brought to the US. However, it was felt this might allow a substantial number slip from our grasp, especially as the Soviets were up to the same thing in the east. The whole affair was thoroughly unacceptable to the institutions that would both outlast and then have to deal with the consequences of a Presidential decision that wouldn't survive beyond a single term.'

Witten paused again, taking another sip and appearing entirely uncomfortable disclosing what he probably considered state secrets, but which amounted to nothing more than the cost of doing business in the modern world.

'The JIOA was forced into circumventing the President's order and recruiting the scientists, anyway. To remove any sense of impropriety, those evacuated were provided with false political biographies and employment, essentially cleansing their records before transportation to the US under what was known as 'Operation Paperclip'.'

'A good story,' Daniel said. 'But it's well known what the Allied intelligence apparatus was up to.'

Witten looked relieved. He shrugged. 'I suppose an operation of that magnitude is impossible to keep under wraps for very long. The best we could hope for was to keep it out of the public domain for a few years.' He wrung his hands together.

Daniel could see the tension return to the young man. He'd obviously not heard the worst part. Witten continued without looking Daniel in the eye.

'Over the past couple of weeks, three of those scientists have been murdered. We need to get to the bottom of it, and we'd appreciate your help.'

Daniel first thought was that Witten should have offered him something stronger than coffee. A moment of silence divided them before Daniel cut through it.

'Hasn't the FBI enough agents to investigate domestic matters like this?'

Witten looked uncomfortable by the question and reseated himself again.

'Of course, there are agents stationed in all our field offices right across the country, but they're engaged in other activities.'

Daniel tilted his head, quizzically.

'Organized crime, civil rights. Top of our list right now is espionage. We're kept busy.' Witten said.

Daniel could understand that. The Soviets were doing the same thing on the opposite side of the Atlantic, but they'd been at it for a lot longer than the Americans.

'We'd like to take you on in a consultancy capacity,' Witten went on. 'Just a short-term contract you understand, to help us tidy this mess up quickly.' He looked directly at Daniel, practically begging him to accept.

'It's an interesting offer,' Daniel said, at length. 'How long have I to consider it?'

'I need to know before you leave today,' Witten said. 'Dead bodies need to be laid to rest, and we don't know if others might turn up… we need to prevent that from happening.'

Daniel regarded the man. Despite his uncertainty, and Daniel didn't know why he would be so when on home turf, he spoke very well. University educated, at a guess, maybe even a post-grad of some kind, then directly into the FBI without ever having had a taste for the tribulations one suffered in the real world. Daniel had seen his type before; a young man being fast-tracked to greater heights within an institution that would become his life until retirement or before if nature intervened. That said, Daniel knew an assignment such as the Witten had loosely described could quickly derail a promising career. Daniel wondered if maybe Witten had any lingering reservations about bringing him in in the first place. Using outside personnel wasn't without risks, but it wasn't without benefits either, deniability being top of the list. As for Daniel, he'd have to weigh both and, it seemed, didn't have much time to do it.

He looked over his shoulder at Alona who'd busied herself with a paperback.

'Mind if I discuss it with her?'

Witten hesitated but acceded with a gentle nod.

Daniel went out and beckoned Alona to follow him out of earshot.

'What do you think?' he said.

'Not what you normally do -'

'But opens up new doors,' Daniel finished. He looked around the office again. There were even fewer people than when they'd arrived. He glanced at a clock. It was after 4.30 p.m.

'Money wouldn't be the same,' he said.

'We've enough money.'

'And you think I should do it?'

'It's a fresh start, a clean slate.'

Daniel still had reservations. What if he couldn't complete the assignment to the FBI's practiced standards? Would that ruin the chances of being offered work with the agency again? But then, he ran that risk with every assignment he undertook.

'It doesn't sound too dangerous,' he said.

'You don't even have to leave the country.'

'That has a certain appeal, alright. You know anything more than what he told me in there?'

'If he didn't give you any specific details, then you know as much as I do.'

Daniel set his jaw and nodded. 'OK. Come back in with me, and we'll hear the rest.'

'I'm not part of the deal.'

He stared at her. 'Then, there is no deal.'

He turned to re-enter the office and waited at the door to allow her to pass. She hesitated before making her way into the room.

Witten stood, confusion stamped on his face.

'You hire us both, or I walk,' Daniel said, pre-empting any discussion.

Witten sat down, clearly considering the change in terms. Daniel and Alona patiently stood while he weighed the options open to him. He stood and without a word walked out the door, coming back a few moments later with another chair.

'Take a seat, Ms. Peers, and we'll go through the rest of the briefing.'

Looking back, it'd been all very quick, unlike any other operation he'd experienced, but then nobody anticipated the same level of danger as might usually have been the case. Typically, Daniel planned his assignments meticulously. Every imaginable permutation calculated and a contingency put in place to safeguard a successful outcome. But, before the clock had struck 5 p.m. on the 16th March, both Daniel and Alona had signed open-ended contracts for the duration of the investigation. How long that would be was anybody's guess. Either they caught the bad guy, or the FBI decided they'd wasted enough energy, time and money and put a real agent on the case.

Witten had briefed them on the investigation to date. Three murders. The first in Washington State where Karl Hasse's body had been found on a mountain trail, the second and third in Nevada where Andreas Lenz had been found with two gunshot wounds to his head and Jonas Otte was found stabbed to death on his hotel room. Despite the varied methods, Witten explained why the FBI believed the three murders were connected – Daniel thought they were getting ahead of themselves on that score but didn't pass comment. He had been handed an FBI Badge (fourteen-carat gold on fourteen-carat stock) complete with an eagle on top, Lady Justice in the center and the words 'Department of Justice' at the bottom. He was given a set of credentials identifying him as an 'FBI Consultant'. Witten had also provided him with a license to carry a firearm which would have been useless on its own, so he also gave him a six-round Smith & Wesson Model 30 with a four-inch barrel and a couple of cases of .32 caliber ammunition. He even threw in a light-brown, leather holster; maybe he'd been feeling generous.

Daniel had been full of hope when Alona had come to him with the prospect of a new beginning and, more importantly for his sanity, a way out of a career that he had grown to despise as the years had worn on. It had been what he wanted, the universe granting him his wish if he believed in that sort of thing, but now, after only a couple of days on the case, he wasn't sure he had made the right decision.

In truth, Daniel hadn't known what to expect when he agreed to the assignment. He had never been a policeman and never trained in the art of investigation. The only life he had known since childhood was one of hunting, killing, and evading, all of which might come in useful if the need arose, but he knew more was required in this line of work. His limitations aside, over the years he had acquired a great many skills from which he could draw, and more importantly, assembled a network of contacts across the globe that might prove useful in his newest venture; it was these that Alona had used to persuade him to take on the task. Besides, what he didn't know now, he could probably learn on the job.

And so, he had already traipsed through the wilderness of Washington State to get to the first crime scene and, the stunning scenery aside had seen nothing but bear shit, which only confirmed to him that they really did do it in the woods, after all.

The local Sheriff, a man named Joel Reed, had been his guide. He was a lean, deeply tanned man not much older than Daniel, and looked like he'd been born, lived, and would die on the side of a mountain. Reed had told him they were lucky to find the victim, after a young teenager with a small troop of scouts on their first outing of the year had wandered off the trail to relieve himself. By the time the authorities had arrived at the scene, there wasn't much of a body left to identify, most of it eaten by predators hungry after a harsh winter. An unloaded Mauser hunting rifle a few yards from the body proved to be the only method of identification. It had been hired from Harry's Gun Depot a few miles away in the city of Granger, just off Highway 82. A follow-up visit to the gun store matched the weapon with a man named Karl Hasse, a German national, who had been to the store six days before what remained of his body was discovered. Although Harry wasn't there himself, his wife Dorothy, remembered Hasse as being a tall, attractive man in his early to mid-fifties. She described the clothes he wore, which matched what little fragments had been found at the scene. Reed had informed Daniel that a Federal Agent out of Seattle had shown up at the station within twelve hours of him reporting the incident. He'd thought it strange at the time, as there was nothing to indicate a crime had been committed, let alone something that would warrant FBI involvement. One look at the file on Hasse and the agent had left without bothering to investigate further. Reed had voiced his curiosity when Daniel arrived a few days later, but Daniel had declined to comment.

The waitress appeared beside him, bringing him back to the present. She slipped him a gentle, but knowing smile, notepad, and pencil at the ready.

'Ready to order, honey?'

Daniel watched her scribble his order in some unintelligible scrawl.

'Does the staff eat here?' he asked, once she'd finished.

'Everybody 'cept the chef,' she said, her smile widening to a grin that bared a set of stain-free teeth, framed by a thick pair of flaming red lips.

Daniel glanced into the kitchen and wondered if the guy knew something the diners didn't.

'Can I get a jug of water, too?'

'Drop it right over, honey.' She placed a set of cutlery and some napkins on the table in front of him and walked away to take another order.

He slipped the menu behind a set of mismatched condiment dispensers and scanned the faces of the other customers. Most were in their mid-twenties and, if he had to guess, were from someplace other than Vegas. Judging by their doleful expressions, lady luck hadn't visited any of them during their stay. Besides, if she had, they would probably be eating someplace other than here.

Daniel's meal, a bowl of goulash and bread rolls, arrived quicker than expected, accompanied by another welcoming smile from the waitress. It looked good and smelled great; this place was filled with surprises.

He was about half-way through when the bell above the door tinkled, and a white-haired man in his late fifties entered. His eyes breezed across the faces of the patrons before settling on Daniel. He strolled across, nodding to the waitress as he passed by. He sidled into the bench opposite and placed his hands on the table, his fingers interwoven.

'So, you're the kid they sent from DC?'

Daniel regarded the man before responding. Underneath a dark, beige jacket, the guy wore an old, chequered shirt, slightly frayed around the collar, somewhat stained around the unbuttoned cuffs. A strong odor of cigar smoke clung to his clothes which failed to mask the smell of stale sweat. Day-old grey stubble coated his face, but it was the man's hands that were most noticeable. The size of small shovels, they were deeply tanned with several blood-streaked cuts along his knuckles.

'Sheriff Collins,' Daniel said. It wasn't a question, but rather a statement of fact.

Collins sat back, his forehead creasing into a frown. 'Bloody Brit. What're the fuckin' Feds playing at?'

Daniel drew a breath before replying. 'I was told the FBI had called ahead. You knew I was coming?'

'They did. They didn't tell me you were a fuckin' Tan though.'

Daniel recognized the reference, a bleak and imminently forgettable period in Britain's colonial history. The comment revealed a lot about Collins. A Gaelic bloodline with the hatred of an 800-year-old oppressor passed down by generations of ancestors. Daniel could have disclosed his Celtic ancestry, but he couldn't be bothered. If he were to justify his existence to everybody who disliked the British, he wouldn't have left the island, so he let it slide.

'I was told I could expect your full cooperation.' He looked at Collins, who had set his jaw firmly and started chewing the inside of his mouth. 'You'll have it, but I don't have to like it,' he said, eventually.

Daniel swallowed a mouthful of tea and watched as Collins' eyes traced the route of a scar on the left side of Daniel's face, which for him acted as a permanent reminder of the fragility of life.

'You seen action?'

Daniel nodded.

'Europe?'

'Most of the time.'

Collins grunted. 'One of those SOE boys, I bet.'

Daniel didn't reply. He saw no point in either confirming or denying anything to do with the part he played in the war or if he'd been a member of Britain's Special Operations Executive. Besides, he wasn't here to make small talk and didn't plan on hanging around Vegas long enough to build anything resembling a meaningful relationship with the local law enforcement.

Collins stared at him and exhaled hard. 'Alright, then. If it's gonna be like that, then let's get outta here, so you can do whatever it is the Feds want you to do.' He slid along the bench. 'Dorothy, stick that on my tab.' He thumbed back towards Daniel, who polished off his tea, but reluctantly left the half-eaten goulash.

CHAPTER 10

Daniel grabbed his belongings and followed the sheriff outside, bowing courteously to the smiling waitress as he slipped past.

Collins opened the driver's door of an off-road patrol jeep that looked like it might have seen action in North Africa in '43. He slapped the roof. 'Hop in.'

Daniel tossed his bag into the back and slid into the passenger seat next to Collins, who had already started the engine.

'Where'd you wanna start?' Collins asked, pulling onto the road.

'Thought I'd go to the two crime scenes first, then the morgue and take a look at the bodies. I presume they're still there?'

Collins half-smiled. 'Morgue freezers been broken a few days. Had to move the bodies to one of them large freezers in the Sahara Hotel; otherwise, they'd be stinking up the place.'

Daniel glanced across at him. 'You're joking.'

'I never kid around... not in this town.'

Traffic had died down, and Daniel stared at the road ahead which was more or less open, save for the handful of slower-moving cars heading away from Las Vegas, the occupants, no doubt, with their opportunistic tails set firmly between their legs. On either side of the road, the buildings started to thin out until soon they were charting a course across a boringly sandy desert mottled here and there by the odd patch of desiccated fauna.

Collins slowed down and took a tight left, continuing along a rutted dirt-track that looked and felt more like a dried-up riverbed. Much to Daniel's relief, he came to a stop a minute or so later.

Collins hopped out, with Daniel in tow. He walked a couple of yards off the track and stopped to light a cigar.

'This is where we found Lenz,' he said, flicking a finger towards the dirt in front of him. 'Not much to see.'

Daniel's eyes swept across the ground, as he strolled around the general area Collins had indicated. He methodically stepped out a grid-like search pattern, but couldn't make out anything that resembled a crime scene.

'Desert winds the past few days probably wiped the place clean,' Collins said before Daniel could say what was on his mind.

He didn't respond but kept pacing about, his eyes scanning the surface, searching for anything that might look out of place: nothing stood out.

'You get photos?'

'Yep,' Collins said.

Daniel nodded. 'I'll take a look at them later.'

Satisfied he had seen everything he needed to see on the ground, he turned his attention to the cityscape. Even in the hot light of day, the place looked wildly impressive with the main strip about 4 or 5 miles away.

'How'd you discover the body all the way out here?'

'One of the locals, an old-timer named Jed Harris, came into the station raving about seeing flashes while he was on his way home.' Collins nodded away to the right.

Daniel turned and, shielding his eyes from the glare, spotted a small bungalow nestled at the foot of a gentle incline.

'You think we could have a word with him?'

Collins stared at the city, the cigar dangling from the corner of his mouth, a steady spiral of smoke drifting in the windless air. He glanced toward the sun. 'Won't find him there this time of day.' 'Daisy's' be our best bet, I reckon.'

Daniel ran a hand over his hair. 'I'd like to take a look at his place first.'

'Sure. I got nothin' better to do today.'

Daniel couldn't tell if the comment was genuine and didn't care either way. He jumped back in the jeep and watched as Collins flicked his exhausted cigar onto the ground.

After a couple more minutes of teeth-shattering driving, they came to a shuddering stop at Jed Harris' home. It was little more than a run-down shack maybe, Daniel thought, an abandoned dwelling left behind by some prospector who had followed the gold rush westwards. The structure was wooden with a pitched roof. As seemed to be the norm in Vegas, a couple of dust-covered windows sat either side of a closed, windowless door that stood atop a shaded stoop, upon which sat an aging unvarnished rocking chair next to a small, beat-up, circular table. Several empty bottles of 'Jack Daniels' lay scattered about the deck.

'I should set up a window cleaning service here, make a damn fortune,' Daniel said.

He glanced at Collins, who appeared not to be listening, and proceeded to climb the three steps to the porch. He tried to peer through a window, but it was like trying to see the bottom of a polluted lake on a moonless night. He walked around the home, appearing next to Collins a minute later. Daniel looked back at the place for a few more seconds.

"Daisy's,' you said?' He turned and saw Collins already getting back into the jeep.

They pulled up outside a bar a short time later, the drive over conducted in silence. Daniel hopped out first, but let Collins lead the way.

It was dimly lit inside with whatever light there was failing badly to penetrate the stagnant veil of smoke that hung heavily over the handful of drunks who slouched around the bar, nursing their drinks. Collins didn't pause to look around. He strode away to the left, toward a secluded booth at the back near the toilets.

He slid in opposite a dozing, older man whose grizzled chin grazed against the top of a clutched beer bottle that moved in time to his slowly rising and falling chest. Daniel slipped in next to the sheriff.

'Afternoon, Jed,' Collins said.

The old man stirred slightly, sweeping his free hand across his face as though he was swatting away a bug.

Collins knocked on the table; it didn't elicit much more of a response.

He reached across and touched the man's hand lightly, which made the old geezer start suddenly. His eyes opened partially, then closed again. He pulled the bottle closer like a child would a teddy-bear and settled back into the seat. Collins glanced at Daniel before reaching across and snatching the bottle from the old man's grasp.

Harris's eyes shot open, a flame of anger sweeping across the two intruders. He waved his arms about wildly and half-shouted, half-mumbled some kind of protest that Daniel couldn't understand. At first, he didn't seem to recognize either of the two men, but his drunken gaze soon rested on the Sheriff.

'Glad I got your attention,' Collins said, placing the man's beer on the table. 'Wanna ask you a couple of questions.'

Jed righted himself in the seat and took a slurp before running a grubby sleeve across his mouth.

'Aw sheriff, what you want this time of day?' His voice rasped like his throat was lined with sandpaper. He took another swig of beer.

'Want to ask you about the night you found the body out near your place,' Collins said.

Harris glanced uneasily at Daniel, seemingly uncomfortable answering questions in front of somebody he didn't know.

'My brother-in-law,' Collins said. 'In for a few days to lose some money at the casinos.'

Harris didn't budge.

'Hey Danny, grab us a couple of coffees will you,' Collins said. He didn't take his eyes off the old guy.

Daniel was annoyed at the request, but it was Collins' show, and he knew how best to run it. Unfortunately, it could mean he might not be able to ask any of the questions to which he wanted answers. He looked around for a waitress.

'Ain't no fancy floor service here.' Harris smirked a toothless smile. He nodded toward the bar. Daniel shot Harris a scowl before removing himself, keeping a watchful eye on the pair while he ordered. By the looks of it, the old man had started to warm to the intrusion, his initial irritation replaced by joy as the old guy started to relax.

Daniel returned and slid a steaming mug of coffee in front of Collins and dropped a bottle of Schlitz in front of Harris before settling back into his seat with a beer of his own. Collins glanced across at him but didn't pass comment.

'You tellin' me she just slapped him across the face, in front of the whole bar?'

Harris chuckled. 'I wouldn't 'ave believed it if I hadn't been here. You shoulda seen it, Gabe. Mulroney's face turned redder than a beetroot. Don't think anybody ever stood up to him in public before… 'cept maybe you.'

Collins smiled, his hands cradling the coffee mug. He looked at Daniel.

'Old Jed here was just tellin' me 'bout what happened Sam Mulroney last night. Sam owns this fine establishment and a scoundrel if ever there was one, that right Jed?'

Harris nodded his acknowledgment, flashing a cheeky grin.

'Seems his missus found out he'd been seein' somebody else. So, she drops in last night, and the fireworks, well, they did fly.' He sipped his coffee. 'Don't know who I'd be scared of most, to be honest, Sam or Cheryl Mulroney.'

The three men sat quietly for a couple of moments before Gabe interrupted the silence. 'So, Jed. Can you go over what you said to me a couple of nights ago?'

Daniel watched the smile slowly disappear from Harris' face. He fell back in his seat.

'About what you found in the desert,' Collins prompted.

Harris tilted his head and hesitated before recounting his story.

CHAPTER 11

THE GLOOM OF THE BAR was in stark contrast to the blinding light of an afternoon sun that threatened to burn the city and its inhabitants for its sins. Daniel remained locked in thought.

Although his investigative career was in its infancy, he'd already been tossed onto a plane headed west without really knowing what to expect. He had very few acquaintances within the law enforcement community and had lost contact with most of those he did know; fighting men who'd gone into the business after the war. Even so, he wouldn't have had time to reach out for a crash course in detective procedures, and he doubted they'd have the time to pass on any salient tips anyway. If he were to continue this path, he'd have to wing it from here and try to absorb as much as he could over the coming weeks.

Two essential elements had struck him almost as soon as he'd stepped off the plane in Washington State: building relationships with the local police on the ground and utilizing the contacts they'd fostered over the years. He'd witnessed this first-hand when Sheriff Reed and the owners of Harry's Gun Depot spoke openly and plainly about their dealings with Haas, and again when Sheriff Collins and Jed Harris chatted like two buddies sucking back suds at a local tavern. Although he could never hope, nor would need, to have the same type of rapport that the sheriffs had with those in their jurisdictions, he knew he would have to cultivate a cooperative bond with those he dealt with directly. He thought back to his initial encounter with Sheriff Collins in the diner and realized he'd have to rectify the mistakes he'd made if this was going to work. He glanced sidelong at Collins.

'Never been to Nevada before, didn't expect it to be this hot.'

'There's a cooler behind the seats, got plenty of water in there if you're thirsty. You wanna grab a couple of bottles?'

Daniel did so, appreciative of the respite.

The short ride across town to the hotel where Otte and Lenz had stayed before their demise was slightly more pleasant with refreshments taken; the same couldn't be said of the hotel itself. Well off the beaten track, and the opulence of the Strip, Daniel found himself in front of a rugged, stone building that might have predated the Alamo. He followed Collins inside.

On the counter, a single whirring fan failed miserably to disperse the air which stank of stale smoke. Through the fog, a fat man lounged behind a desk, reading a tattered newspaper and chewing on the butt of a crooked cigarette. It was impossible not to notice the large sweat stains under the armpits of his light-green shirt; the source of the other odor that affronted Daniel's senses. The guy swept the crumbs of a recent lunch off his chest as they approached.

'Anyone in rooms 210 and 211?' Collins asked.

Daniel thought that an odd question given the circumstance; he was sure Collins would have sealed both rooms until the investigation was concluded, and certainly ahead of the FBI's arrival.

The guy shook his head, which led Daniel to believe that Collins' question had been asked more out of courtesy than any incompetence on the sheriff's behalf. He struck that down as another lesson on how to handle the locals.

'We're gonna head up there, give it one last look over before I release it back to you. That ok?'

The fat guy puffed his cheeks and let out a bored sigh which seemed to enrich the malodor in the room.

'Got the keys right here.' Collins jangled a pair and left.

Daniel hurried back out the door, glad that the lack of small-talk had allowed him a breath of fresh desert air. He followed Collins up the out-door stairs and along a balcony corridor to a room crudely stamped with the number 210. After fiddling, then swearing at the lock, Collins stepped aside, allowing Daniel to enter alone.

It hadn't been what he'd expected.

Except for a low, unmade double bed and a small locker on one side, the room was sparsely furnished. Two plastic chairs sat against the wall under the window, each with a small unopened suitcase on top. Gaudy, floral wall-paper that looked like it had been hung when the hotel first opened, peeled away in small sections as a mosaic of watermarks splashed across the ceiling caused, no doubt, by the infrequent but torrential desert rains. Near the back, a door stood slightly ajar leading, Daniel assumed, to the bathroom. The smells and stains left behind by past occupants and their transgressions assailed Daniel's senses, not least of which was the most recent. The carpet sucked at the soles of his shoes like quicksand, as he tread as lightly as he could across the room toward a large, dark stain on the floor. He leaned down, the rusty scent of Jonas Otte's dried blood rising to greet him. His eyes scoured the rest of the floor, but nothing distinctive stood out. Perhaps, Daniel thought, evidence had already been collected which he could examine back at the station. He stood and took a step back. He placed a hand on the unmade bed which felt so solid Daniel doubted there were any springs in the mattress.

He moved cautiously to the back of the room, careful not to stand on anything that might be considered evidence or, more likely, infect him. He pushed the bathroom door aside and peered in. It smelled of dampness and, like the rest of the room, didn't have any form of ventilation, not even a window. Other than a shower, a sink, a toilet, and a chipped mirror, it too was empty – not even a toothbrush.

He went back to the suitcases and unzipped them one at a time. He looked through each but didn't see anything in either that vacationers wouldn't have brought with them. He zipped them closed and went back to the main door. He took one last look around before joining Collins outside.

'Let's take a look at the other room,' he said, leading the way.

Collins opened room 211. Daniel took one look inside from the safety of the doorway and turned away. There were no signs of anyone, including a maid, having been in the room for several weeks, so nothing to see there.

As the Sheriff locked the door, Daniel leaned against the railings and looked at the jeep below then at the rest of the empty car park. He looked to his left and counted the row of doors which no doubt led to other rooms of similar squalor. To his immediate right, he counted the fourteen steps to the ground floor.

Collins drew up alongside him. 'What next?'

'I'd like to take a look at any evidence you gathered.'

'Sure.' Collins started to walk away.

'A lot of blood in there,' Daniel said.

Collins stopped. 'Sure is.'

'And Otte was found there?'

Collins started to light up a cigar and nodded. 'What you think?'

'Looks like both men stayed in room 210 but rented 211.' Daniel looked at Collins, who simply nodded.

'Homosexuals.'

Daniel detected no malice or disgust in the Sheriff's voice, just indifference. In fact, since Daniel's arrival, he would have described Collins's attitude to the two murders as almost casual, like a man who had seen more dead bodies than anybody ever should. Daniel could relate to that; at least they had that in common.

'Anything else?' Collins asked.

'Assuming we're looking for a lone killer, it'd be difficult for a single man, even armed, to subdue two grown men. He runs the risk of being overpowered, and the roles reversed.'

He slid his foot slowly through a fine layer of sand on the balcony floor.

'Maybe he kills Otte here, so he only has to deal with Lenz on the way out to the desert. But why not just kill both here? What did he have to gain by separating them? It's a lot more dangerous to transport a man to his death after he'd just seen his lover killed.'

He paused.

'Unless the two weren't together when Otte was murdered.' He tickled the handrail with his fingertips, as he thought. 'Otte is killed first, and the killer waits in the car park for Lenz, or maybe that sequence in reverse.'

A glint of appreciation sparked in Collins' eye. He almost looked impressed with the assessment, which made Daniel feel like he hadn't said anything too ridiculous. He looked beyond the car park toward the nearby hotels that lined each side of Las Vegas Boulevard.

'Wonder why two relatively wealthy men would stay in a dump like this so far from The Strip?' he said, before immediately answering his own question. 'Maybe, so they didn't attract any unwanted attention, and have you haul them off for breaking sodomy laws.'

He turned to Collins. 'You think maybe this was a hate crime? Somebody who wanted to rid the world of a pair of queers?'

'It's a possibility, can't rule it out.'

It certainly seemed to fit but then, why had he been told that these two murders were linked to that of Hasse in Washington State? Other than the fact that all three men were from Germany and had been brought to America by the government, they had nothing else in common. Even Hasse's autopsy had failed to determine a cause of death. So, what did the FBI know that they weren't sharing and, more importantly, why weren't they sharing it? Was Daniel's involvement merely cursory, an investigative deception performed for the sole purpose of appeasing a superior? Maybe, it was why they had asked him in the first place, to hire somebody with no experience in this field, so they could point the finger at his incompetence when he returned empty-handed. But, that didn't make sense either as his failure would reflect poorly on their judgment to contract him in the first place. There had to be another unseen dimension to the investigation that might reveal itself as he progressed.

'We done here?' Collins asked. 'Suppose you wanna see the bodies?'

'I suppose so.'

They pulled up outside The Sahara Hotel a couple of minutes later. Collins left the jeep running for the valet and made a bee-line for the concierge inside. He asked to see the manager who didn't have them waiting long.

Denis Johnson was a tall, tanned man who had more hair on his chin than on the crown of his head intentionally shaved which projected a powerful and frightening image to any who might happen across his path; any who did never found it an enjoyable experience. He wore a sharp, crisp suit, shirt, and tie, all black which made him stand out from the two men who flanked him; their shirts were white.

He slipped his hands behind his back as he approached, choosing to greet Daniel and Collins with a scowl that would melt steel.

'Get those bodies out of my hotel.' His voice hissed. He had kept it low, but not low enough to prevent a couple of nearby guests flash concerned looks before realizing they were too close to a conversation that, perhaps, they shouldn't overhear. They shuffled away without looking back.

Daniel thought it unusual that a man with a vested interest in the entertainment business should be so reckless by any negative public relations. He glanced sidelong at Collins who didn't seem unduly displeased by Johnson's ferocity. In fact, it looked like he was quite enjoying it.

'Only a day or so more, Denis. We gotta guy working on the problems at the morgue.'

Johnson shot a venomous look at Daniel. 'This him?'

'Nope. He's an investigator from DC, come down to give us a hand.'

'You bring a Fed into my place, Gabriel?'

Daniel could feel Johnson's disgusted gaze hover over him and, sweating through a tee-shirt he had put on more than twenty-four hours ago, suddenly felt underdressed for the occasion. An awkward silence settled across the group, disturbed only by the artificial sounds of musical slot machines, coins tinkling metal trays, and a lone pianist playing to a handful of disinterested drinkers in a nearby bar. Johnson looked back at Collins.

'Billy will take you to the fridges.'

Daniel looked between Denis' two sidekicks and tried to tell to which of them he was referring; he would have been better off tossing a coin. The guy to Denis' right stepped to one side.

'Please follow me, gentlemen,' he said, his tone not in keeping with the general hostility bestowed upon them by his boss. He started to walk away with Collins and Daniel a couple of steps behind.

'If they're not out of my hotel by the time I've finished breakfast tomorrow, I'll bury them in the desert myself,' Denis called out. That sent another couple of guests scurrying in the direction of the blackjack tables. Collins waved a dismissive hand.

Whatever about Denis Johnson's antagonistic way with the local law enforcement, he seemed to run a pretty tight ship in the Sahara. As they marched through the hotel, Daniel watched smartly-dressed waiters deliver trays of piping hot delicacies to the tables of the hungry, as pretty, short-skirted waitresses flitted about the casino, depositing free drinks next to the non-playing hands of the smoking gamblers, all of whom seemed hell-bent on allowing themselves to be legally robbed for an opportunity to beat the house. It was a curious thing Daniel thought, very few came away with more money than they had entered and yet everybody smiled. It seemed the handing over of their savings was the price they paid for that enjoyment.

As Billy led them through the kitchen doors and to the refrigerators beyond, Daniel regarded their guide. He must have been almost six and a half feet tall and a couple of hundred pounds. In his experience, men like that weren't hired for any specific skills other than intimidation; in some lines of work, it was better to prevent an aggressive action rather than become embroiled in one, especially where the outcome might be less than assured. Besides, although bulk had its benefits, it also had its drawbacks.

They moved through the kitchens, where scores of white-coated chefs swarmed between tables of raw vegetables and meats in various stages of preparation. Billy led Daniel and Collins to the last in a line of industrial-sized fridge doors. He grabbed hold of a large, metal handle and, with ease, pulled the door aside, allowing a rush of cold, but not freezing air to escape.

The inside looked exactly like every other hotel refrigerator Daniel had ever seen; large and rectangular with shelved walls upon which sat unopened cans and boxes of fruit and vegetables. What made it different were the two gurneys in the middle of the walkway upon which was the only meat.

'Don't care much for contamination?' Daniel said. He glanced at Billy, who replied with only a smirk. Collins didn't add anything, so Daniel pushed on towards the first covered body. He pulled the plastic sheet away and revealed the late Andreas Lenz, which meant the other one was Jonas Otte. He moved in for a closer look.

He scanned Lenz's naked body for distinguishing marks, his eyes settling on a small tattoo on the inside of the man's left arm. Continuing, he allowed his eyes to dwell for a moment on what remained of the man's face. As he placed his hands on the head, Collins reached out.

'Can't touch the body, I'm afraid.'

'This'll only take a second,' Daniel said, ignoring the Sheriff's instruction.

Collins paused before allowing Daniel to continue. Daniel twisted the head to one side so he could see the back.

'Entry wound. Small caliber bullet. Close range. See here,' he said. He made a circle around the perimeter of the hole. 'Singed. Coroner should be able to get residue from there. Gun was placed right up against the guy's head.'

'Made sure he wasn't gonna miss,' Collins muttered. He shot Daniel a disdainful glance as though he had never considered it.

Daniel returned the head to its initial position and looked at the exit wound, a cavernous hole a little larger than a clenched fist on the left side of Lenz's face where the cheekbone and eye would have been. Particles of light grey brain tissue clung to tattered edges of the skin that had been ripped aside as the bullet had exploded from within, mining its way through the head. It was little comfort, Daniel thought, that the man wouldn't have suffered, save for the emotional turmoil he would have endured in the moments leading up to the pulled trigger.

'Here's what we collected at the scene.' Collins grabbed a small plastic bag from the end of the trolley and deposited it on the side.

Daniel held it up to the light streaming in from the kitchen outside. He could make out bits of an eye, some bone attached to lumps of skin, more brain tissue, and a mixture of blood and other fluids. His attention was momentarily drawn to the look on Billy's face, the kind that somebody would have if they were pleased with their handiwork. He said nothing and continued his examination.

'Were the bullet and cartridge recovered?' he asked, switching his attention back to Collins.

'Being processed back in the lab.'

'That's good.' Daniel was impressed. He had thought Vegas too small to be capable of performing ballistics tests of its own. He passed the bag back to Collins and glimpsed a smirk splash across the Sheriff's face. 'Was that funny?'

'This isn't DC. The lab isn't what you think it is.'

'I haven't seen any other, so can't compare,' he said, running his fingers down the body and leaning in to examine Lenz's legs. After a moment, he stood back. 'Now, that is unusual.'

'I thought so too.'

'Both Achilles tendons have been sliced through.' Daniel tilted his head to one side. 'I guess it's difficult to run when that happens. OK. That's enough of Mr. Lenz.'

He pulled the plastic sheet back over the carcass to protect what was left of the dead man's modesty and turned to the other body. He uncovered Jonas Otte.

Daniel stopped.

His eyes were immediately drawn to the man's groin and in particular, the bloody gaping hole where his genitals should have been. Daniel shot a startled look toward Collins.

'This wasn't in the report.'

'No. Thought I'd leave it until the coroner finished up.'

'Important detail. Makes it look like a sex killing.'

Collins stuffed his hands in his pockets and grunted. 'Maybe, that's all it is.'

Daniel didn't reply. He looked back to the body. Unlike Lenz, Otte had received multiple stab wounds to his chest and abdomen, any one of which might have been the fatal strike; an expert would have to decide which one. Daniel searched the man's arm for the same tattoo that Lenz had but came up short.

'Good looking guy,' Daniel said to himself. 'Kept himself in shape, just like Lenz.' He shook his head. 'Nothing else of note here.' He recovered the body.

Collins shrugged and started outside. He patted their escort on the arm. 'Thanks for your help, Billy. You can tidy up. We'll let ourselves out.'

Billy didn't look all that sure about leaving the Sheriff and his side-kick meander about the hotel unaccompanied, but both Collins and Daniel had moved to the kitchen door and were gone before he could object or make a move to stop them.

They retraced their steps in silence before re-entering the casino floor. Daniel stopped.

'Look, Sheriff, I don't know what's eating you, but I've been sent here to help get to the bottom of these murders. I'm not here to step on anybody's toes.'

Collins turned to face him. 'And the big wigs in DC don't think we're capable of doing that by ourselves?'

Although his voice was calm, Daniel still detected an underlying resentment; perhaps, his investigative skills were improving, after all. He gently rubbed the back of his hand along the underside of his chin, weighing up an appropriate response that wouldn't annoy Collins further; he had to build bridges and work with the guy, somehow.

Daniel thought for a moment. Special Agent Witten had instructed him not to disclose anything of the murders, and what linked them, to

anybody. But, what was discussed in the confines of a Washington bu-
reaucrat's office didn't necessarily translate into what had to be done in
the field. Every situation had to be taken on its merits, assessed, and the
appropriate action taken. It didn't take him long to decide it would be
advantageous to bring the sheriff in on some of what he knew; people
always responded well to knowing things that would remain secret to
others.

'There's more to this than you know.'

'Really? Like I hadn't figured that out as soon as I got off the phone
with Special Agent 'whatever-the-fuck-his-name-was' yesterday. We
rarely have the privilege of a visit from the Feds, so when they come
snooping, I'd like to think they're not wasting either my time or theirs.
So, it's generally for a damned good reason, and I'd like to know what
that is.'

He stared hard at Daniel, who didn't show any emotion. If Collins
thought playing the bad cop routine was going to intimidate the younger
man into divulging some nuggets of information, then he was wasting
his time. Daniel had faced tougher interrogators than that of a small-
town sheriff, leaving them crimson with exasperation, his secrets intact.
But, Collins wasn't an enemy and, like Daniel, was trying to get to the
bottom of the killings, even if his motivations were different.

'Sheriff, can I call you Gabe?' Daniel waited for a reply, but getting
none, pushed ahead. 'The Feds think there's a serial killer on the loose.
The two killings in Vegas are the second and third murders they've been
able to link.'

'You saying there's another outside the town?'

'Outside the state.' Daniel paused. 'I can't imagine what goes on
out here. Hundreds of miles from anywhere, this place really is the
last frontier. I bet you see all sorts. But, you're only seeing a small
part of what might be going on.' He paused again, biting his lower
lip. 'I'll tell you what I know. Maybe, we can work the two cases
together?'

Collins nodded after a time and led the way out of the hotel. Despite his scowl at the valet who scurried off to retrieve the jeep, he seemed a little more pleased than before.

'Back to the station?'

Daniel nodded. 'Sure. I need a coffee to cleanse my palette after that.'

Chapter 12

The night air had dripped with moisture, until the deluge swept in from the east, removing the dampness and forcing the airborne insects that infested Georgia at this time of year to seek temporary shelter, insects that would return to hunt, and feed, and mate as soon as the downpour subsided.

Parked in the darkness between a pair of street lamps, a man sat in a car, an inconspicuous 1951 black Buick Special; inconspicuous, that was, compared with other vehicles that edged the tree-lined boulevard.

Across the street, nestled behind a freshly trimmed lawn, sat an ornate, two-story American Foursquare. A large willow wept away to one side, its branches swaying lightly, brushing leaves against the side of the house, licking it with rain-water.

He had been staring at the house since the couple had entered. That'd been before the rain had come. He mapped their progress as, one by one, lights and lamps were turned on from porch to landing. The bedroom had remained in darkness, the only sign of life, the faint silhouette of clothes being eagerly discarded.

That was more than an hour ago.

The man glanced at a half-pack of Junos on the seat next to him, but he turned away. He couldn't risk revealing himself, so he would wait until he had done what he had come to do. Through the refracting film of water on the windscreen, he scanned the road again. The neighborhood was quiet and at peace. He checked his watch. If the man stuck to his routine, he would be done shortly, maybe another fifteen minutes, slightly longer if he showered and washed away the other woman's scent before going home to his wife.

A car approached, its tires squelching on the soaked asphalt. Making no sudden movement, the man slowly sunk into the shadow of his seat. It passed, the grizzly hum of its engine fading as it disappeared into the night.

The rain began to lighten, and his eyes fell to a small pool of water on the 'sidewalk' – an American expression, they were footpaths everywhere else.

He hated the Americans.

Barely touched by the war a decade before, they had jitterbugged as Europe and Asia had burned. He found it ironic if not hypocritical that one of their dead presidents had referred to a sunny December day as a 'day of infamy'. What would he have said to the hundreds of thousands who had died at his country's hands in the blasted cities of Dresden, Hamburg, and Hiroshima?

His mind began to drift, and he did nothing to prevent it. His thoughts went to his family as they always did when he had time to reflect. He knew he thought about them more than he should but equally knew that their everlasting memory and the accompanying grief allowed him to maintain focus whenever he felt himself waning from the task. He had met Lena in Cologne in 1935 before enlisting in the new Wehrmacht. Pregnancy followed a whirlwind romance, and so he had done the decent thing and married her before she gave birth to their son Felix. Two years later, and they were blessed with another child, who they named Claudia. The perfect family, people, had said. They were taken away from him on the morning of 31st May 1942. The flame of pain he felt the day news came to him of their deaths still burned as bright today as it had then.

He slid a hand into a jacket pocket and pulled out a folded photo, the edges slightly tattered, a single creased line down the center. He had many photographs, but this was his favorite, the one he carried with him everywhere. He ran a finger across the yellowing matte finish, tracing the austere face of his wife, their infant daughter cradled in her arms, and their smiling son standing next to her. He could feel the anger build; his chest tighten, his breathing become shallow.

He allowed it to consume him

He was wrenched back to reality by a light spilling from an open doorway to his right. The man was leaving. He slipped the photo back into his pocket and prepared himself.

Anton Segal turned around and looked at the woman. 'Tomorrow?'

Alice smiled, the corners of her eyes curled with a temptress' sparkle. 'Take me somewhere nice for dinner, then we'll see,' she said. She reached out, pulled Anton closer, and kissed him.

Her full, soft lips, the taste of her lipstick, and the scent of the expensive foreign fragrance he had given her fused with a hint of after-sex sweat to form an electrifying aphrodisiac. The sexual energy that had been expelled minutes ago, coursed through Anton's body once again. He leaned in closer and wrapped his arms around her, his fingers searching beneath the pastel-colored negligée, caressing the smooth curves of her lower back.

She pushed him away. 'You have to go,' she said, still smiling.

He took a reluctant step back toward the path, his hand lingering in hers for a moment. He withdrew it slowly, as Alice backed away to the shelter of the doorway. He bowed gently before trotting away, his jacket slung across his shoulder.

He always felt the same whenever he left her, an old man reborn, revitalized with the enthusiasm of a youth passed; what he wouldn't give to change his life to that which better suited his needs and desires. He had thought about it too, more than he should have, more than was good for his marriage or what remained of it. Whisking her away in the dead of night, leaving his wife and the foreign government for whom he now worked. He could use his contacts, close acquaintances from his birth country of another era. Like him, some had managed to obtain safe passage to faraway places, unlike him, their manner of travel had been much different.

He retrieved a set of keys from a trouser pocket and jumped into his car, stowing his jacket on the seat next to him. He started up the engine and pulled out onto the road.

It would only take a couple of phone calls, a few well-chosen words with the right people, and he would never be found. He could live out the rest of his life in luxury with a woman who captivated and exhilarated him in equal measure.

After several blocks, he took a left, followed by a right.

But then, perhaps his life wasn't all that bad either. He had a wife he tolerated, a mistress he could fuck whenever he desired, a well-paid job he enjoyed most of the time and a spacious and elegant home provided by his employers. He wanted for nothing – the Americans had seen to that, they had made him comfortable, but had they made him soft? Was he too old to care anymore?

He stopped at an intersection, and through the tunnel of trees, looked left, then right before making the turn. A car glided past him, causing him to swerve and slow down before he resumed his journey home.

He thought it ironic that, despite all the security protocols in place, he could still manage to communicate easily with his old friends. The rage and bitterness for the Germans that had exploded less than a decade before had been replaced by the fear of a color that represented an ideal antagonistic to that held by the Americans. Their focus had shifted and relieved some of the pressure he had felt when he had first moved here.

He pulled up next to the curb and shut off the engine. He looked sidelong at his home. The living room light was still on; she was still awake. He felt dampness under his armpits, and he swore. He rolled down the window and allowed the cooler outside air to enter. It carried with it the cacophony of nature's night-time orchestra, a distant dog's bark, and a melody from a radio or television someplace.

Anton stared at his keys and promised himself he would only wait a little while, maybe until she had turned off the lights and he had allowed her sufficient time to prepare for bed and fall asleep. He hated her. He hated this place, hated his new life. He wanted to escape. He would start making plans tomorrow, making calls to his old friends, get things moving, and start anew.

He glanced back toward his home but froze, his eyes wide in terror.

The man pulled the trigger. The suppressor hissed. And Anton's head rocked sideways, blood, brain, and pieces of skull speckling the inside of the car. Anton's lifeless body slumped onto the passenger seat, as blood leaked from him, pooling in the footwell.

The man quietly returned the gun beneath his jacket. He paused as though admiring his handiwork, before reaching in and snatching the keys from Anton's fingers. He ripped the key-ring off and tossed the bunch back into the car. Bringing it closer to his eyes, he studied it. He had never considered collecting trophies, but a blood-red metallic disc with a black Swastika emblazoned on a white background would be an excellent place to start.

CHAPTER 13

THEY ENTERED THROUGH THE REAR of the station, the jeep parked out back. The same deputy, sitting in the same position, reading the same paper, barely acknowledged their arrival. Daniel couldn't make out if he'd even turned the page. They walked to the back of the building and around a corner, out of sight of any would-be customers.

'Coffee?' Collins headed over to a counter that sat next to a wall and poured himself a mug from an old stainless steel pot.

Daniel took one look at the sludge that seeped from it and declined. He watched Collins empty the last of a canister of sugar and stir it in with a partially chewed pencil he'd found lying on the counter.

'Probably an Earl Grey kinda guy,' Collins said, under his breath, but loud enough for Daniel to hear. 'OK, this way.' He led Daniel past a pair of rooms that faced each other labeled 'Interrogation Room 1 & 2', to an office that had 'Sheriff' written neatly on the door.

Daniel took a moment to look around as Collins sat behind a desk that was slightly too large for the space in which it stood. It faced the door and anybody who entered having business with the Sheriff. Behind Collins, and to one side, a small wooden bookcase stood against the back wall, displaying a host of classics by Dickens, Tolstoy, and Wells, to name only three. A variety of reference books ranging from 'The Penal System and Recidivism' to 'A Handyman's Guide to Fixing Your Car' stood by themselves on a lower shelf. A couple of grey, paint-chipped filing cabinets each with four drawers stood on the other side – the top drawer labeled 'Ongoing' was partially open. An old couch lay against the wall to Daniel's right and next to it, a small wooden locker; it's door ajar. Inside, Daniel spied some folded up blankets and a small pillow. He guessed Collins probably spent more than a few nights a week curled up here instead of going home if indeed he had a home. Hanging on the wall above the couch, the only spark of color in the room was an oil painting of the Grand Canyon, depicting a sunrise or a sunset; difficult to know which. Daniel's eyes moved to the desk which had a reading lamp, a large notepad, and an assortment of pens and pencils and, oddly, a copy of James Joyce's 'Ulysses', open, but face down. Daniel wondered if it was deliberately on display, as he knew of few people who had managed to get through the first chapter, let alone claim to have finished the entire thing.

'You reading that?' Daniel asked.

Collins followed Daniel's eye line. 'Trying. My Latin isn't so good.' A wry smile swept across his face. 'The product of a Catholic education. My school didn't teach Latin, so it fell to my father who had learned from his father before that.'

Daniel could feel Collins watch him over the rim of his mug. 'You?'

'Catholic, same as you, no Latin in my school either,' Daniel said. 'I went to a small village school with one teacher per year. Their range of subjects wouldn't be extensive, but what they knew, they taught well.' He shuffled on his feet. 'If you want to read Joyce, maybe try 'Portrait of the Artist' or 'Dubliners'?'

Out of the corner of his eye, he caught Collins try to hide a smile.

He scanned the other walls and the framed black and white photos that adorned them. Walking closer to one, he admired the duo standing either side of the Sheriff; Jerry Lewis and Dean Martin. His gaze floated across another photo of Collins draped in the glittering fashion of Liberace, the world-famous pianist planting a kiss on the shocked-looking Sheriff's cheek. He couldn't tell if the reaction was authentic or faked for the camera. There were other photos too all of the Sheriff and somebody else that Daniel didn't recognize.

'You get your photo taken with every celebrity who comes to town?'

'Sometimes.' Collins sipped his coffee. 'You were going to tell me a story? You said there was another killing that the Feds think is connected to the two I got?'

Daniel scanned one or two other photos before taking the seat opposite Collins. He placed his bag carefully on his lap and crossed his arms on top before telling the sheriff about his trip to Washington State and what he'd learned there.

After Daniel finished, Collins sipped his coffee, set his jaw, and shook his head. 'I don't get it? What connects my two bodies to your one? You don't even know if yours was a murder. Could've been a suicide or maybe the guy was attacked by a bear. The mountains can be dangerous places if you don't know what you're doing.'

'I guess if the two bodies hadn't cropped up here, then the Feds might have drawn the same conclusion. But something has them spooked. They moved fast to send me out west.'

'You haven't told me how they're connected?'

Daniel leaned forward, his face stern and severe. 'All three were German scientists during the war. The government relocated them here as much to prevent the Soviets from getting their hands on them as to use their intellect to help further any scientific programs that were being worked on here.'

'I'd heard rumors,' Collins said, 'and read the speculation in some of the bigger papers. We don't get a lot of those out here though, so I never kept up with the story.'

Daniel made a small slacking sound with his tongue. Thirst had crept up on him caused, he figured, by the desert air.

'Cooler over there,' Collins said, nodding just out the door to his right.

Daniel put his bag on the ground and slipped out, filling and drinking a full cup before refilling and returning to the office.

'They're serious, alright. They've put security on any others they believe to be potential targets.'

Collins sat upright. 'That's a lot of effort even for the Feds. They must've identified a solid connection between the living and the dead, and if they've made the connection, then they must have some idea who the perpetrator is.'

'That's what I thought too, but they're not sharing much more.' Daniel looked beyond Collins. 'I'm expendable.'

They fell silent for a moment, the only sound coming from the whirring fan out in the main office.

'You're not a fully signed-up agent?' Collins frowned. 'I'm guessing some kinda contractor hired to dig around a bit and report back?'

'Yeah, I'm just here to investigate what I can, examine the evidence, and report what I find to Washington.'

Collins gulped another mouthful of coffee and ran a hand across his bristling head. Daniel could feel an awkward question brewing.

'They could've sent anybody if all they wanted was a run-of-the-mill investigation. There's something you're not telling me.'

Daniel sat back, focusing on Collins. 'I get paid to do a job. I'm briefed, told what to do, and what's required of me. I don't ask questions.'

'OK. Maybe they haven't told you anything else, or maybe you're not going to tell me anything, but this doesn't feel right.'

'It never feels right,' Daniel said. He looked down.

The people who usually hired him played a game that had rules they abided by until they no longer worked to their advantage. That's when they tweaked them or invented new ones that suited their needs better. It was a necessity. They maintained their distance, never exposed themselves, and continually manipulated circumstances for their benefit, steering clear of the dangers they imposed on those who did their bidding; people like Daniel. The game was about power, maintaining it, and staying one or, indeed, several steps ahead of the competition. As for the opposition, they came in many forms, cropped up in many places, sometimes emerging from within the same organization. There was a time when he loathed the game, hated himself for playing it. But, in truth, he didn't play. He was moved about; an insignificant pawn marooned on a global chessboard of deceit and deception.

He ran a hand across the back of his neck and made a move to stand. 'I'm going to check in at my hotel and grab some food. How long for ballistics to come through?'

Collins checked his watch. 'Too late now, it'll be tomorrow morning.'

Daniel sighed, and Collins sat forward. 'Look, these two homicides aren't the only things I'm dealing with at the moment. Some fuckers still think it's the wild west out here and they can do whatever the hell they want. And, sometimes they try to do just that, that's where I come in. I maintain order in a society intent on lawlessness. I juggle so much shit I should work in a sanitation plant. So, when a couple of dead bodies show up in the middle of the desert, I investigate as much as I can and pass it along for the white coats to do their bit. If something turns up, swell, but I won't lose sleep over either those lost souls or whatever errand you're on. We're detached from the bureaucrats in Washington, a remote outpost that nobody gives a fuck about.'

'Until now,' Daniel said. He held up his hands, conceding the point.

'Until now.' Collins agreed. 'You got somewhere to stay?'

'Yeah, they put me up in the Flamingo.'

'Spared no expense,' Collins said, and with a smirk added, 'Maybe ask around some, you might find out something over there.'

Daniel gave him a knowing look. He'd done his research before he'd arrived and knew all about the people who owned and ran the hotels and casinos. He'd even gone so far as to gather information that wasn't on the record. What he'd found hadn't surprised him given the money that was being generated in the city by an entire range of enterprises the legality of which depended on how busy the Sheriff was. In other words, keep doing what you're doing if you don't get caught. He picked up his bag and headed for the door.

'You could catch a show while you're in town, maybe get your photo taken too,' Collins said.

Daniel could hear the sarcasm in Collins' voice but didn't respond.

It took less than the time to boil an egg for Daniel to hail a cab and have it drop him outside the Flamingo. It didn't seem all that far from the

Sheriff's office, which was another reason for Collins to be happy, Daniel thought. As soon as he entered the foyer, he again felt underdressed. All the male employees wore black bow-tie suits, which in this weather said a lot about the image the owners wanted to project. Check-in at reception was swift, with the receptionist barely noticing Daniel's ragged appearance.

As soon as he opened the door to his room, he threw his bag on the bed, climbed out of his sticky clothes, and headed straight for the shower where he spent the next twenty minutes cleaning twenty-four hours of grit and sweat from his pores. His skin was red when he stepped out.

He walked across to the French windows which opened onto the balcony and stood naked, drying in the shade of a large, potted palm tree that hid his modesty from the sunbathers down by the pool. If anyone saw him, he'd be having an altogether different conversation with Sheriff Collins.

He'd been given a room on the top floor of the hotel, which meant it was on the second floor; Las Vegas was no New York; that was for sure. It was a city that'd taken roots in the flats of the Nevada desert, an enormous sprawl with large swathes of desolate and unbroken land between the hotels that'd already been built. As Daniel looked around, he did not doubt that expansion would be swift both outwards and upwards. He didn't envy Collins the job he'd have controlling the accompanying increase in crime over the coming years. The small police force would have to grow in line with the city, and he wondered if maybe this was where a new opportunity lay. He thought about it but shook his head. It was just too damn hot.

Once he'd dried off, he went back into his room and slipped on a pair of boxers. He lay on the bed, the lace curtains, fluttering softly in the warm breeze.

And so, seventy-two hours, three and half thousand air miles and a few meager hours shut-eye later, Daniel closed his eyes and drifted away with a clear conscience.

CHAPTER 14

DANIEL WAS AWAKENED BY A sharp knock on the door. He looked around the darkened room, twisting his arm and struggling to see his watch in the small amount of light coming through the windows.

The knocking came again.

A red-faced young woman faced him when he answered.

'Hi, I'm Julie from reception. We've been trying to call you, but we kept getting an engaged tone.'

Daniel looked back to the cabinet beside the bed and the phone which rested next to the cradle – a failed attempt to ensure some quiet now that the receptionist had called to his door.

'Sheriff Collins called. He asked that you go back to the station to-night.' She was a young woman, barely out of her teens and, judging by her bluster, either not used to dealing with the local authorities or having to knock on guest's doors.

Daniel nodded. 'Can you arrange a courtesy car?'

'Of course.' She turned and walked away, a little bounce in her step as though she'd single-handily averted an international crisis.

Daniel arrived at the station less than fifteen minutes later. There was a different deputy seated at the muster desk, an older man who looked like he wouldn't have been out of place puffing on cigars and swilling brandy at an 'old-boys' club in central London. Unfortunately for him, he was working the graveyard shift in the Las Vegas Sheriff's Office, instead. Daniel asked for Sheriff Collins and was shown through to his office.

'You had a call from, Ms. Alona Peers,' he said. 'You've to call her back.'

Daniel detected curiosity in the man's voice. He wondered why she hadn't called him at the hotel and figured she had new information about the investigation that he could share with Collins. He checked his watch. It was almost 11 p.m. local time, which meant it was nearly 2 am in Washington; she was working late. He debated waiting until morning, rather than disrupt a sleeping home, but she'd called and woke him up, so it was only fair that he reciprocate.

'May I?' He indicated the phone on Collins's desk.

'You want me to leave?'

Daniel shook his head. 'Might be useful for you to hear what she has to say.'

He dialed the operator, who patched him through. Alona answered on the second ring. After a quick exchange of pleasantries, Daniel told her that Collins was in the room.

'Fine. What I have concerns him too.'

Daniel listened while Collins waited for the update.

'The FBI has identified a further two missing scientists, an Aurik Bauer, and an Erich Werner, neither have been seen since Thursday 12th March. Both had been relocated by the JIOA in 1946. Their bodies haven't turned up, yet.'

'That's over a week ago.' Daniel said. 'What the hell has the FBI been doing?' He sighed and closed his eyes. 'Why do the Feds believe these are victims, too?'

Alona paused before answering. 'I'm told that both were men of routine, punctual to a fault. They haven't shown up to work and haven't been seen by their wives. Nobody has had any communication with them.'

Daniel looked across at Collins. His head was down as he picked at his fingernails. He could feel the enthusiasm to solve the two Vegas murders dissipate from the older man. If he hadn't known before that the FBI was in charge, he did now. With his shoulders sinking, he looked a deflated and beaten man.

'Where were they last seen?' Daniel asked.

'They both worked for Pittsburgh Medical School, researching vaccines for whooping cough, diphtheria, and polio, but that's not important. Both attended a card game at a colleague's house, but never arrived home after it'd finished.'

'And the colleague?'

'Howard Andersen. He was questioned by local police, but they released him without charge as his alibi held up to examination.'

'Which was?' Daniel said.

'He was at the emergency department with another colleague, Norman Swain, who had been at the same card game. It seems Swain had drunk too much and vomited blood and pretzels all over Mr. Andersen's living-room floor.'

'No chance Andersen and Swain could have worked together and killed Bauer and Werner before their trip to the hospital?'

'No. As I said, both Bauer and Werner were men of habit. They always stopped off at an all-night café for tea after the card games. This was well known. The waitress there was questioned by the police, and she confirmed she'd served them at a time which matched that of the emergency department admissions clerk for Andersen and Swain.' She paused a moment. 'Oh, hold on. There's another call coming through.'

The line went silent.

Daniel recounted the story to Collins. 'What do you think?'

Collins sighed. 'This is bigger than I thought it was going to get,' he said. 'A couple of queers getting stabbed and shot is all it seemed to be. Looks like a helluva lot more than that, now. There's not much I can do 'cept try and gather more evidence from my two homicides. Hopefully, it'll help you with the other cases.'

Daniel noticed that Collins's tone had become less frosty, detecting an almost conciliatory quality in his voice. He could see now that the man was simply a small-town Sheriff who was struggling to get to grips with a growing crime rate in a place he clearly loved, but which had outgrown him. He was a proud man, but it looked like he was about to throw in the towel and let a younger generation take over. He was powerless to slow down what others called progress as the world he knew slipped away. He was a laboring dinosaur, and his world was on the verge of extinction.

The line crackled to life again.

'That was Witten. There's been another one, a shooting, this time in Atlanta. He just got the call from the local field-office leading the investigation down there, so he hasn't any more details yet. They told him they would pass on regular updates once they had more.'

Daniel leaned back in his seat and ran his hands through his hair. He looked across at Collins and mouthed 'another one' and could tell what the older man was thinking. How come the FBI hadn't secured all the scientists they'd relocated to the US by now? Collins didn't look like he was going to add anything to the conversation, so Daniel decided to wrap it up.

'OK, Alona. It's late. You get off to bed. You'll be up early with Anthony.'

'What are your plans now?' she asked before hanging up.

'Not sure at the moment. The Sheriff and I will talk a bit. I'll ring you in the morning with a plan.' He was tempted to add an 'I hope'.

They signed off, and the two men looked at each other for some time.

'Any chance I can get one of those coffees you offered?' Daniel asked. He needed time alone to think.

Collins smiled for the first time since Daniel had returned to the station. He slipped out, leaving Daniel to ponder both the direction of the investigation and the sudden increase in body count.

With the murder in Georgia, the two missing men (presumed dead) in Pennsylvania, and the killings in Oregon and Nevada, the victims were scattered right across the country. For the first time, Daniel agreed with Witten in assuming they were related and committed by the same person or group, particularly when compared with the deaths to date of all those who'd been transported from Germany after the war. When they'd met, Witten had said that of the 1,500 who'd made the trip, only thirteen had died before the start of this year. Excluding one guy who'd been mangled in a car crash, and another who'd broken his neck on a skiing trip, the remaining eleven had died of natural causes. The FBI had been right in taking over the investigation from each local police department, as they were the only government agency with the jurisdiction and manpower to collate the evidence gathered from each murder scene in the hope of finding a link that would lead them to the capture of the killer.

Collins reappeared, carrying two mugs. He handed one to Daniel.

'So, what do we know?'

Daniel sipped the coffee, which looked and tasted like sweetened tar and, like last time, he wondered how long the pot had been left stewing. He didn't pass comment.

'The number of dead is on the rise, and I've no reason to believe it won't increase,' he said.

'The FBI that bad at protecting people?'

'Seems so. Maybe the urgency of the situation wasn't fully appreciated by the various field offices charged with ensuring their safety.'

'Maybe some couldn't give a rat's arse if a bunch of Germans was killed. There's still a lot of hatred towards them since the war.'

Daniel shrugged. He wasn't aware of anyone openly despising the Germans for having dragged the world into a war, but a lot of Americans had died in the European theatre of operations, so it wasn't unreasonable to assume that there were those who still harbored grudges. Whether they worked for the federal government and would disregard a direct order from Washington was another question.

'What are you going to do now?' Collins asked.

'I've seen all there is to see I think, and you've got the investigation here covered, so I'm wasting both our times hanging around.'

'You gonna head to Atlanta?'

'It seems the reasonable course of action,' Daniel said. 'It's the most recent crime scene, and I could learn something that might not be in the official report sent back to Witten. That wasn't meant as a jibe.' He smiled at Collins.

Collins placed his coffee on the desk and picked up the phone, which he cradled after a brief exchange with somebody, Daniel assumed, out at McCarran Field.

'First flight out of here is 6.15 a.m., which goes to Los Angeles,' Collins said. 'You can't get a direct flight to Atlanta, but there is a United Airlines DC6 departing 8.07 a.m. for Meacham Field, Dallas. You should be able to pick up a connection to Atlanta from there if you ring ahead.'

Daniel stood. It was near midnight and, despite the caffeine, he still wanted to get some sleep before being subjected to the misery of another attack of jetlag; he was pretty sure he hadn't fully recovered from the flight to the west coast in the first place. He extended his hand, which Collins shook warmly.

'Nice to meet you, Sheriff. I'll update you with the rest of the investigation if anything new turns up.'

'Like another dead body?'

'Yeah, something like that.'

'I'll send you on the ballistics and autopsy reports when I get them,' Collins said. 'There may be something useful in there.'

The two men said their goodbyes and Daniel left for the Flamingo to pack his bag.

CHAPTER 15

STANDING ON THE RAISED TEE of the Par 3 2nd of the Old Colonial Golf Club bestows upon each player a magnificent view of the Potomac, as it streaks south-east through Virginia and into Chesapeake Bay, passing through the nation's capital, Washington DC, along the way. It was here that Yuri Karatsev stood on top of the gentle incline, his eyes sweeping across the surface of a low-lying mist that rolled across the obscured contours of the land below, as twilight inevitably gave way to the dawning day. Sounds of the awakening countryside floated through the air, as unseen creatures began to stir in the manicured undergrowth and budding trees overhead. In the distance, the faintest sound of a ship's horn departing the Washington docks for the Atlantic frightened a pheasant from its resting place, taking temporary flight before coming to ground nearby. The air was still and crisp which reminded him of Ust-Izhora, his birth village, that lay on the banks of the Neva River to the south-east of Leningrad.

His smile faded.

It'd been almost a decade since he'd been home and he wondered if the village still stood. Even if it did, he doubted he'd recognize it, the places he used to play, and the shops from which he used to steal while growing up in the 1920s.

It was late summer 1941 and, as hundreds of thousands of people, mainly women and children were evacuated east ahead of the approaching fascists, Yuri's family had opted to move into Leningrad, instead. His paternal grandparents, who owned and lived above a small haberdashery store on Telezhnaya Street, had been delighted to take them in, especially, as it meant seeing more of their grandchildren than they usually would. However, the atmosphere quickly changed when the Luftwaffe and German artillery started their bombing and shelling campaigns in the early autumn – he'd later learned it had taken the Germans and Finns only a couple of months to completely encircle the city and begin what became the costliest siege in human history, claiming over 1.4 million lives. With all routes into and out of the city severed, the demand for food soon became everybody's top priority, especially, as temperatures began to plummet to 30° Celsius below. The besieging armies had thought that capitulation would be swift. And, such was his confidence, Hitler had printed invitations to hold a victory party in the city's Astoria Hotel. But, the Russians resisted for eight hundred and seventy-six days.

Some supplies did, however, make it into the city once the 'ice road' across Lake Ladoga became operational in November. With limited supplies coming one way, some civilians tried their luck by heading in the opposite direction. Yuri's family was no different. His father, mother, younger brother, and sister, along with his grandmother, started across the ice. However, Yuri, as an infantry soldier in the 4th Rifle Corp of the 7th Army on the Karelian Front north of the city had a duty to remain. His grandfather too chose to stay. Unfortunately, the old man, well into his seventies, had withered throughout the next year and died the following winter. After the war, Yuri spent months searching for his family but found no trace, forced to concede they had perished either during the lake crossing or elsewhere as the war took its toll. In truth, he never really stopped looking or gave up hope, using his position within the Soviet regime to keep searching. Equally though, he knew that war didn't discriminate between its victims so, as the years wore on, his effort declined.

He took a few slow practice swings before preparing himself for the stroke. His head hovered over the ball; he settled his breathing. He drew back the club, twisted and struck the ball. He watched, as it sailed into the clear-sky before it eventually began its gradual descent. He didn't see where it landed because his eyes were focused on the enormous building several miles to the south on the other side of the Potomac that was home to the US Department of Defense.

Construction of The Pentagon had begun in 1941 mainly because the US War Department, which was responsible for administration within the US Army, had been scattered across several locations in Washington, bringing with it an inherent lack of cohesion, direction, and effective communication. Although the US wasn't directly involved in the war at the time, ranks within the Department had swelled mainly because it was believed that entering the war with Germany was inevitable; a war on two-fronts however, had never been envisaged.

He moved to one side to allow his playing partner his turn.

Nikita Morozov placed his ball on a tee, glanced quickly at the target and swung.

Yuri shook his head. 'Lost another one?' He didn't even bother to see where Nikita's ball had ended up.

'Who cares?' Nikita said. He stashed the club in his bag and slung it across his shoulder.

'You could at least pretend to enjoy the game. Don't I pay for your membership?'

'You could give me the money instead.' The younger man, dressed in a blue short-sleeved shirt and beige slacks led the way down the slope to the green.

'You'd only spend it on whores and vodka.'

'Whores yes, vodka definitely not. My mother's piss is stronger than what the Americans sell in their bars.' Nikita stomped off, clearly trying to shorten the time he'd have to spend on the course.

Yuri strolled behind, his bag slung across his back, unwilling to allow himself to be hurried. He had always enjoyed the outdoors, the smells and the sounds of a natural world that was oblivious to man's meddling, except, that was when it was impacted by them; nature could be pillaged by the greedy without seemingly offering any resistance. As a result, he looked forward to his weekends and trips away from the office. He found the confines of an office and the associated dress code far too restrictive. A small part of him longed to return to a time when he could operate with little supervision, when assignments could be completed any way he cared, so long as the desired outcome was achieved. For him, and more importantly, his bosses, the end completely justified the means. But, time's arrow moved only one way, and other opportunities had presented themselves. He could, of course, have decided to maintain his status quo and keep doing what he was good at, but he'd seen what had happened to those who had dithered too long within the profession. Laziness, perhaps even arrogance, had set in. They assumed nothing could go wrong simply because nothing had ever gone wrong.

That amused him.

It reminded him of 'Silas Marner, The Weaver of Raveloe' who, Elliot had described, hadn't locked the door to his home in the mistaken belief that because nobody had ever broken into his home, it was unlikely ever to happen. In his old life, Death's scythe had occasionally flashed before him but had never managed a clean strike.

He'd been approached by some Colonel, whose name he couldn't recall, about becoming Special Intelligence Liaison to the Ambassador in America and had jumped at the chance without even having read the job description. In fact, the post offered him more than he could ever dream. Whereas before, he was an instrument of death, now he was the bringer of death. Initially, he'd wanted to end all those whose dossiers had crossed his desk, but thankfully he hadn't been handed the reins from the get-go and been allowed unfettered savagery. Superiors at the Kremlin had ordered a handover period with Sergei Kosh, the man he was to replace. Kosh tempered the young Yuri's thirst for blood and showed him the value of not only selecting a particular target but also deciding when (and sometimes how) to eliminate the target for maximum effect. Looking back, he would have said his guidance was too short. He had so much to learn. It had been impossible for Kosh to condense almost two decades worth of experience in the time allowed.

'I'm in here,' Yuri said, finding his ball in a shallow bunker to the left of the green. He looked across at Nikita who had started swinging a club at the undergrowth inside a small wooded area in search of his ball. He looked back up the slope at the tee and the two men who were waiting for them.

'I'll ask them to play through.'

Nikita stopped and looked up at the two federal agents.

'Let them wait.' If anything his scowl seemed to darken the morning even as the sun started to peek above the Maryland horizon to the east.

Yuri stepped into the bunker, deciding not to wait for Nikita to locate his ball. He took a couple of practice swings before landing his shot to within a few feet of the hole. He brushed the sand off his pants that had deposited during the swing and saw another ball arc high into the air and land almost as near to the hole as his own. He shrugged at Nikita's blatant cheating.

Both men met on the putting surface.

'How many has he eliminated?' Yuri asked. He sized up his putt.

Nikita's face brightened at the change in topic.

'Six. Four this week alone.'

'In a week? Productive. I want more.' Yuri hit his putt to within a few inches and groaned.

'The Americans have linked them and initiated protective measures for the others,' Nikita said. He lined up his putt and rolled it in without displaying any satisfaction.

'That's a lot of men to protect. I'd have thought it difficult for the Americans to mobilize security personnel for them all so quickly, especially in a country so vast.' Yuri looked at Nikita, his smile and cheerful voice replaced by the harder, more demanding tone of a superior fearing their progress might soon slow down.

'I didn't say he was finished. He has the list and is going through them in the order we requested. He should manage a couple more before it becomes impossible for him to continue.'

Yuri stood on the green and looked back at the two agents who were patiently waiting on the 2nd tee. He thought for a moment.

'Do you think we should change the order and get him to target more prominent figures?'

'Only when he's prevented from progressing will he deviate from the order.' Nikita walked across to his bag.

'I thought he would've got to more by now. I fear he may not be able to continue and that we have wasted a good opportunity. Maybe, we should have used more men like him?'

Nikita shook his head. 'Don't second-guess yourself, Yuri. The plan is sound. Killing one is a good result; killing six is very good.'

'I was aiming for excellent not 'very good'.'

'Men like Sieber are hard to find; he isn't one of us.'

Yuri acknowledged that with a slight shrug. He knew that to use their men would have risked drawing attention to themselves, which would further increase tensions between the two superpowers or perhaps push both toward a war for which neither had an appetite, not yet anyway. Nikita was right. The plan was indeed, sound. Using the German to carry out their objective had been the intelligent thing to do.

'And the Americans are investigating?'

'Naturally. Local law enforcement at first which was expected. Some Federal Agents have become involved more recently.'

'Can we do anything to slow them down?'

This time it was Nikita's turn to stop and think. Yuri watched him. The younger man shook his head.

'Not without exposing ourselves. Perhaps, when the time comes, we can use the German to divert attention from us.'

'Be sure to maintain regular contact with him just in case it becomes necessary to do just that.' Yuri's frown softened. He looked down at his ball and rolled it into the hole with his toe.

CHAPTER 16

A COLD, DAMP DRIZZLE FELL across the city, and on a dimly-lit street somewhere between Little Italy and Chinatown, a man dressed in dark clothing kept to the shadows, his head down, his ears listening, his eyes watchful. It was after midnight when Tomas Sieber entered the ground floor of an old, ramshackle tenement that stood sandwiched between others in a row of similar buildings that'd been erected more than a century before. The heavy wooden front door scraped along the threshold, as he leaned against it, snapping the lock in place. He paused and stared into the darkness, listening for any sound that might be out of place in a building that was settling for the night. He slowly ascended the staircase to the first floor.

He came to a solid, paint-chipped door, like all the others in the building, and stood for a moment outside the room provided by his employers. He ran his fingers gently against the door and frame, feeling for, and finding, the slip of cardboard he'd placed there over a week ago. He let out a controlled breath and felt any residual anxiety disappear, knowing that nobody had entered his lodgings while he'd been gone. He took an old brass key from his pocket and entered the room, quietly shutting the door behind. He removed his shoes and padded softly along the floorboards to where he knew the bed to be. His hand searched for the small lamp which rested on a wooden crate next to the bed. The light dazzled him momentarily before his eyes became accustomed. He looked around the room, checking all was as he had left it, and then at the heavy, black drapes, which allowed light to neither enter nor escape through the large window that overlooked the street below. Aside from a bag that sat on a wood-wormed sofa propped against one of the walls, the room was as bare as every other in the house. He'd discovered this on his first evening in the city, as he familiarized himself with the layout of both the building's design and the warren of intertwining streets of southern Manhattan.

Happy that all was as it should be, he reached under the bed and carefully withdrew a smaller, more precious bag. The mattress squeaked as he sat. He placed the bag next to him. From inside, he removed a notebook and pen. He opened it to the last page, staring at a list of more than a hundred alphabetized names. He ran his fingers along each in turn, his mouth mumbling as he went. Four times he stopped and struck a name from the list. He leaned back and stared at the page.

He was pleased with what he'd accomplished in the few short weeks he'd been in America.

He'd already scratched a further two names from the list a week earlier, bringing his total to six, and in doing so, had destroyed some of those he'd come to hunt. Of course, many remained and, he believed, were still unaware of what awaited them should he be allowed to continue. Those who had brought them here had, after a brief time of vigilance, become careless with their acquisitions and allowed them to roam the country and go about their daily lives, for the most part, unchecked. America was a vast, industrious land, and with their indigenous scientific community spread throughout, it had led to the authorities scattering the new intellectual property that had been plucked from post-war Europe as their needs demanded. Their strategy of scientific decentralization had so far proved highly beneficial for him as he'd gone about his work. He also believed it unlikely that the Americans would be able to establish a link between the six killings, given the apparent randomness, spread, and the country's already high murder rate. However, it had made completing his mission slower than anticipated as travel between kills had taken time which might increase his risk of detection the longer he continued. However, he'd found that once on American soil, he hadn't had to carry any form of identification. He believed the Americans were either naïve or reckless when it came to national security (perhaps even both); which was something his Fatherland or his employer's Motherland could never be accused.

That was probably the only thing the opposing ideologies had in common.

As he read through the list of names again, he wondered who would be next. Of course, he recognized some as being the most highly prolific scientists of the modern era, famous for their ingenuity, innovation, and creativity. He had even met some throughout the war, having had occasion to dine with them at many prestigious Nazi Party functions. However, in accepting a new life in the New World, he deemed each a traitor who deserved the fate that would follow. The choice of who lived and died, though, was not his to make. His employer would make that decision.

His employer.

Zorin Sokolov was certainly not that, yet he found it difficult to label the man as anything else. The Russian had called himself a 'partner' when they had first met, but Sieber had disliked the term as it proclaimed some level of equality which he completely dismissed (although he hadn't said as much to the communist at the time). Sokolov was merely a means to an end, a willing party within a symbiotic relationship of provision and reception to be maintained until such time as their mutual objectives were achieved. Sokolov had provided him with safe and undetected passage to America, a small supply of personal weapons and, in this room in downtown Manhattan, a base from which he could operate. He did not need any financial aid, although Sokolov had offered. The war had been generous to people like him, people who had squirreled away some of the spoils and grown modest savings from which they could live out the rest of their lives in some comfort.

The irony too that some of America's intelligence services lay in such proximity wasn't lost on him. Foley Square was within pissing distance of his hideaway. The American authorities, though, had decided that, with the war over, a new enemy had to be faced and so, had willfully sought one out. Hoover searched everywhere for those 'damned Reds', thus allowing him to go quietly about his business.

He closed the notebook and dropped it and the pen next to him on the bed. He walked across to an adjoining door and entered a small bathroom. He placed his hands on the sink and, in the faint light of the bedroom lamp, looked at himself in the mirror. Throughout his life, he'd borne witness to more worldly events than most of those who roamed the planet. He leaned in closer and wondered if it somehow showed on his face, might anybody who looked close enough be able to see all that he had seen, experience all that he had been through, witness all that he had done. He took off his shirt and vest, and splashed a handful of cold water on his face, running his damp hands through his short, bristling hair.

He had been lucky.

He'd come through the war unscathed, without any physical scarring, but then, he hadn't served on the frontline like many of his fellow country-men not, that was, until the spring of '45. By then, he and others knew the game was up. Despite reassurances from Der Führer, he had been making good his preparations for escape before the noose tightened around both the country and his neck. Besides, he had no love for Hitler; his loyalty and allegiance lay with another.

He looked at his reflection and admired his body for a moment. He was in good shape for a man his age. He maintained a healthy, balanced diet, and continued to pursue the aerobic exercise regime instilled in him by his Drill-Seargent during basic training. His eyes moved to his left arm, and the small tattoo painted there. Ironically, it was a mark that had been designed to save his life during wartime that might now, during peacetime, herald a death sentence. His printed blood type would forever label him a member of the Waffen SS, one of Germany's most exclusive clubs and be a permanent reminder of his past and the ideals he still held dear. He remembered having seen newsreel footage a couple of years ago, as lines of topless German soldiers, their arms aloft, trotted past their Allied counterparts who looked for the same printed blood type tattoo. Any men caught were hauled away for interrogation, and later, for some, execution.

Tomas had avoided that. He recalled the last day he'd spent in Germany.

It had been late evening and, even with dusk still more than an hour away, they had risked traveling the roads in the staff car. Sieber knew the last roll of the dice, a request that Himmler be permitted to join Donitz's interim government and maintain law and order in a post-war Germany had been declined. He sat next to his Master, as the Mercedes headed south out of Flensburg towards well, he didn't know where they were going. The entire world was coming apart. The vision and promise of a one-thousand-year Reich had only days left as it drew its dying breaths. He chanced a glance at Himmler, expecting to see outrage at this recent slight, but instead saw a curiously calm superior who had now accepted his fate.

The car trundled on towards Friedrichskoog, a second car behind carrying four personal bodyguards. Neither car traveled particularly fast. The mood inside was somber, the view outside serene. They passed through the town without incident and continued southwards. They crossed the Elbe at Wischhafen and continued west for a few more miles.

Eventually, Himmler leaned forward and ordered the driver to pull over.

Both cars slowed, and the passengers disembarked where they stretched their legs and relieved themselves in the ditch. One of the guards passed around a flask of whiskey. Everybody took a sip. The seven men knew each other well or as well as any who had been brought together by circumstance. They were a close group who had worked alongside and enjoyed each other's company for many years. They were more than acquaintances or friends. They had shared a turbulent part of their young lives and in doing so had forged an everlasting and unbreakable bond – that too would change.

Himmler leaned into his car and emerged with a bottle of Louis XIII Remy Martin. He instructed his driver to get seven snifters. The little group drew close, as Himmler poured the brandy. Cigarettes were passed around, and conversation was sparse, consisting only of passing comments to which nobody listened.

Sieber stared towards the falling sun, partially obscured by a smattering of clouds, the sky an ever-changing array of color, and wondered what the future would hold for him.

Darkness had closed in by the time they'd finished the bottle. Himmler divided the group into two. He would take two men south into Lower Saxony while Sieber and the other three would go west. After that, each could go where he wanted. They knew this would be the last time any of them saw each other.

Himmler told them to dispose of their uniforms and destroy their vehicles at the first opportunity. Once the order had been given, Himmler took Sieber aside and gave him a small leather-bound pouch. No words were exchanged. Sieber looked into his Master's eyes before Himmler nodded and, unsmiling, turned away to join his group.

Some miles further down the road, Sieber's car drove into the small village of Belum. Here, they changed into civilian clothing acquired from one of the residents at gunpoint, compensating him the staff car they'd been driving for the truck they also took.

They drove on west through Otterndorf and turned south towards Bremerhaven where the group had planned to break up, each to go his own way. Sieber would aim for the coast and try to board a ship bound for anywhere out of continental Europe.

They'd only made it as far as the city outskirts when they happened upon an American checkpoint. They offered false documentation, which, in the darkness, Sieber hoped wouldn't be scrutinized as thoroughly as should be the case.

He was wrong.

The four men were ordered out of the truck and forced to the ground at gunpoint. They were restrained, searched, tossed into a lorry, and taken to a nearby jail.

Sieber couldn't remember how long he'd been in the cell when the American came to him.

'Are you hungry?' the man said.

Sieber didn't reply.

'Thirsty?'

He looked away.

The man opened a folder and placed it on the table. He sat down.

'Says here your name is Norbert Richter, a fisherman from Kiel.' He stopped and stared at Sieber.

'You're a long way from home Herr Richter. Why is that?' He took a sip from the mug of coffee he'd brought in and waited.

Sieber knew how the game went; he'd seen it and played it many times, but never from this side of the table and so was unsure how to act. Should he try to reason his way out of the situation or stay quiet in the hope that the American would tire and release him. He knew though, that in the end, the interrogator always got what he wanted, and so, was left wondering if there was any point in prolonging the inevitable. He turned to face the man, his mouth half-opened to say something. The man was holding the speech given to him by Himmler.

The silence in the room tightened around him.

'How did you come by this?' The man spoke plainly, without malice or anger.

Sieber thought about the best response. A lie would lead him down an avenue where every word he uttered would be examined and analyzed for irregularities while the truth would eventually indict him. But, what had the Americans got on him, anyhow? He'd been a loyal soldier to his beloved Fatherland and as such afforded all the protections provided by the Geneva Convention.

Being truthful, no matter how distasteful, would set him free.

Over the next few hours, while the American sat quietly and listened, he told his story or as much as he felt he could disclose. No notes were taken, no recordings were made. Once he had finished, he'd been given food and water and placed in a cell by himself until the American returned two days later.

'We're rounding up men like you all over Europe,' he said.

Sieber disliked the term, as though the men he'd fought with were dumb cattle grazing the countryside.

The man stared at him, his eyes fierce.

'Some will be released back into civilian society while others will be prosecuted and serve time for what they did. There are those, however, who will go to the gallows.'

Sieber sat motionless, his head hanging, his eyes staring at the floor.

'But, there is an alternative.'

Sieber looked up cautiously. He didn't understand what the man had said.

'I'm in a position to be able to offer you protection… well, protection isn't the correct word.' He scratched his head, searching for the right phrase.

Sieber knew it to be an act, the throwing of a lifeline to a condemned man.

'A way out of this mess,' the man said. The corner of his mouth creased into a slight grin. 'If it's wanted, of course.'

The two sized each other up for several moments, the growl of army vehicles passing on the other side of the jail walls, the only sound.

'How would something like that be accomplished?' Sieber said, eventually.

'We'd enter into a mutually beneficial arrangement.'

For the first time, Sieber smiled. With all the rhetoric about righteousness, it appeared the Americans were no different from the Germans. Spoils of war would be gathered by the victors regardless of language, nationality, ethics, or morals.

Looking back, the American had asked for only a modest amount to secure his release and relocation, but it had been worth it. A truck had taken him from the jail to an airfield in Holland where he boarded a flight to Spain. He remained there for a little over a month until the American returned and provided a travel itinerary and falsified documents, including references of character that'd been notarized by an eminent member of the Catholic Church. A transatlantic flight to Cuba and another south to

Belize had followed. He'd also been given a list of possible destinations from there, places where he would be 'comfortable'. He hadn't known what that meant until he arrived at one such location, a German-speaking community in Bogota.

Only after he had left Europe had he become aware of the hunt for Party members and soldiers like him. Many had indeed been rounded up just as the American had said; some though had not survived. In the eyes of the victors, they had committed the worst atrocities mankind had ever witnessed, and they were made pay with their lives.

Of course, Sieber disputed this assertion.

Man had possessed a predilection for killing his kind for millennia by perhaps even worse methods than he and his countrymen had employed. The only difference was the industrial magnitude with which they had gone about their craft.

Although Tomas was incredibly proud of the small part he had played, there had been times over the following years when he had cried himself to sleep for glories so nearly attained, and yet unachieved.

He spent a few years with the German community, apprehensive at first about divulging too much about himself. But, over time, he found that many of those he met had made similar journeys once they'd paid the going rate. Having accumulated much wealth during the war most didn't have to work, and so lived the lives they had been promised by Der Führer, albeit, in the southern hemisphere. They wanted for nothing. They ate and drank until early morning, waking in the afternoon, to do it all over again. But for Sieber, this existence became humdrum. He didn't want to live out his life merely living off that which he had plundered. His Master had been a shrewd man of cunning and intellect and had provided Sieber with an agenda to be undertaken when the time was right.

He dried himself off with a small hand towel and put his vest back on. He went back into the other room and removed from his bag the same small, black, leather-bound pouch that Himmler had given him. Inside, he found his most treasured possession. He lay down on the bed, his head propped up by a crumpled pillow, and started to reread the speech he had read a thousand times before. He drew breath when he came to one particular section. He closed his eyes, placed the pages on his chest, and began reciting the remainder of the text by heart.

'I am now referring to the evacuation of the Jews, the extermination of the Jewish people. It's one of those things that is easily said: 'The Jewish people are being exterminated', says every party member, 'this is very obvious, it's in our program, elimination of the Jews, extermination, we're doing it, hah, a small matter.' And then they turn up, the upstanding 80 million Germans, and each one has his decent Jew. They say the others are all swine, but this particular one is a splendid Jew. But none has observed it, endured it. Most of you here know what it means when 100 corpses lie next to each other, when there are 500 or when there are 1,000. To have endured this and at the same time to have remained a decent person — with exceptions due to human weaknesses — has made us tough, and is a glorious chapter that has not and will not be spoken of. Because we know how difficult it would be for us if we still had Jews as secret saboteurs, agitators and rabble-rousers in every city, what with the bombings, with the burden and with the hardships of the war. If the Jews were still part of the German nation, we would most likely arrive now at the state we were at in 1916 and 17.'

He opened his eyes, flicked ahead to the end of the document and ran his fingertips across where his Master had signed his name. It was a speech, made in Poznan that had been given to Tomas as a farewell present, a token of gratitude for years of devoted service.

Tomas pulled the covers over him and quickly drifted away into a peaceful sleep, happy in the knowledge that he was some way to completing Himmler's last wishes.

CHAPTER 17

IT WAS NEAR IMPOSSIBLE TO book a meeting room at the CIA office in Foggy Bottom. This was due primarily to a burgeoning sense of duty and patriotism within an agency sworn to protect the country against those 'damn Commies' who had occupied Eastern Europe after the war. As a consequence, staff numbers had swelled across all departments, which had led to something of a dystopian existence with overcrowding on every floor and desk space at a premium. The Agency had smaller satellite offices scattered about the capital that might, on occasion, have some available space, but it was rarely, if ever, guaranteed.

Consequently, Leon Knox chose his meeting places to suit the occasion, agenda, and participants. Sometimes, he would use an outdoor venue, lunch on the steps of the Lincoln Memorial or coffee on the benches at the far end of The Mall near The Capitol, as both provided an informal setting with impressive views should he tire of the conversation. If the weather were inclement, then a hotel lobby or one of Washington's more exclusive restaurants would suffice, especially if he wanted to impress the other attendee.

He would choose none of these today.

He drove across Memorial Bridge, which spanned the Potomac between DC and Virginia, and continued along Memorial Avenue into Arlington Cemetery. Taking one of several circuitous routes, he wound his way respectfully along the rising road that bisected the hundreds of rows of white headstones that sprouted from the landscaped gardens, until he came to a small pebbled car park next to Arlington House. He cut the engine and paused for a moment before stepping out of the car. He always liked visiting the cemetery. It was a place of solitude and reflection, peace and remembrance. He walked across the pebbles, gazing at the building that had once been home to Robert Lee before he joined the Confederacy in 1861. Back then, the US Government, realizing they couldn't allow the Lee Family estate to fall into enemy hands, immediately seized it and the surrounding lands, which it never relinquished.

It was a dull, overcast day and a threat of rain hung in the clouds like an unkindness of ravens perched overhead, but even still Knox had decided not to wear an overcoat; he didn't plan on being outdoors for too long. He took a path that led down a gentle slope, crossing the freshly trimmed grass between graves toward a large copse of trees, the distant hum of a mower, the only sound. He came to a stop and lit a cigarette, tilting his head back and blowing a funnel of smoke into the air.

'I didn't think you'd come,' a voice said from amongst the trees.

'I was intrigued by your note,' Knox said. He didn't look back.

'So, you don't know why I contacted you?'

Knox discreetly shook his head and took another drag, his eyes continually roaming the landscape ahead of him, searching for unwanted eyes. He'd deliberately chosen this location for that very reason; favoring both the privacy and secrecy it offered. From here, he could maintain a watchful eye on the approach roads and be on the lookout for anyone with more than a passing interest in a visitor to the cemetery and mansion. He'd only had cause to use it as a meeting venue a handful of times over the past number of years but had felt it appropriate today given the nature of his discovery earlier that morning.

The note had been slipped under his front door during the night which he'd handled carefully and read slowly, digesting its contents. He'd recognized the initials immediately, despite not having had any contact with the individual who'd signed it since after the war. Memories of people met, and places visited had trickled back before other more vivid experiences flooded his mind which he'd wished would have remained largely forgotten. He'd also recognized the contact number scrawled at the bottom which he'd later called from Sweeney's, a local bar on 21ˢᵗ Street known mostly for the anonymity afforded its clientele. The receptionist at the St. Regis Hotel answered promptly, and Knox asked to be put through to room 212. While he waited, he thought about how the man hadn't bothered to use an alias. Perhaps, it'd been an oversight due to the hurried nature of the business at hand and the discussion to be had, but he doubted it. As a former Commandant of the Vatican Swiss Guards, Michal Valent was far too experienced a man to overlook such matters. The commandant had wanted Knox to know who was intruding into his life after all these years. But, Knox wasn't going to accede to the rules of the Italian's game like he had done at the end of the war. And so, with the meeting arranged, here they stood together, again. This time though Knox was on home territory, the tables turned, the rules reversed.

'I was led to believe you Agency types were intelligent,' Valent said.

'And there I thought you had come with another proposition. After all, our last venture proved quite fruitful.' Knox waited and could almost hear Valent smiling behind him.

Apart from the mower, there was a brief silence before the Italian spoke. 'We may be exposed.'

Knox's face hardened, but he gave nothing away. He held his cigarette in front of him for a moment before licking his fingers and extinguishing it. He placed it back into the pack and turned around, coming face to face with a man he hadn't seen since Rome, 1945.

The years had been kind to the Italian in some respects, but bad in others. His hair was a coiffed, bright grey, and the age lines about his eyes had elongated and deepened. He'd put on weight, two trouser sizes if Knox were to guess. His tanned sallow skin was the only feature that had remained the same, that, and the unwavering dark eyes which stared at Knox now.

'Is that right?' Knox said. 'How so?'

'You've a serial killer on your hands.'

Knox didn't reply. He would never discuss an ongoing operation with anyone it didn't concern, either inside or outside the agency, but that was about to change.

'I believe I know who it is.'

Knox tilted his head to one side, as he sized up his old acquaintance, for calling him a friend would be a stretch; Knox didn't have any friends. Should he believe him? Perhaps. After all, why would he have come all this way and arranged a meeting like this unless he was sure? More importantly, though, should he trust him? Years in the service had taught him many valuable lessons, learned, it had to be said, by observing the experiences of others and thus not making the same mistakes.

'Go on.'

'Tomas Sieber.'

The name didn't register with Knox but then, how could it. He had met thousands of men throughout his lifetime. The unknowing look on his face betrayed this.

'He was one of those we helped relocate to a better life after the war.'

Knox felt his stomach tighten and his face grow taut in equal measure. How could something like this have happened? Safeguards had been put in place to prevent old foes and new friends from ever coming into contact with each other. There were people whose job it was to report on any activity that might be deemed suspicious, anything that might unravel the thick web of deceit that cloaked the past.

No.

Valent was wrong. Dementia brought on by old age, or paranoia, perhaps even both. Maybe his life had become banal and meaningless. Maybe he was trying to remember and relive past glories; more money than anyone could spend in ten lifetimes might do that to any man.

Knox shook his head.

'You doubt me?'

'The thought is crossing my mind. Nobody else has come to me, yet.'

'I'm coming to you now.' Valent's tone was one of pent-up anger.

Knox took a slow step back and calmly scanned the graveyard.

'There is nobody close by, nobody you need be concerned with anyway,' Valent said.

That didn't fill Knox with any measure of comfort. It meant the old man hadn't come alone and if not, then he was bluffing. He leaned down to retie a shoelace, allowing some time to think. If a horse had bolted, then it didn't matter who had left the barn door open. What mattered was getting the beast back and making sure it was securely locked up for good. He stood up.

'I'll look into it.' He adjusted his tie.

'See that you do.'

The pair regarded each other for a moment.

'The killing of Father Hernandez was unfortunate,' Valent said.

Knox's face turned to stone, remembering the flow of expressions that had crossed the priest's face after he'd been shot; astonishment, then disbelieving, and finally acceptance. 'We witnessed many unfortunate events. Let's not relive the past.'

'Unfortunate and reckless.' Valent nodded his head, staring past Knox at the quiet cemetery beyond.

'It was necessary.'

'But for my intervention, we'd have been discovered.'

'Am I to be grateful?'

Valent shook his head. 'Repentant, perhaps.'

'That'll have to wait until I'm prepared to meet the Divine.' Knox tipped his hat and walked away from the Italian.

'You'll contact me?' Valent called out.

'If I need to,' Knox said without turning back.

*

Knox pulled up outside a bungalow on Exeter Street in an area of Baltimore known as Johnstown. He'd been careful while making the drive from

Arlington, taking a haphazard, zigzag route, continually checking for a tail by doubling back several times. He was sure he hadn't been followed. He waited for a minute before climbing out and approaching the door, slipping a key from his jacket pocket and entering.

He stepped from the small hallway into what was once the living room. It was dark inside, lit only by a shaft of light that illuminated part of the floor and a small wooden table stained with circles from a time when those who used to live here had gathered and enjoyed mugs of tea or coffee together.

The house had been unoccupied for almost five years. It had been owned by the Mother of Oscar Benitez, a soldier with the US 3rd Ranger Battalion that'd landed in Sicily in the summer of '43. Unfortunately, Oscar had stepped on a land mine on the beach, and he'd died before he'd seen his twenty-second birthday. Camila, his mother, had died a year later when she'd driven her car into Baltimore Harbor. Officially, the authorities had ruled it an accident, but it'd happened on the 1st anniversary of her only son's death. As for the father, he had left the family home by agreement before the war had broken out, which was to say that Oscar had witnessed him punching his mother and, after taking the leg of a chair to the man, had left him bleeding on the floor with a busted jaw and several missing teeth. Oscar threatened to kill him if he ever came back to the home. He never did.

Knox had learned that the house had been left derelict and so bought it using a shell company he owned under one of his many assumed names. He held several properties about the Greater Washington area that served his many purposes. He had fingers in many pies, and so it paid to have contingencies in place.

The neighborhood wasn't what he would consider working class, but it wasn't delinquent either. The people who lived here were good, decent folk, who always looked out for their own. To that end, he'd arranged to have the property taken care of by members of St. Benedict's Community Centre in return for a more than generous annual payment which they used, he learned, to keep the elderly in dinners during the winter months when they daren't leave their houses for fear of breaking a hip. The kids from the Centre washed the windows every month, mowed the lawn when needed, and painted the house once a year. So, even though nobody went in or left through the front door, it gave the appearance of being lived in, and so remained undisturbed.

He went back into the hallway and to the kitchen at the rear of the house. He took another key from his pocket and opened a door that led to a stair to the basement. He stepped inside and closed the door behind him, careful to ensure the lock had snapped back in place. He reached across to a shelf at the top of the stairs and grabbed a flashlight he kept there.

He flicked it on and went down.

The basement was musty but not damp, and specks of dust darted about the flashlight's beam as though startled by the intrusion. He scanned the rows of shelves that still housed some of Mr. Benitez's workman's tools and other items collected over the years (although, Knox had disposed of any flammable materials soon after he'd made the purchase). All was as it had been on his last visit over eight months ago.

He walked across to a large shelving unit at the back of the cellar and pulled on bolts that secured the top and bottom. Gently pulling back, the furniture arced away from the wall on small wheels revealing a steel door. Knox entered a six-digit code into a mechanical combination lock, twisted a small steel wheel, and heard the internal mechanism unlock. He pushed the door and went into the room behind. Here, he could turn on a light, as he'd arranged to have power for this room siphoned off the main grid that ran along the street outside.

As soon as his eyes had adjusted to the sudden brightness, he moved toward a set of filing cabinets to his left.

It was here that he had stored all the documentation accumulated during his time with the Office of Strategic Services and later, the CIA. The room held many files; dossiers and reports already known to many in the business, but it also held secrets known only to him and a few others.

He stood for a moment, thinking.

As with every operation undertaken during the war, he had given the project he'd conducted with Michal Valent, what he considered to be quite an apt codename, given its nature. His hand moved across the alphabetized drawers until he came to 'V'. He opened the drawer and flicked through the files there, his fingers resting on 'Veil'. He opened the thin folder and scanned a four-page type-written document that he hadn't opened since he'd deposited it there in the spring of '46.

Both pages had four columns of words; a date (in ascending order), a name, an alias, and a reference number. He mumbled the name Valent had mentioned. 'Zieber', or was it, 'Sieber'? Perhaps it was some other spelling. His finger ran along the second column until it landed on 'Sieber' near the bottom of the third page. He quickly checked the rest of the document for any similar name but found none. He went back to the third page and noted the reference number that was next to Sieber: PW-0116. He placed the document and folder back in the drawer and shut it. He turned around and stared at the opposite wall.

Eight rows of shelves, each one bending in the center under the weight of its burden, ran from the doorway to the back wall. There was still some space on a couple of rows for new documents should he need to add to his collection, but not much. For a moment, Knox thought perhaps a little 'spring cleaning' could be done to be rid of any excess material but recoiled at the idea; it'd be too much work. He'd be better off acquiring another property and adding to his collection there. Besides, one never knew which documents might become valuable over time.

He scanned the files until he came to those beginning with PW. His fingers tickled the spines of the numbers as he went along until he arrived at the one he needed. The air was dry down here, and he felt his throat tighten.

He swallowed gently.

Knox removed the file and took it to a small desk at the rear of the room. He sat down and prepared himself before opening it.

CHAPTER 18

DANIEL HELD THE DOOR OPEN for Alona, and they entered the same cubed-shaped building on I-Street they'd visited six days earlier.

After he had returned from Las Vegas late Friday evening, they'd taken the weekend to run through events as they'd unfolded, analyzing the sequence of murders, the timelines, locations, and methods employed by the killer (or killers). It'd been late Sunday evening by the time they'd drawn conclusions and developed a working theory that they'd present to Witten this morning.

But, they knew they had to be careful.

While they were new to investigative procedures, the FBI was not. They would have to gauge the flow of the upcoming discussion cautiously as they didn't want to jeopardize either the outcome of this case or any future work that might come their way. However, they also knew that if it came to it, they might well be made scapegoats to protect the reputations of any long-standing Bureau officials who might be embarrassed by the lack of a collar. Not that they were incompetent. Inexperienced maybe. But, they were only two people, working alongside an agency of several thousand, and if sacrificial heads were required, then theirs might be offered.

As before, they rode the elevator to the 4th floor and walked toward the same meeting room. It was early morning, and the office bustled with the renewed vigor a weekend break provided, something the place had lacked the last time they were there.

Nobody looked in their direction. Everybody was too busy.

This time there was an older gentleman seated next to Witten, and it was clear from the outset that he was the man in charge. Witten stood as they entered; the other man did not. Straight away, Daniel knew it would be a challenging but not a terminal discussion. If they were to be fired, the man in charge wouldn't have been present. He'd have left it to Witten to deliver the news alone. This man wanted to see what his tax dollars were buying, so their performance had to exceed his expectations.

Daniel felt the older man's gaze wash over him and, for the first time in a long while, felt uncomfortable. He recalled immediately the last time he'd been in the presence of somebody who had radiated such fearsome authority. It'd been almost eleven years ago in a gentrified office in the heart of Whitehall, London. Having arrived in the dead of night unannounced, he'd felt apprehensive when discussing with Bronson Browne his exclusion from a mission to Stalingrad. That night, he'd laid all his cards on the table and managed to change Browne's mind, even if his argument had been supported when the preferred operative had broken his foot, courtesy of a falling aftershave bottle.

He glanced sidelong at Alona who didn't appear to be showing any signs of nervousness. In fact, she seemed to have barely registered the older man's presence. Perhaps, she knew him through the many dealings she had with the various government agencies and knew what to expect. Maybe nothing frightened her anymore after all she'd been through.

They shook hands with Witten and took the seats opposite.

'You didn't travel to Atlanta?' Witten's tone was questioning rather than accusatory, and Daniel had anticipated it, though perhaps not so soon in the conversation.

'I didn't feel the need.'

'Why was that?' Witten hadn't missed a beat.

'The investigations in Oregon and Nevada, although informative, didn't reveal much more than what was in the official police file we'd received. I believed it best not to waste any more time, energy, and money in chasing after a killer long departed.'

'And you didn't feel the need to continue building on what you'd learned at the coal-face, so to speak?' It was a withering comment, designed to throw an interviewee off his stride.

Daniel was undeterred.

'No. I preferred to discuss the investigation face to face and completely with Alona,' Daniel said, making a gesture towards her, 'rather than piecemeal with the authorities in each jurisdiction.'

'Even though we're running the investigation in Atlanta?'

'I thought my time would be better served evaluating the investigation in its entirety rather than bringing the Georgia FBI up to speed with the rest of the case. Besides, they have access to the same reports I have. If they need to look beyond their murder case, they can start reading.'

Daniel noticed Alona's shoulders drop and knew she wasn't happy with his response. He was sure Witten had seen it too, but it remained to be seen whether he would ask the obvious next question.

He did.

'Why would we hire an independent contractor if we could have put one of our men on the case from the start?'

Daniel knew he had to tread carefully now. What he said over the next few minutes might determine how much more investigative work he got out of the FBI.

'We wondered about that, but it didn't take us long to figure it out.'

Witten, who had been hunched forward, sat back into his chair, his head tilted to one side, his arms crossed. Daniel continued.

'The FBI is charged with investigating and, where possible, preventing crime within the jurisdiction of the United States. Any inquiry that might take it across a border would mean cooperating with other agencies both foreign and domestic. If that were to happen, you can't be guaranteed any measure of efficiency as language barriers, international protocol, perhaps even the self-serving intentions and motivations of others, who might not be as righteous as yourselves. They might look to slow you down, maybe even derail the investigation completely. You need somebody who can avoid the red tape and can relentlessly pursue the assignment to the end.'

He exchanged a glance with the man seated next to Witten, who remained poker-faced. Daniel refocused on Witten.

'The knowledge, expertise, and contacts we've gathered over the years are an invaluable resource at your disposal.'

Witten set his jaw and looked down at the small stack of folders before him. Daniel knew he'd hit the nail on the head. The FBI needed him just as much as he needed them. Witten nodded and glanced at the other man, who had listened silently to the exchange.

'And have you discussed the case since your return?' Witten asked, the irritation he had exhibited, now gone.

Daniel nodded, but it was Alona who spoke.

'We've assumed there is only one killer because more than one would require communication and coordination. Six murders in four states spread across the country is quite an achievement, especially in such a short space of time. Given the distances and timelines involved, the killer has chosen to fly, which doesn't present any problems, as the number of internal flights is substantial. Sifting through pages of manifests searching for a common passenger would take weeks for an army of administrators, by which time the killing spree might well have come to an end, especially if all potential targets have been secured by the FBI. In any event, the killer probably has false documentation. He likely changes his name for each flight, which means any manifest search performed would have been pointless.'

Witten played nervously with his wedding ring, twisting it on and off his finger. Alona continued.

'Then, there are weapons. The National Firearms Act of 1934 allows somebody to carry a concealed pistol or revolver without a license. However, he is prohibited from carrying a weapon on board an aircraft. Security at airports may not be as tight as it could be, but we assume that he wouldn't want to risk being stopped and searched and then answer any unnecessary and awkward questions. We've not received the ballistics report from Las Vegas yet, but the two from Pennsylvania and Georgia don't match. That means different weapons. So, he has to get them somewhere. Either he buys them at a local gun store, or they're being provided through some other support structure within the country. If it's the first option, it could indicate he's working alone, but if it's the second, then it poses a greater difficulty as this indicates a conspiracy. But, I'll come to that in a moment.'

She reached across to take the glass of water from in front of Witten. 'May I?'

He nodded and continued to listen when she continued.

'The fact that the killer has been able to find his victims with relative ease means he has a list. Names and addresses, maybe even other details like their daily routines. That information is not easily acquired. He may be working for the government in some capacity and has access to confidential information. We should be looking at all federal employees who have this level of security clearance and cross-check against holidays or sick leave. He may be one of the scientists who were liberated from Germany under 'Paperclip' and, for some reason or another, has fallen out with his former colleagues and decided to kill them. All those who came here after the war were well debriefed. You should have access to those files. Cross-checking the victims' records for commonalities such as projects they worked on and intersecting travel during the war might prove fruitful. We should look to see if any of their paths crossed during their lifetimes, places of birth, where they grew up, all of that.'

She took another sip of water and ran her tongue over the back of her teeth. Across the table, Witten's breathing had become labored, and Daniel knew Alona's assertions were more than a fictitious concoction imagined in his apartment over the past few days. She carried on.

'Then there is the conspiracy element. We contend that somebody or some organization has specifically targeted these men with the sole purpose of disrupting scientific advancement in America and is using a contract killer as their tool. They are directing him. They have provided him with a shopping list, and he is going about his business, perhaps needing little or no contact with his employers, which they no doubt prefer. Which brings me to the burning question: who has most to gain from the murders?'

She sat back, and the room fell silent for a short time before she continued.

'The only groups who benefit are those in direct competition for what-ever it was the victims provided. That could be any business that researches in the same areas, pharmaceutical companies, small corporates, trying to level the playing field. However…' she paused. 'With exception of the two Pennsylvania victims, all others worked in diverse areas of science. There-fore, there can be no common link between competitors. We believe it's improbable that a cohort of organizations cooperated, colluded, and devised a plan to eliminate competition from within their respective industries. So, if it is not several organizations, then it is one. It is either one organization or one country.'

'And that may explain why this assignment was given to us.' Daniel said. 'As I said, we can cross borders with relative ease, if needed. And, with my proficiency in languages, I can travel to many countries where English is not commonly spoken.'

The room went quiet again, longer than before. Witten broke the silence.

'Could you give us a few minutes to gather our thoughts?'

He looked from Daniel to Alona. They shared a glance before getting up and leaving the two FBI men alone.

'What do you think?' Alona said when they were out of earshot.

'I'm impressed with how much your English has improved,' Daniel said with a smile. 'I think they'll be impressed that you said all that without the aid of notes. I think we're in a good place. If they thought they were going to pin a failed investigation on us, then that ship has sailed. Not that I'd ever suspect our new employers of such a thing.'

He looked back to the meeting room, where it appeared as though the two men were engaged in a tense conversation.

'What do you think is going on in there? And, who was the other fella'?' he asked.

She shrugged. 'I've never seen him before. As for what they're talking about, maybe they're going to give us access to more information. We can't be sure they've told us the full story. Not that I would ever believe that of a new employer either.'

They both laughed.

'I'd die for a beer,' Daniel said. He looked around as though he'd be able to find a bar hidden away somewhere on the floor; all he saw were the tops of heads, their owners hunched over their desks. 'Let's take the rest of the day off and get pissed, charge it as 'further investigative discussion'.

He caught sight of Witten at the door, beckoning them back. 'We're on again.'

With the door closed behind them, they retook their seats. Witten and the other older man sat in silence as though deciding how best to open the next part of the discussion. Daniel didn't know what they would say although he had an inkling. Straight away, though, he detected a more affable ambiance in the room, the older man stood and introduced himself for starters.

'Nathan Simmonds, Assistant Director of the FBI.' He shook both Daniel and Alona's hands. He now wore a broad smile, clearly aimed at putting his guests at ease, but Daniel wasn't to be fooled.

'We'd like to thank you for your efforts to date,' Witten said, once everybody had sat back down. 'We realize this has been difficult from the start, especially for you coming into the assignment cold, as it were. So, what are our next steps?'

Simmonds sat motionlessly; his eyes closed, his hands in front of his face, his fingers forming a steeple as though he was praying.

It was a question designed to prod, to see just how far Daniel and Alona had considered the investigation, not only as an evaluation of the facts but a measure of their ability to take imaginative leaps forward and draw conclusions.

Daniel and Alona looked to each other, and her expression told him she wouldn't be fielding that particular question. He turned back.

'We're chasing our tails trying to catch a killer when we have no idea where he'll strike next. It's a big country, and we don't have the manpower. We need to get ahead of him. We need to be there when he strikes next.'

'But, we've taken everybody under a protective umbrella,' Witten said. 'Right now, there is nobody alive from Paperclip who hasn't got eyes on them.'

Daniel must have looked skeptical because Simmonds nodded solemnly in agreement.

'How would you feel about luring him to us,' Daniel said.

'You want to set a trap?'

'Sure.'

'Nobody in their right mind would agree to that; the risks are enormous.'

'Not if it's planned properly and everybody does their job correctly,' Daniel said. 'It'd also be better if the bait isn't aware of the operation. We need to ensure the killer doesn't suspect anything, and edgy bait would do just that.'

Daniel saw the look on their faces, both were unconvinced, and he didn't blame them. After all, it was a thought spoken in the heat of the moment, a proposal that gained credibility the more he thought about it.

'Look, you can't keep everybody from 'Paperclip' secure indefinitely and who's to say that the killer won't just wait you out and strike again as soon as your back is turned. You'd never know where or when, and we'd be right back here discussing the same problem, wishing we'd taken a chance to snare the guy.'

Everybody sat back and pondered the suggestion before Simmonds spoke up.

'It would have to be someone the killer would find impossible to pass up, even at enormous risk to himself.' A grin slowly started to appear on his face, and Daniel was reminded of his father's look when there was devilment in the air.

Witten, on the other hand, looked drawn. He glanced uneasily at Simmonds, his face growing paler the more the older man smiled, but he didn't say anything.

'Let's think about that some more,' Simmonds said. 'We'll be in touch in a day or two.'

With that, he tapped Witten on the arm, and both men stood and left the room, leaving Daniel and Alona to look at each other.

'How about that drink?' Daniel said.

She nodded. 'I'm buying.'

CHAPTER 19

CLANDESTINE GATHERINGS ARE FRAUGHT WITH danger whether it be from the person one is meeting or, depending on the circumstance, a law enforcement authority charged with preventing a criminal act; the very nature of the affair is generally peppered with suspicion and paranoia.

And so, when it was time for Sieber to meet his Russian contact at the pre-arranged time and place, he had arrived ninety minutes early to stake it out. He sat on a bench under the little thicket of trees at the intersection of Chambers Street and West Broadway, pretending to read a discarded newspaper that he'd fished out of a nearby bin.

It was overcast, and there was a stiff breeze coming in off the east river, tunneling right along Chambers. Sieber had wrapped up warmly in a long, dark, woolen winter-coat that reminded him of the sort he used to see dispatched by the carriage load to the Wehrmacht fighting on the eastern front. He pulled the collar up around the back of his neck and shrunk snugly into it.

'Marty's' was a small delicatessen on the corner of Chamber's and Broadway, slap bang in the heart of Tribeca and far enough from Foley Square and Wall Street as to not be frequented by either law enforcement or stockbrokers. It was a mostly residential district, so any retail premises in the area chiefly made their money at the start and end of the working day as people went to and from their places of employment. Now, only mothers, pushing their pre-school children, and other passing trade availed of their wares.

It was here he would meet Zorin Sokolov.

He had disliked the man the moment he'd set eyes on him, which had been expected given that he loathed all Soviets without exception. But, his abhorrence had been magnified as soon as the man had opened his mouth. Right from the get-go, Sieber had felt as though Sokolov believed he was in charge, passing on mission sensitive information as though doing him a favor, speaking to him as if he were an infant. Sieber could tell the man had never served in the Red Army and had him pegged for the son of a medium-ranked Kremlin official who'd managed to maneuver within the right political circles with the sole intention of elevating his prominence within the Communist Party.

Sieber had been given a list of Germans who'd come to the United States under the protection of a US government agency. It was short, prioritized and included a recent photo of each man, which led Sieber to wonder: if the communists had gone to the trouble of taking photographs then, why hadn't they just executed the subjects at the same time. Each name came with a small biography, no longer than a paragraph, detailing each man's specialty, family members, leisure activities, along with any lurid predilections which Sieber believed had been included to disgust thereby providing further motivation (if any were needed). As far as he was concerned, each man was a traitor to his beloved Germany and the Reich, and so should and would receive the appropriate sentence.

He was particularly sickened by what he'd read of Andreas Lenz and Jonas Otte, scarcely believing it until he saw the two together in Las Vegas. Of the six men he'd eliminated, their executions had been the most gratifying. He smiled as he remembered Lenz, the weaker of the two in his opinion, comforting his lover after he'd slashed Otte's Achilles tendons and preventing him from walking. With that single act, he'd inflicted terror into their minds and incapacitated both. He'd bound and gagged Lenz and flung him into a corner of their squalid room, forcing the man to watch as he set about stabbing Otte to death on the bed.

When done with him, he'd bundled Lenz into the boot of his rented car and driven out into the desert. He'd thought the man might struggle more than he had, but all he heard was the pathetic whimpering and sobbing of a coward who knew he would die for his crimes against The Fatherland.

He'd found it peculiar that both men had instinctively known they were going to die as soon as he'd forced his way into their hotel room, which was in contrast to the withering wretches he'd seen in the camps he'd visited across Europe during the war. Hope had seemingly been etched on their emaciated faces right up to the point when they realized that both it and their lives were slipping away; within them, it had always been the last thing to die.

He checked his watch as a cab pulled up to the curb a few doors from Marty's and, over the top of the paper, eyed the passenger as he got out.

Sokolov was early.

The Russian paused on the pavement and lit a cigarette. He took a couple of drags and glanced around, his gaze resting on a car that'd stopped on the opposite side of the street. He smiled, gave the occupants a little wave followed by the finger. His smile turned to a scowl, and he flicked the cigarette in their direction before heading into the deli.

Sieber looked back to the car and wondered who the men were. Judging by Sokolov's behavior, they weren't exactly on his Christmas card list, and if they weren't friendly, then they must be Americans sent to follow him. He thought about that for a moment, and it made sense. The American intelligence community wouldn't allow a Russian citizen, regardless of occupation, the freedom to wander about the city without knowing exactly where he was at all times. He wondered how much manpower the Americans had invested in tailing 'persons of interest' across their country. Had it been ten years earlier, and on a different continent, anyone who warranted such attention would have been whisked off the street and most likely never heard of again.

He smiled and shook his head in pity. In this land, it would be the freedom the Americans cherished so much that would eventually prove their downfall. How did they ever hope to succeed against enemies who despised their ideals and yet could so readily hide within the very protection offered by those same principles?

But, now he had a dilemma. With the Americans tailing Sokolov, should he abandon the meeting, in the hope that the Russian would make contact again at a later time, or be bullish and meet as planned, anyway?

Sieber thought for a moment. He hadn't seen anybody follow Sokolov inside, so he could assume he wouldn't be spotted if he went in through the rear, away from the prying eyes of the Americans out front. But, what if the Americans had anticipated Sokolov's destination and planted somebody inside?

He doubted it.

Sokolov had known they were following him and so wouldn't have led them to the meeting. Besides, he knew not to use the same meeting place more than once so how could the Americans have anticipated the location.

Sieber decided it was a risk worth taking.

He rechecked his watch and, after a moment of second-guessing himself, headed for the alley behind Marty's.

*

Nobody likes to pull a double shift, but Douglas Carter had rung his boss to say he wouldn't make it into work after his wife had finally given birth to a bouncing bundle of joy, having been three weeks overdue. And so, Rodney Goudeau had drawn the short straw and been ordered to replace the new father for today's assignment. He wasn't particularly pleased about it, having completed a full night tailing some foreign asshole from the Chinese embassy the length and breadth of Manhattan only to find himself back on the same street he had started out on more than ten hours earlier with fuck all to report other than the length of time his quarry had spent at various locations, who he'd met, what he'd had to eat and when and where he'd taken a dump. He looked across at Scott Peterson in the passenger seat.

Peterson had returned from Europe after the war, sometime in the winter of '45. A year earlier he'd landed on Utah Beach with the 4th Cavalry Group, had seen action in the Normandy hedgerows during June and July, and the Hurtgen Forest during the Battle of Bulge, where he'd received the

Distinguished Service Cross, the army's second-highest personal award. He'd been transferred to the Military Police in February '45, where he'd served out the remainder of the war.

Goudeau looked across at Peterson again.

'What?'

'You're making that damn noise again,' Goudeau said.

'Yeah, well it's hot. It's burning my lips.'

Goudeau raised his eyes to the roof. He rubbed them and stifled a yawn.

'You want some?' Peterson asked, offering the cup.

'Don't much care for the stuff.'

'It'll help keep you awake.'

'You're doing a grand job of that all by yourself.'

'I'm real sorry you had to come out with me today,' Peterson said.

'Can't be helped, not with Carter's kid 'n all.'

'Yeah, but you were real unlucky. I'd been all set for a relaxing day of paperwork until this guy jumped off the plane at LaGuardia. Only for him, you wouldn't have to be here.'

'Don't I know it?'

'Here.' Peterson thrust his cup into Goudeau's hand and reached behind him for the file on their newest assignment. He flicked through the threadbare details. 'Christ, we've fuck all on this guy. Two pages, that's it?'

'That's why we're here. To bulk up this dickhead's profile.'

Goudeau looked across the street at Marty's, as Peterson read out some of what was in the file.

'Zorin Sokolov. Russian, works for Novosil Oil and Gas Exploration up on Broadway and 19th. Bounces back and forth between New York and Washington, lobbying the bureaucrats down there. Young guy...'

He tossed the file behind him and took his coffee back.

'Makes you wonder,' Goudeau said. 'Guy gets on a plane, travels what... a little more than an hour to New York, hasn't any baggage, doesn't stop off anywhere as he's on his way to some deli in Tribeca, doesn't even go to his own office in Midtown. Just doesn't make sense to me.'

'Maybe Marty's does the best bagel in Manhattan?'

Goudeau looked at him with contempt. 'How long you been on this detail? Star and Shamrock do the best bagel in this town.'

'I know that. I was only messin' with you.' He slurped his coffee again.

Goudeau shook his head. He didn't know who to feel sorry for most, him or Carter, who had to put up with Peterson every other day.

A loud bang sounded nearby, like a small explosion except sharper and without the usual scattering of detritus that usually followed. It made Goudeau jump, and he bumped off his partner.

'Fuck.'

Goudeau looked across and smiled when he saw the coffee spilled over Peterson's legs. 'And beige pants too,' he said with a grin. 'That'll stain.'

'Not funny. I only bought these at the weekend.' Peterson looked around for something with which to wipe himself, but there was nothing to hand.

'Shit, that's hot.'

He opened the door and stepped out, doing a little jig as he pulled at the trousers, pulling them away from his skin. He looked around and spotted a hot dog vendor at the end of the block.

'I'll be back in a second.'

'Hurry up. We don't know when this asshole's goin' to leave.'

Goudeau watched Peterson shuffle down to the vendor and grab some napkins from him. He stopped after a few dabs and looked back towards Goudeau, shrugging forlornly. He glanced to his left and raised a finger to indicate he wouldn't be long before he disappeared from view.

'Jesus,' Goudeau muttered under his breath. He checked his watch and looked across at Marty's again. From where he'd parked, he couldn't see inside what with the reflection from the windows, but he hadn't seen anybody of note either enter or leave. He also had a full view of the alley entrance behind the delicatessen and Sokolov hadn't tried to ditch them by leaving that way. It was a good bet he was still inside eating his bagel, or for whatever it was he'd gone in.

A minute or so later, the door to Marty's opened and Sokolov came out. He waved across at Goudeau again before flagging down a cab. He jumped in, the car heading west down Chambers.

Goudeau didn't waste time thinking about what to do. He started the engine and took off in pursuit. As he passed, he glanced into the shop that Peterson had entered, but couldn't see the younger man. He carried on, swearing under his breath.

When Peterson eventually emerged, he discovered both Goudeau and the car were gone. A sickly feeling washed over him. What would his boss say when he showed up at Federal Plaza alone? More to the point, what would he do? He'd been absent from his post and allowed a suspect to escape and why? All because he'd spilled coffee on a new pair of trousers.

Out of the corner of his eye, he spotted the door to Marty's opening. He took a step back against the shop he'd just left. He saw a man exit and hail a passing taxi. Even with the hat, he was sure he'd seen the face before, but he couldn't place it. Maybe, it was somebody he'd met during his FBI career; he'd met so many people over the past eight years. He shook his head and paid it no further mind.

All he could think about as he walked back to the FBI Field Office was how, after a flawless and decorated military career, he might well be finished with the Federal government. How could he have been so fucking stupid? One lapse in concentration, that's all it had taken, and his life in counter-intelligence was over. If his superiors wanted to make an example of him to others, he'd be moved to another division like planning or strategy and demoted at the same time. His career would never recover. He'd be better off resigning and starting up a golf driving range somewhere in Nantucket.

He pulled his jacket tightly around his body, attempting to keep the cold at bay, the breeze smacking him in the face, perhaps as punishment for his transgression. If that were the only price he'd pay to avoid a reprimand, then he'd gladly suffer it.

He turned left up Broadway, then right on Duane Street, stopping off at a small café to buy another coffee to replace the one he'd spilled over himself. After some time, he found himself at Foley Square where he sat on a bench and waited for an appropriate amount of time before deciding to bite the bullet, go in, and come clean.

He was walking towards the building when he heard his name called out. He looked around and saw Goudeau stroll toward him.

'You didn't get it all out.' He motioned towards Peterson's trousers. 'Sorry, I had to let you walk back,' he said. 'Russian guy left just as you went into that shop. I looked in but didn't see you, so I followed him on my own. Fucker headed straight back to LaGuardia, hopped onto a waiting plane, and flew back to Washington. Here.'

He handed Peterson the notebook they'd been keeping of Sokolov's activity.

'I'm done for the day. Anybody needs me, tell them I'll see them tomorrow.'

Goudeau turned to leave but stopped. 'By the way, nobody needs to know you missed the last bit of the tail. Nothing happened. So we're good, yeah?'

'Sure,' Peterson said. 'Thanks. I owe you.'

He watched Goudeau walk away before calling out.

'Maybe I'll buy you a bagel in Marty's? They're obviously pretty fuckin' good.'

CHAPTER 20

THREE DAYS HAD PASSED SINCE he'd met with the FBI, and nobody had called, or more to the point, Alona hadn't called to say they'd been in touch. Daniel was beginning to wonder if maybe he and Alona had overplayed their hand, declaring outlandish theories of corrupt governments and if now, the FBI wanted to put some distance between themselves and their consultants before eventually terminating their arrangement. As the days passed, he became more convinced that the next call he'd receive would be a request to hand in the firearm and his credentials with a polite 'thank you' for your service, 'your check is in the mail'. As a consequence, he'd started thinking of other lines of work he could get into.

It was Thursday, 26th March and St. Patrick's Day had passed him by, so he'd decided to celebrate belatedly with an expensive six-year-old bottle of 'Chateau Pichon Longueville'. In the background, Mahler's 2nd Symphony played on the turntable.

Earlier that day, he'd been to see an advance screening of Hitchcock's latest thriller 'I Confess', starring Montgomery Clift, and Anne Baxter. A friend, who knew a guy who knew the wife of another guy, who ran a small cinema, had been given the movie reels by the distribution company a week before the official opening. In the true spirit of entrepreneurship and capitalism, the guy who ran the cinema spread the word quietly, and one could gain entry for a few bucks and the promise to keep your mouth shut.

Long live the 'Great American Dream'.

So, as Daniel sipped on his third glass of the evening, he sat staring out his window at the passing traffic. As the shadows crept up the buildings opposite, his thoughts drifted to a career without the FBI.

Of course, his propensity for languages and real-word experience would certainly help in any future endeavor. Perhaps, something in the United Nations? Having been created only eight years ago, it was an organization still in its infancy, each nation jostling for position and power beneath its diplomatic umbrella. But it was growing every day. If ever there was a place that could use the skills he had to offer, that was it. Location though was the main downside. He'd been to New York a handful of times and hated the place. Too many people, too many cultures crushed together on a tiny island, like bacteria on a pinhead. And, as for the weather, it was colder in winter and hotter in summer than Washington, and neither extreme appealed to him.

Then, there was England. He could always go back to London and get a job with one of the intelligence agencies there. There he had plenty of contacts, people he'd met fleetingly or otherwise during both his wartime and post-war activities. Encouragingly, he'd managed to piss-off only some of them, so there were options if he was willing to return. But, then there was the weather – a temperate climate of grey drabness along with the need to carry a raincoat every day of the year didn't do anything for him.

His thoughts drifted north and to his home in a small Yorkshire village. Apart from the house, there was nothing for him there anymore. Both his parents were dead and his older brother, Alex, had fallen before he could reach Dunkirk's beach to stare upon the horizon in the hope of salvation. He didn't think of his brother often, but when he did, the memories were bright and vivid, better than any Technicolor newsreel footage. He wondered if Alex's death had meant anything in the grand scheme of things and mused that the bullet that got him would probably have ended up in the back of some other fearful Tommy scampering through the French hedgerows, fleeing the Blitzkrieging Nazi's. He wondered if it had been worth it and with that, had any of the killings he'd committed made any difference. The world still turned, and the majority of the people on it still made poor and selfish decisions, willfully, it seemed, refusing to learn from past failures.

He sipped his wine and rested his head against the side of the armchair.

He considered making a list of employment options, their pros and cons, and scoring each out of ten. He wasn't a fussy man, but he'd been through enough hardship in his life to believe he'd earned the right to choose what he would do next.

He turned his head and saw a little red beret appear around the corner and under it, Gail, carrying a couple of shopping bags. Even at this distance, she looked tired. She plodded slowly, as though stumbling towards a desert oasis.

Daniel thought for a moment before standing up and lifting the needle off the record. He grabbed a second bottle of wine from the fridge, slipped his apartment keys into his pocket, and trotted down the stairs.

He was just out the front door by the time she'd started climbing the steps of her home on the other side of the street. He skipped across and put a foot on the bottom step.

'Hi.'

She half-turned and smiled wearily, but a smile, nonetheless.

He raised the bottle in his hand

'Read my mind,' she said. 'Help me with these?'

Daniel skipped up the steps and took the heaviest bag from her. She fumbled with a bunch of keys before finding the right one and pushing her way through the door with her hip. She led him down the hall and into the kitchen at the back, putting the bags onto a table. Daniel did the same.

'Glasses?' he said.

'In the cabinet over there.' She nodded across into the kitchen area and started to unpack.

Daniel poured then put the bottle in the fridge. He walked across to the window at the back of the apartment. It wasn't anything that might be described as a decent view, only the side of the apartment block (no more than ten yards away) that opened onto P-Street. He looked up at the building, but couldn't see the sky. On the ground between, somebody had attempted to cultivate a small garden but seemed to have given up once the fruitlessness of it became apparent.

Behind him, the sound of Count Basie's Orchestra began to fill the room. He turned and handed a glass to Gail as she walked across to him.

'You like jazz?' Daniel asked.

'It relaxes me.'

'Really? You don't look like you need any.'

'Stress resides deep inside me. Jazz helps bring it to the surface so that it can be expelled. Do you like my taste?' She cocked her head and pushed her hair behind her ear.

'I like classical, but can be persuaded to try different things.'

She sipped the wine. 'Gosh, that's good. Don't think I've tried it before.'

Daniel smiled. 'Probably not.'

She kicked off her shoes and into a corner, and sat down, her legs folded in under her. She patted the space next to her on the sofa. Daniel joined her.

'How come you're home drinking, and on a workday too?'

'I'm not at work today.'

'What do you do?'

'Consultancy stuff.'

Her eyes explored his face, searching for clues of what might lie beneath. 'All very vague and mysterious.'

'I don't mean to be.'

'Sure you do, it adds to the intrigue.'

Daniel looked around the room. The layout was a mirror of his place, which was somewhat disconcerting, the architecture identical except the opposite. She'd chosen to paint rather than paper her walls, the colors, dark and vibrant; Daniel wondered what, if anything, that said about the sort of person she was. Did it offer a greater insight into her personality? To his right, an unset fireplace stood dark and empty in the center of the wall with an alcove on either side. In one, an old bookcase rose floor to ceiling, its shelves packed and buckling under the weight of books of varying sizes, thicknesses, and topics. A floral dress was draped over an armchair in the other, a pair of discarded nylons and stilettos next to it.

'What do you do?' he said, returning to face her.

'I'm a reporter.'

'Are you going to ask me questions? You should know I'm good at handling interrogations.'

'My life is all about questions.' She smiled.

'What about answers?'

'Not all the time.'

'An investigative journalist so?'

'Oh, I wouldn't go that far.'

'What does that mean?'

Gail went quiet for a time, her smile disappearing. 'It's a man's world.'

'The world in general or just journalism?'

'I suppose it can be applied equally to both.' Her smile returned.

They sat quietly, sipping their drinks, as the lyrical strains of 'Oh! Lady Be Good', preventing any awkwardness that silence might have promoted. Daniel leaned back into the sofa and closed his eyes.

'I love your accent,' Gail said after a time.

'I've had it all my life.'

'That's funny, me too.'

'Really? You don't sound like you come from Yorkshire.'

She gave him a playful dig.

'Let me try and guess what you do,' she said.

'Sure.'

She turned to look at him full-on, taking a long sip of wine, her lips resting tantalizingly on the rim of the glass for a moment.

'The facts first. You're from England but live in Washington. You haven't lost your accent, so you haven't been here all that long. You can afford, and have a taste, for fine wine, yet you don't care what time of day you drink it.'

'You're good.' He laughed.

'You have a scar.' She leaned across and traced her finger from his eye to cheekbone. 'It's not all that old, maybe a war wound. You have good healing skin, so it's difficult to see unless up close and were looking for it.'

Daniel could smell the perfume on her wrist, a warm, exotic scent that complimented her. 'You've enough to go on,' he said.

She pursed her lips and nodded. 'You're the British Ambassador's estranged husband who, having had enough of your drunkenness and general bad behavior, kicked your ass out on the street after you tried to attack the head chef at The Jefferson for overcooking your steak.'

Daniel laughed out loud this time.

'The poor man, of oriental origin, and very handy with knives, had been slaving in a roasting kitchen all night when you and your wife strolled in after the kitchen had closed and demanded to be served. You threatened to have the place shut down; you are, or were, very well connected, after all. The chef is quite tempermental, as all head chefs tend to be, and attacked you with a cleaver. He was able to strike once before being restrained by your wife's bodyguards.'

Daniel looked across at Gail, his eyes wide.

'How'd I do?'

With a sheepish grin, Daniel shook his head almost imperceptibly.

'Not even close. For starters, the British Ambassador is Sir Roger Makins, and he's happily married to Alison Brooks Davis, daughter of Dwight Davis, founder of the Davis Cup. You are right, I do like my wines, and as I can afford to pay for them, I like to think I can drink them anytime I chose, day or night.' He laughed. 'As for the scar, you got that part is right.'

'You were attacked by an Asian chef?' She stared openmouthed.

'No. An old war wound.'

'How'd it happen?' She leaned forward, her interest piqued.

Daniel went across to the counter and refilled his glass, offering more to Gail – she shook her head.

'I was dumb enough to get caught in an air raid.'

'The Blitz?'

Daniel nodded. He walked to the window again, his mind flitting to the girl who'd lost her life that night. No matter how hard he tried, he hadn't been able to recall her face since. He changed the subject. 'You really should move to a place with a better view.' He could feel Gail's eyes watch him and knew she wanted to hear his story. The room grew silent, the record coming to an end, the player resetting itself. Finally, he heard the sofa sigh as she fell back into it.

'Not on what I get paid.'

'You mean they pay you to stick your nose into other people's business?'

'Not very well.'

'It's a living, I suppose.'

'My parents say that too then they shrug their shoulders and change the subject.'

He turned back to her. 'Why did you come to Washington?'

'How do you know I'm not from here?'

He laughed. 'Nobody is actually from Washington. Everybody comes here to work. The place shuts down at the weekends. Besides, you're not even American.'

'I didn't think you'd know the difference.'

'Between a Yank and a Canuck? Hear that?' He cupped a hand behind his ear. 'Everybody north of the 49th parallel just let out a collective groan.'

Gail smiled, cradling the glass in her hands, looking at the bubbles rise and explode when they broke the surface. 'I didn't want to be a reporter in a hick town across the border where the breaking news is how many apple pies Ms. Perkins baked for the school fundraiser.'

'So instead, you came to Washington where you're trying to make a name for yourself, reporting on world events.'

'Yes. If something happens anywhere in the world, you can bet somebody here is involved, knows about it, or has an opinion about it. After decades of isolation, America stands at the forefront of global politics. The decisions made here affect everybody on the planet. Isn't that worth reporting?'

Her voice had taken on a serious tone, and she looked soberly at Daniel.

'Sounds like you've got it all figured out.'

'You say that like it's a bad thing.'

He shook his head. 'I guess I'm still trying to figure out what I'm supposed to be doing with my life.' He turned back to the window and craned his neck to peek up at the sky.

'Do you think the answer is up there?' Gail stood beside him. She touched her hand off his, her fingertips brushing his.

'Answers are everywhere; I just need to see them.' His head dropped.

'Maybe I could help?'

He turned and gazed into her eyes. 'I'd like that.'

CHAPTER 21

THE AIR WAS CLEAN AND crisp as Sieber walked north along Broadway, the grey clouds that had unloaded their burden the previous night, having cleared away inland, replaced now by flurries of brilliant-white puffs of cloud that chased each other playfully between the skyscrapers. The ground was still saturated, but the streets would soon dry if the rain clouds failed to return. Creeks of rainwater flowed along the gutters and trickled into drains, flooding the sewers beneath Manhattan.

He walked in the shade of the buildings until he got to the corner of 19th Street, where he leaned against the wall and lit a cigarette. He inhaled deeply, tilting his head back to enjoy the burst of nicotine surge into his body. He glanced up at the 4th floor of the building that stood on the corner opposite and saw the blinds had been lowered on the three rightmost windows.

He smiled to himself, feeling a prickle of excitement sprout from within.

He'd looked at the same windows for the past five days, hoping to see the signal, but none had been displayed; all blinds pulled to the top. So, each day he'd been forced to backtrack to the accommodation provided him by the Russians to wait another twenty-four hours. Today, thankfully, was different. He continued north a spring in his step as he passed the Flatiron building and turned onto 5th Avenue.

He didn't light another cigarette until he arrived at the corner of 41st Street, where he admired the two lions that stoically guarded the entrance of the New York Public Library at Bryant Park. He had come to believe that 'Fortitude and Patience' had symbolized the spirit of his mission and thought it fitting that his Russian co-conspirators had chosen this location as their drop point.

He stubbed out what remained of the cigarette and crossed the road, climbing the steps and entering the building. He showed his card to the librarian at reception and took the stairs to the 3rd floor where he walked along a shined, parquet floor until he came to the end of the corridor. He turned left and headed to the 'Genealogy' room at the back of the building.

The room was deserted, as it usually was so early in the day. Shelves laden with books of various sizes, weights, and origin lined the walls. Between sections of shelves stood numerous busts and figurines of once-famous but now deceased people of which Sieber had never heard. He crossed the room and walked to the corner furthest away from the entrance, his hand running along the fourth shelf, seeking out an old, bulky reference book that detailed families who lived in Massachusetts between 1820 and 1870. He slid it from the rack and brought it across to a reading table. He took a seat facing the entrance and flicked through to page fifty-three. There, he found a slip of paper that had been left sometime before. He committed the details he read to memory: a name, a date, a time, and a location.

After replacing the book, he made his way back downstairs and out onto 5th Avenue, rereading what was on the paper one last time before shredding it, and tossing it into a nearby bin.

While he walked back to Little Italy, he thought about the name he'd been given. It was the name of one, if not the most, famous German who had been repatriated to the United States after the war and, for Sieber, epitomized the reason he had decided to embark upon his crusade against those he deemed traitors to his beloved Fatherland.

Wernher von Braun had been both a Nazi Party member and a Lieutenant in the SS. He had sworn oaths in the '30s only to recant the day he surrendered to the Americans. In doing so, he had turned his back on those who Sieber himself had adored. Even if it were the last, Von Braun's scalp would be an appropriate addition to those he had already taken.

As luck would have it, the man was due to visit New York this coming weekend. He would be the keynote speaker at an event to be held in his honor at the Waldorf Astoria Hotel on the evening of Friday 3rd April, a few days before Easter Sunday. Honor, the very idea that the Americans could confer such an accolade on a man who, through his actions, had displayed anything but, rekindled the fires of hate in Sieber's soul. It would be a pleasure to execute such an individual, especially at such a public forum. He smirked. It would be a Good Friday indeed.

It bemused Sieber that the American Press had not made mention of the other deaths he had inflicted over the past month, and wondered if the American authorities had gagged them. Perhaps, the Press was unaware of what he had done, that his deeds had until now gone unnoticed or unconnected; that would certainly change this weekend. He'd ensure the whole world would know what became of traitors once uncovered.

*

Daniel despised wearing anything around his neck, but the occasion demanded he dress appropriately, which meant a black tuxedo and matching bowtie. But, he'd had to call the hotel concierge to ask for assistance, having never wrapped such an accursed thing around himself before. Now that it was securely in place, he felt as though it might constrict the blood flow to his brain. He swallowed hard and wriggled his head back and forth to loosen it a little.

He stood back and admired himself in the mirror. Even if the night failed to lure his prey, getting dressed up in this garb might prove fruitful with any single ladies who might happen to be in attendance, although he doubted there would be many, if any, given the topic for the evening.

He checked his watch. It was time to head down to the ballroom.

The FBI had already placed personnel in the hotel, scattered about the venue in various guises from waiters to attendees. They'd been obliged to supplement von Braun's usual protection contingent with a handful of additional agents, so as not to make the target too inviting, and thereby arouse suspicion that this was anything other than a genuine event.

It had been a gamble that Simmonds had mulled over for several days before giving the green light. The irony wasn't lost on Daniel, as the FBI had backed itself into a corner by providing additional security to those they had relocated, thereby preventing their quarry from continuing his killing spree. And so, in hosting tonight's gala dinner, Simmonds had been obliged to create a chink in the protective shield he'd erected in the hope that the bait would be too great to pass up.

As Daniel skipped down the stairs, his thoughts moved to what they would do if tonight's event went off smoother than anticipated. He was all out of ideas if the killer didn't take the bait and he was pretty sure the FBI was equally perplexed.

They were betting the house on a single roll of the dice.

The ballroom was beautifully decorated, with large floral bouquets placed at regular intervals around the perimeter. At the far end of the room stood an elevated platform and podium, and between it and the main exit, where Daniel now stood, were more than thirty circular tables that would seat twelve guests each. Silver cutlery and fine-cut, crystal glasses sparkled, adding to the sense of grandness that $100 a dinner would buy. For authenticity, Simmonds had been compelled to invite guests from New York's high society and political elite. Tickets had been snapped up, which had caused him still more heartache as, not only was he responsible for the safety of von Braun but also, those who would attend the charade.

At that moment, the only people in the room were a handful of waiting staff who were putting the finishing touches to the tables, and some tuxedo-wearing security guards who were completing one last sweep of the venue before the main event. Arriving guests were invited to sip champagne and gossip in an ante-room off the main foyer before being called for dinner. Daniel didn't bother to scan the faces of those already there, as he felt sure the killer wouldn't turn up as a regular paying customer.

He headed for the kitchen instead.

Even before he opened the door, he felt a pang of hunger as a rich and savory aroma tickled his senses. He went in.

It was a large area filled with smartly uniformed chefs, toiling between arrays of metallic counters and shelving units. Despite the frenzied activity, there was little by way of conversation as everybody seemed to be working in unison to a clear and well-rehearsed plan. If the killer were here, he would have been easy to spot, so Daniel decided to look elsewhere.

He completed a cursory search of the hotel's ground floor, noting the faces of some of the guests and staff as he went. Pretty soon, and with few exceptions, each blended into one another, and he felt sure he wouldn't be able to recognize somebody who he hadn't seen before. He wondered if he should discount all the women, but thought that might be foolhardy. However improbable, there was always the possibility the killer was a woman – he'd witnessed that when in Russia.

As for von Braun, he wouldn't arrive until after the guests were seated, no doubt entering to a standing ovation which Daniel found bizarre in itself. He would be accompanied by his wife, Maria Luise. They would dine with the Mayor of New York and his wife, both of whose names escaped him at that time, although he seemed to recall they sounded Italian.

At the stroke of eight, Daniel heard a tinkling bell and raised voices from the ante-room as waiters called the guests to dinner. Over the next ten minutes, the ballroom began to fill with a cacophony of conversation, chairs being moved, and glasses being dished out and clinked with whatever complimentary drinks were on offer.

Daniel took up an innocuous position in one corner which provided him a full view of the ballroom. While he waited for the room to settle, he wondered how many of them had even heard of the man they were here to honor, let alone know the role he played in the regime of which he'd been a member-only eight years ago. Not all old wounds could be healed by the passage of time, but then maybe that was a matter of perspective. On the face of it, the night seemed to be more about wearing the latest fashions and being seen with other New York socialites, rather than bearing grudges. Maybe for these folk, it was more about social aesthetics than the returning coffins of those they'd sent to war.

A momentary flurry of activity to the left of the platform caught his attention. A middle-aged man with a pretty woman on his arm stood taking instructions from another equally well-dressed man who Daniel knew to be the Master of Ceremonies for the evening. They were surrounded by four extremely serious-looking gentlemen, who had eyes on everything and everybody but the man they were guarding. Daniel had met them yesterday along with those other agents who had been carefully embedded amongst the guests, so everybody knew whose side they were on if it came to any shooting. He'd come out of that meeting feeling a lot more confident of the plan than he had before he'd entered.

The MC smiled to von Braun, shook his hand warmly, and marched to the podium. On cue, the room went quiet.

'Ladies and gentlemen, Wernher von Braun and his wife, Maria Luise.' Simple and effective, Daniel thought.

As predicted, those seated stood as one, and the guest of honor entered to rapturous applause. Mostly everybody smiled; Daniel focused on those who didn't.

Once the von Brauns were seated, a small squad of waiters swarmed like cockroaches from the kitchen and dished out hor's d' oeuvres – everybody tucked in.

Daniel made a mental note of where all the agents were in the room and tried to recognize those who'd been glamorized for the evening; at least they were getting a free meal while he watched on.

The main courses followed, and everybody gorged, except von Braun, who looked a little apprehensive. As far as Daniel knew, the man was unaware that he was the worm on the hook, so presumed it was just pre-speech nerves.

Desserts came next, but not everybody ate, most waiting for tea and coffee to finish off their meal. By now, Daniel's stomach had started to rumble, but he resisted the urge to disappear and grab some leftovers.

When the time came for the main event, von Braun's mood had changed. For starters, he smiled and waved to the crowd when called to the podium like a condemned man displaying a defiant act of bravery but who knew there was no escaping his fate.

Daniel's awareness level, having risen steadily throughout the night, now peaked. He looked at the exits on both sides of the podium and scanned the crowd and waiting staff. He tensed and slowly shifted from one foot to the other.

New York's Mayor, whose name Daniel still struggled to recall, gave a quaint introductory speech before presenting von Braun with some expensive glass creation, which might well have cost more than it had to feed an entire table. Von Braun placed it gently to one side and addressed those gathered.

He began with his childhood. Born in Poland, where initially he'd had no great love for science, but rather fancied himself as a musician; apparently, he played piano and cello to an acceptable standard – a talent unknown to Daniel but which still did little to redeem the man. He went on to talk about how his life changed after he'd read a book about rockets and space travel. And that was where the biography came to an end. There was no mention of what he did during the war, his Nazi Party membership, his association with the SS, or how he used concentration camp inmates to progress his experiments at Mittelwerk and Peenemünde. And, Daniel couldn't blame him for attempting to bury or at least try and hide his past. The remainder of the speech was about how everybody should follow their dreams as he had, and how he was now working to help get the Americans into space. Von Braun spoke eloquently and with passion and, despite the German accent, had everybody hanging on his every word.

When finished, von Braun took another round of applause, louder and longer than that previously received, proving to Daniel that any memory of heinous deeds committed can be easily vanquished by poetic rhetoric. Von Braun left the stage, and Daniel scoured the room for a hint of anything out of the ordinary. He saw nothing and began to wonder if the bait would be taken at all.

The band that had been quietly playing in the background during the meal started to ramp things up with a Strauss waltz. Couples began to emerge from the carnage they'd left at their tables and dance.

It was more difficult for Daniel to keep an eye on von Braun with so much more movement, which forced him to move closer to the German. He meandered between tables, keeping one eye on von Braun and another on those who approached seeking to shake the man's hand, and there were many. It seemed the man had a great deal of admirer's.

It was almost midnight when it came time for the von Brauns to depart. They'd danced some, ate some, and spoke a lot. Handshakes were offered all round as the four men charged with his security waited patiently at the same door they'd entered through hours earlier. The von Brauns left with Daniel following at a discrete distance.

The route to the car took them through the bowels of the hotel, the parts most frequented by staff and, oddly enough, as a means of secure exit for the hotel's more important guests. Despite that, it was here that Daniel felt the killer would have the best opportunity to strike. It was quiet, there were multiple entry and exit points, and sections of the meandering route were shaded in pockets of darkness, affording a-would-be assassin the perfect location for an ambush. He felt his heart quicken, and he stepped up his pace, shortening the distance between him and the entourage. He looked ahead and to the sides of the party, as it snaked its way underground towards a waiting car.

When they emerged in the car park beneath the hotel, von Braun paused for a cigarette as his wife slipped into the back of the car. No more than a minute passed before von Braun shivered in the damp air, discarded the butt, and joined his wife. One of the agents opened the passenger door and was about to step in when there was a loud crack.

Everybody froze.

The agent slumped to the ground, clutching his stomach as the car containing the von Brauns sped away, the passenger door swinging loosely. Daniel and two other agents gave chase, the sound of their vehicle sparking to life from behind. Everybody had their guns out.

Gripping the steering wheel in one hand and with a handgun dangling the other, Sieber accelerated up the ramp, skidding to the left at the top, the chasing agents disappearing from view behind him. The streets were virtually deserted at this time of night as he tore through red lights, and swerved around the odd pedestrian who'd strayed onto the roads.

'What is this?' Von Braun said his voice a combination of fear and outrage.

Sieber said nothing, his foot pressing hard on the accelerator, pushing it to the floor.

'I demand you stop immediately and let us out,' von Braun said although his tone was now uncertain.

Sieber smiled and spoke in German. 'Soon, Herr von Braun. We haven't far to go.'

Behind him, von Braun and his wife exchanged frightened glances and clutched each other's hands.

The car tore westward through Park, Madison, 5th and 6th Avenues before turning left onto 7th, and heading south. The streets were busier here as Broadway theatre-goers meandered about the streets, slipping in and out of bars; a nightcap after their evening's entertainment.

Sieber slowed down, coming to a stop near 47th Street and gently nestling the car against the curb at Times Square. He turned to the von Brauns and waved the gun in their faces.

'Out.'

They hesitated, each looking furtively to the other, desperately seeking an alternative in one another. Sieber didn't offer them one.

'Out now, or I'll blow your fucking heads off where you sit.'

They both reached for and fumbled at the door before stepping out onto the road where Sieber was already calmly waiting for them.

'That way,' Sieber said, motioning them onto the street.

Some nearby pedestrians, their smiles quickly fading, moved off to the side of the pavement nearest the buildings like sheep moving to the side of a pen to avoid a fox that had found a way in. Sieber ushered his elegantly dressed hostages across the street and onto the center island between Broadway and 7th.

Once on the path, Sieber spoke again. 'On your knees.'

A look of horror was carved on the von Brauns' faces, their mouths half open, both still in shock. Maria Luise began to cry. She tried to say something to her husband, but only gasps of air escaped her moving lips. Sieber smiled, thoroughly enjoying the terror he was inflicting.

'Don't worry. It'll be over soon,' he said. 'On your knees.' He struck von Braun across the face with the gun, and the man crumpled, his wife dropping to the ground next to him, holding him close, whimpering into his chest.

Unhurried, Sieber moved the handgun back and forth between the couple, as though deciding which to shoot first. The gun eventually stopped on the wife. A cruel smile creased Sieber's face. He took a deep breath and tightened his finger on the trigger.

A shot rang out.

Sieber bucked in surprise and held his leg. He swung the gun around, but bucked twice more, as several more shots and screams from the passersby resonated throughout the Square.

Sieber fell to the ground, the gun slipping from his hand.

Daniel was the first to reach him. He kicked Sieber's gun to one side, as three agents, their weapons drawn, circled the wounded man. He looked down at the moaning man.

He was young, his hair a tight crew cut, his complexion pale and coated with sweat, his eyes frantic. He screamed hoarsely in German, words that Daniel couldn't make out. Judging by the blood on his clothes, he'd been hit three times, once in the leg, twice in the torso. It was impossible to tell if any would be fatal.

One of the agents retrieved the assassin's gun, while another took the von Brauns back to their car, comforting them along the way. The third agent wrapped cuffs roughly on the wounded man, as a flustered police officer hurried alongside, brandishing his revolver. They identified themselves, and asked him to call for back up to control the growing crowd of interested onlookers, and for an ambulance to take their charge to the hospital.

Daniel crouched down and went through the man's pockets, finding a handful of dollar bills and two keys. One looked like it might fit a front door latch, while the other, a large brass key that one might use for an internal door. He wondered why the man had chosen this place to execute von Braun. Had it been the publicity of the killing that had been denied him thus far by the FBI, all he craved? Had he wanted to ensure his death at the same time? Daniel resolved to find out as, in the end, neither had happened.

Daniel watched over the killer, as they waited for the medics to arrive. He wanted answers and knew his best, and maybe only chance was by getting in his questions first.

CHAPTER 22

THE MAN HAD SUSTAINED THREE gunshot wounds during the skirmish; one of the agents had hit him in the upper, right leg, while Daniel had placed two in the abdomen. As guessed, none were life-threatening, all three having passed straight through without hitting bone, arteries or any vital organs, although one had sliced through his appendix which may have saved him a minor surgery somewhere down the line. Daniel couldn't quite believe the guy had only been hit three times given the volley of shots that'd been fired. For that matter, he was equally amazed that nobody else had been caught in the crossfire in the packed Time Square. Sure, there'd been dozens of other minor injuries to some, mainly cuts and scrapes after they'd dove to the ground once the shooting had started, but nothing that antiseptic gauze and a claim off the Federal government wouldn't heal.

Daniel had insisted on traveling in the back of the ambulance for the short trip to Lenox Hill Hospital up on East 77th Street. The man had slipped in and out of consciousness as they'd spoken, where Daniel had learned only his name. Oddly, Sieber seemed relieved at having been captured, an uncharacteristic calm settling over him, while he lay on the trolley, perhaps believing he would soon die. Daniel had seen soldiers with wounds far worse than those sustained by the German, so knew he'd pull through when the doctors set to work on him.

If Daniel had had his way, he would have made the ambulance drive to Mount Sinai on Madison Avenue as it would have served as a useful demonstration that Jewish doctors and nurses took their Hippocratic oaths very seriously, treating everybody equally, no matter what atrocities they'd committed in the past. But, the powers that be had seen to it that

Lenox Hill would be his destination and so there he now lay, hooked up to both morphine and saline drips.

Ironically, Winston Churchill had been treated in the same place twenty-two years earlier after he'd been hit by a car while crossing 5th Avenue – how different things might have turned out had the vehicle been traveling any faster than it had been.

Daniel had been debriefed by a beaming Agent Witten in a small waiting room just off the hospital lobby for all of ten minutes and then told to go back to his hotel to await further instructions. He couldn't tell if the guy were pleased with how things had turned out, or relieved that the bait had remained alive and ignorant of the role he'd played in the apprehension of the murderer of several of his colleagues.

Daniel declined the offer of a lift from New York's finest, choosing to walk instead. It was a short hike north to the Warwick Hotel on W 54th Street, a five-star he'd selected for the duration of his stay in the Big Apple. The expenses provided to him wouldn't have covered the hors d'oeuvres in this place, but he didn't mind throwing the extra cash towards it himself; the alternative might be a 2-star in Harlem and even he wasn't that brave.

He walked through the hotel lobby and headed directly for the bar. It was the early hours of Saturday morning, and the place was pretty quiet, as most patrons were either coiled up in their beds or still out enjoying the distractions the city that never slept had to offer. He found a stool at the end of the bar far enough from the piano player that he could still enjoy the tinkling ivories but low enough that he could think about tonight's events. He put a twenty on the counter and asked the barman for a double Brandy and a telephone. He rang Alona's number via an operator.

'We caught him,' Daniel said.

'Dead or alive?' She sounded thankful.

'Alive, but full of holes.'

'How many?'

'Six.'

'Shot six times, and he's not dead?'

'Hit three times, they all went through. I got him twice.'

'Aren't you the hotshot?'

'Yes, I am.' He chuckled.

'So that's it. Case closed?'

'I reckon so. All we need to do now is lodge the cheque. How's Anthony?'

'In bed.'

'Hope I didn't wake him.'

'That child would sleep through an earthquake. Where are you now?'

'In the hotel bar.'

There was a pause on the other end.

'Eating or drinking?'

'The latter, although I've just realized I haven't eaten since before six.'

He nodded across to the barmen and put his hand over the receiver.

'Can I get a club sandwich?'

The guy wrote the order on a pad and went across to one of the waitresses.

'Doing both now,' Daniel said.

'Great. It's not good to drink on an empty stomach.'

'You're like my mother. I'll call you in the morning. Can you book a return flight for tomorrow evening?'

'You don't want to stay longer?'

'I wish I was already gone.'

Alona laughed. They said their goodbyes and hung up.

A wave of tiredness swept over Daniel.

'Can I get that sent to my room?' he said to the barman. '612.'

The barman made a note of it. 'Would you like another for the road?'

'Haven't heard that expression in a while. Sure. Make it a double.'

His drink arrived, and Daniel tossed another twenty on top of the first.

'Keep the change.'

Daniel walked to the elevator carrying a Brandy in each hand.

By the time the porter arrived with his sandwich, Daniel was fast asleep.

*

Morozov left the office on foot, forcing one of the agents tailing him to get out of the car while it crawled behind. He walked briskly east down D-Street and waited for the lights on the corner of 7th to change. Crossing, he stopped to admire some shoes in a window before continuing. He went into a neat, little café midway between 7th and 6th, quickly hurrying past the service counter, through to the staff resting area in the back. He pushed through a heavy metal door and stepped into the alley between a few parked delivery trucks in various stages of unloading. His head down, he hurried to the far side and went in through one of the open doors. He brushed past a guy carrying a handful of boxes, through another set of doors, eventually ending up in a haberdashery store. Walking past the retail staff that ignored him, he exited the shop on Indiana Avenue and slipped into a waiting taxi. Without exchanging words, the cab driver pulled away from the curb and drove at a moderate pace up the avenue before taking a right and heading south on 6th Street. A series of lefts and a right later and the cab pulled up at the intersection of Massachusetts and Louisiana Avenues.

Morozov got out and, without looking back, walked casually towards Union Station, confident he had lost his tail. Besides, it might attract the attention he was seeking to avoid, and he was very sure the FBI had agents all over Washington, looking for anybody behaving suspiciously. Paranoia within the American Intelligence Agencies was at an all-time high, comparable, Morozov thought to that of Stalin back in the '30s. However, it was unlikely the Americans would round-up those they feared and distrusted and execute them the way his old leader had. A few days in a holding cell with interrogators would be the worst he could expect, followed by deportation back to his Motherland if they decided to dole out any punishment.

He knew the oil company would be forced to field questions as to his disappearance, but like every other day when he went missing, they would furnish a less than satisfactory explanation that the Americans would be forced to accept. Everybody saved face. He would continue doing what he'd been sent here to do, and the Americans would continue to try and catch him doing precisely that.

It was, after all, a game, one in which he and his comrades played very well.

As he walked, he peered up at the six statues that stood elegantly in the attic above the cornice of the façade. He'd been to Rome a few years before and seen the Arch of Constantine, and so was impressed by the architect's attention to detail in this remodeling.

It was mid-morning, and the working commuters had come and gone, leaving only tourists who'd arrived to visit the nation's capital, businessmen embarking on or returning from rail trips, and a small army of construction workers who were repairing the station's, Great Hall. A locomotive with faulty brakes had jumped the platform back in January and tunneled a path through the stationmaster's office before ending up in the basement, the floor of the Hall collapsing under the train's two-hundred-tonne weight. Miraculously nobody had been injured.

He walked across the concourse to a bank of public telephone kiosks and slipped inside one, shutting the door firmly behind him. Removing his hat, he dialed a number he knew by heart. He faced the wall so nobody could read his lips and waited.

'Hello,' the person on the other end said.

'He's alive,' Morozov said.

'I know.'

'He must not be allowed to talk.'

'Agreed.'

'And your plans?'

'Working on it.'

Morozov frowned. He loathed the nonchalance this particular American displayed. 'Do not take too long.'

There was a pause from the other end.

'It's in all our interests that I don't.'

'How will we know when it is done?'

STEPHEN FRANCIS

There was a chuckle from the other end. 'I'm sure you'll know before I do.'

'And if he has spoken to somebody already.'

'Then I'll take further measures.'

'Good.' Morozov hung up. He scanned the waiting area for anyone taking an inordinate amount of interest in him but registered nobody. He put his hat back on and left.

He caught a cab outside the station and asked the driver to take him to the corner of 6th and C-Street. Upon arrival, he handed over the fare plus tip and got out. He stepped into a small café and bought himself a black coffee 'to go'. He strolled back toward the office on D-Street, passing the car with the agents he'd lost little more than twenty minutes ago. Before entering the building, he turned back to them, smiled, and raised his coffee. Even at this distance, he could see dislike stamped on their faces which only served to broaden his smile further.

CHAPTER 23

THE WALK TO AND FROM the corner shop was one Daniel looked forward to each morning, as it allowed him time to think through any problems that might preoccupy his mind and so determine an appropriate solution. Today though was not such an occasion as there was neither anything pressing nor worth worrying about. The stroll, however, was made all the more enjoyable, as the sky overhead was clear, the air was breezeless, and the temperature noticeably warmer than it had been over the past week. Certainly, Daniel thought, warmer than New York, where the wind had funneled along the streets with such an icy chill and ferocity as to try and freeze him in place while attempting to knock him over at the same time.

He'd bought a Hershey's bar which he'd wrapped inside a folded, morning edition of the Washington Post and swung a pint of milk gently by his side.

The footpath, for he still used the correct English term, was empty. As they usually did, most people had vacated the city for the weekend, leaving the place eerily devoid of human life, save for one or two lost souls who would no doubt also enjoy the onset of spring. Up ahead, he spotted a figure leaning against a parked car, staring back at him, her arms folded.

He waved to Alona, who didn't respond, which didn't bode well. He could tell by her expression that something had happened and his mood immediately changed.

'Morning.'

'Is it,' she said.

'It was.'

'Let's go inside.' She looked around, her eyes darting to a car that drove by.

An anxious tingle flashed along Daniel's spine, but he shook it off.

'Want some chocolate?' He said once they'd entered his apartment. He tossed the paper onto the kitchen countertop and took out a couple of glasses, pouring milk into one.

'Not for me.' She paced slowly back and forth across the floor.

He came around to join her. Shoving a couple of squares in his mouth, he shot her a quizzical look.

'Sieber is dead,' she said.

Daniel stopped chewing.

'What happened? He was fine when I left him, dreaming of the Fatherland, or whatever Nazis dream of when they're doped up on morphine.'

'I got a call from Witten about twenty minutes ago. He said the medical staff had moved him from the emergency department to a private room on the 5th floor. He'd been there almost twenty-four hours and had been getting steadily worse. He died a short while ago.'

'From what? His injuries weren't life-threatening.'

'Witten is waiting on the autopsy. It's been prioritized. He should have the report first thing in the morning.'

Daniel stared out the window beyond her. He shook his head.

'Was he guarded?'

'Yes. Two FBI agents were stationed outside his door at all times, including during the transfer in the elevator. He was never alone.'

'Damn. I didn't expect that.'

'It seems neither did the FBI. Witten asked us to meet him tomorrow to go through your account of Friday night again. He'll be able to share the autopsy results with us then.'

'Going through my story again won't do much good,' Daniel said. 'He was alive when I left New York. Now he's dead. Somebody fucked up.'

'Or fucked him up.'

'Nice play on words.' He half-smiled. 'You're getting better at this.'

She stopped pacing. 'What do you think?'

Daniel sighed. 'Murdered for sure. My guess, somebody covering their tracks didn't want him to talk.'

'I thought the same,' she said, nodding in agreement.

'So, we catch one killer only for another to surface. We'll be busy for a while yet.'

'The FBI may not want us on this one.' She picked at her fingernails, immersed in thought.

'After the success of our last assignment? How could they not.'

Alona looked concerned, and that bothered Daniel.

'What's on your mind?' he said.

'I wonder if the FBI thinks we had anything to do with it.'

'Why would they?'

She laughed the sarcasm evident.

'Look at us. A Holocaust survivor and a former British agent. You can't say we didn't have our motives.'

'Us and a million others.' Daniel leaned back on the seat, his hands behind his head.

'We had opportunity, which rules out most of those million suspects. And, depending on what the autopsy finds, we may have had the skills too,' she said.

'Don't you think you're getting ahead of yourself? Besides, you were nowhere near New York over the weekend. If the FBI is going to look at anybody, it'll be me, and I didn't want him dead, not that bad anyway. Someone else has done this, and if there's one thing I know about government agencies, it's their insatiable desire for containment and continuity. From their point of view, the fewer people who know about what Sieber did, the better. They'll want this wrapped up quickly and without involving too many others. We know, so we're in the loop. They may add a handful of support agents here or there, maybe even the same fellas they used at the Waldorf on Friday. But, for better or worse, we're the guys who can help them.'

Alona still seemed skeptical.

'Mark my words. Now, come sit down and have some chocolate and a glass of milk. I can make you something stronger if you'd like?'

'Herbal tea would be nice.'

*

The weather was foul the following morning with strong winds sweeping in from the Atlantic, the temperature tumbling back into single digits. Forecasters predicted a storm gathering pace out at sea, and the Maryland and Virginia coast guards had ordered all fishing boats back to harbor. Perhaps, it was an omen for the meeting ahead.

As before, Alona had called into Daniel, but this time they took a taxi to the FBI Office on I-Street. They didn't speak during the short trip, each wrapped in their thoughts. The rain had just started to fall when the cab pulled up to the curb.

They took the elevator, announced their arrival to the receptionist, and headed for the same meeting room, but found it empty. They took their usual seats and waited.

More than thirty minutes passed, and still, Witten hadn't shown up.

'Did we get the time wrong?' Daniel asked.

Alona checked her watch. '10 a.m., that's what the man said.'

Daniel stood and stretched his back and legs. He walked to the door and looked up and down the office. Nobody looked in his direction.

'Friendly bunch,' he said to himself.

Daniel returned to his seat. 'What the hell can be keeping them so long?' He exhaled hard and looked around the room. With the only hint of color struggling to enter through the small window in front of them and the absence of anything that might be described as decoration, it really was a bland space, serving only one purpose – to hold meetings for as quick a time as possible so the occupants could leave before they died of boredom.

Witten and Simmonds arrived twenty minutes later. They didn't look pleased, an ominous sign of the discussion ahead.

'Sorry, we're late,' Witten said. 'We were waiting for the toxicology report before we started.' He opened a folder in front of him and read the document to himself as though seeing it for the first time his eyes skipping across the pages.

Simmonds coughed gently, and Witten responded.

'Cause of death was poisoning,' he said.

He read the next few lines of the report out loud, stumbling over some words. Daniel sympathized with the man's struggles, as the language used by coroners and medical practitioners wasn't, in general, something a layman could easily verbalize let alone understand, for that matter. This was further evidenced by the findings of the toxicologist.

'The patient died of complications arising from acute radiation syndrome, instigated by exposure to a large dose of Polonium-210. Given the rapidity of death and additional tests, exposure has been determined as more than 30 Gray. Although the patient did exhibit some prodromes such as tremors and seizures, others, such as ataxia and lethargy, were absent due to the patient being heavily sedated.'

'So, he was irradiated,' Alona said.

Witten nodded and continued. 'An injection mark was found on his left arm. This is believed to be the delivery site.'

He closed the file and placed it on the table between them. He sat back, his hands on the arms of the chair, his eyes looking upwards. He appeared thoughtful.

'Where can somebody get Polonium? I'm guessing it's not something bought in a local hardware store?' Daniel said.

'It's primarily made in Russia,' Witten said. 'But, the Soviets do export to several other countries.'

'So, we could be looking at anybody from Russia to whatever countries buy the stuff from them. Does the US buy from Russia?'

Witten glanced at Simmonds before continuing. 'Officially, I can deny that any such agreement is in place. However, there are certain items that both countries produce that are of interest to the other. It'd be foolish to believe we don't buy whatever we need from the Russians just like any other consumables.'

'So, that's a yes,' Daniel said.

'What about suspects?' Alona asked.

'Lenox Hill kept a register of everybody who attended and visited Sieber after he was admitted. Everybody, including the agents who guarded him, will be interviewed over the coming days.'

He leaned forward and looked directly at Daniel. 'You're obliged to be re-interviewed and tested for trace amounts of the radioactive substance.'

'Sure, I've nothing to hide. If it'll help progress the investigation and eliminate me from the suspect pool.'

Witten nodded, clearly happier to have heard that.

'When will that be?' Daniel asked.

'New York, tomorrow. I'll set it up. You'll have to take the agent-in-charge through the events of Friday evening. He won't want to only speak to you. He'll want you to show him what happened, from the hotel to Times Square, describing the chain of events as you go.'

Alona cleared her throat. Everybody turned to face her.

'We need to figure out why Sieber was killed and who had a motive. For me, it appears as though somebody was trying to prevent him from revealing possible accomplices in the six murders he's suspected of committing. Daniel's original question was, 'where can somebody get Polonium?' A better question is: who can buy the material? It's radioactive and produced mainly in Russia, so it's probably tricky to transport undetected and requires expert care when dispensing. That's not the work of a disorganized gang. We're looking for an intelligence agency or a government that supported Sieber but had no hesitation in eliminating him to avoid exposure.'

The room descended into silence as everybody digested her words.

'What about Sieber?' Daniel said.

Simmonds glanced sidelong at Witten, a fleeting hint of anxiousness appearing, before dissolving into a smile.

Witten paused and took a breath. 'He was one of Himmler's body-guards during the war.'

Daniel could feel Alona stiffen then recede into her chair. He leaned forward. 'Is that it?

Witten shook his head. 'We picked him up in May of '45. He was processed by the relevant authorities of the time and disappeared like a lot of other folks did back then. Probably wanted to forget the past and move on to the future as quickly as he could.'

'That's it?' Daniel shook his head. He could feel his temperature rising as Witten's words stoked the flames of anger that had been dormant for so many years. 'What about reparations? Nobody gets to that level within the Reich without being a member of the Waffen SS. What about war crimes? I'm pretty sure the guy should have hung for what he did.'

The room went silent again, the three men looking from one to another. Only Alona sat motionless, her gaze fixed absently on the window and the scenery outside.

'OK. Let's leave it there for today,' Witten said. 'I'm sure everybody has things to do.' He picked up the file and made a show of tapping the edge to align the pages inside.

Daniel stood and placed his fists on the table. He was about to speak, but Alona reached out and gently, yet firmly, slowly pulled him back. He looked at her. She shook her head.

'Not now.'

He saw the pain she was feeling evident on her face. He cleared a lump from his throat.

Everybody stood except for Simmonds, who spoke for the first time that day.

'A moment Mr. Miller if you would be so kind.' As before, his smile was approachable and compassionate.

Daniel turned to Alona. 'I'll see you outside.'

She shrugged her shoulders and left with Witten, closing the door behind them.

'Please, sit.' Simmonds held out a hand. 'I'm sure you'll appreciate there are certain things we cannot discuss with you.' He leaned forward, placed his elbows on the table, and locked his hands together.

'And this is one of them?' Daniel resumed his seat.

Simmonds didn't reply. He tilted his head to one side and looked at Daniel.

'So much of your father in you. I was sorry to hear of his death.'

Daniel didn't reply, temporarily taken off guard by the comment.

'Thank you,' Daniel said at length, the anger he'd felt earlier beginning to ebb. 'He died near the end of the war.'

Simmonds nodded sadly, and Daniel felt the sincerity in the man.

'I know. I attended the funeral.'

Daniel looked down at his hands, his fingers interlocked. He'd been somewhere in Europe at the time, he couldn't recall exactly where, and hadn't been notified until his father had been interred for more than a week.

'I didn't mean that as a slight of course,' Simmonds said hurriedly, raising a hand by way of apology.

'That's OK.'

'Everybody made sacrifices at that time.'

The room went quiet.

'How did you know him?'

Simmonds leaned back. His head cocked, he smiled, as though recalling a fond memory.

'I was one of those 'Yanks' who'd been 'oversexed, overpaid and over 'ere'. I don't remember cavorting with too many women though, and the money wasn't all that good either.' He chuckled to himself. 'I served my country, although, not on the front line as you did yours. I was in the Office of Strategic Service, working in London, somewhere near Baker Street – I can't recall exactly where. I worked with your father on various projects from time to time.'

'You don't seem to remember much,' Daniel said with a smile. He was starting to warm to the man, which made him wary.

'It was such a long time ago. So much has happened since.'

'For some.'

'Indeed.'

Simmonds looked at Daniel for a time.

'Your meeting tomorrow is purely cosmetic,' Simmonds said. 'The New York agent-in-charge is going to extraordinary lengths to investigate all avenues open to him. I certainly don't see the need to drag you up there, so it appears to be little more than a 'dotting t's and crossing i's' exercise. That said, it does present us with an opportunity to re-examine the scene first-hand, and I'd sooner get the report from you rather than some young buck trying to make a name for himself.'

'And you don't think I'm trying to make a name for myself?'

Simmonds smiled at Daniel's attempt at a joke. 'Your name and reputation were never in doubt.'

'I'm not terribly happy to hear you say that,' Daniel said. 'I'd rather hoped I was flying under the radar.'

Simmonds threw his head back and laughed.

'That's a new phrase. I haven't heard it too many times. Young people are so imaginative when it comes to the English language.'

He bit gently into his lower lip, and his face grew serious. He tapped the table rhythmically with the tips of his fingers before speaking again.

'We agree somewhat with Ms. Peers, which is to say that we suspect foreign involvement in the whole affair. The very idea of a former Waffen SS officer running about our country assassinating his fellow countrymen unaided doesn't make sense to us. Somebody had to supply him with the wherewithal to accomplish what he did. Given the security measures in place and the potential motives, it points to an international dimension.'

'Or somebody in the US government with a grudge to bear?'

'I agree. We must consider that a possibility too, but my money is on the former.'

Daniel looked at Simmonds for some time.

'There's something you're not telling me.'

'There are many things I can't and won't tell you, but none about this case.'

'Why don't I believe you?'

'You decide to believe me or not, but wouldn't it strike you as odd that I wouldn't share with you everything I knew if I thought it'd help us get to the bottom of it all sooner?'

'Sometimes, there are other reasons for not revealing everything.'

Simmonds smiled with a sparkle in his eyes. 'You are so much like your father. He questioned everything until he was happy with what he'd been told. I liked that about him.'

Daniel couldn't recall that about his father. He'd always known him to be a quiet and considerate man, and knowledgeable about many things. He'd never known him to question anything, generally having an answer for everything. Perhaps in that, it was because he'd always quizzed others until he was sure his hard facts weren't somebody else's soft guesses. Daniel found it comforting to know he had been appreciated by others outside his immediate acquaintances.

Simmonds stood and headed for the door, tapping the back of Daniel's chair before leaving him to his ruminations.

CHAPTER 24

SIMMONDS HAD BEEN RIGHT. JEFFREY Ward, the agent-in-charge of Sieber's murder investigation had been all the old man had said he'd be: young, ambitious, and arrogant, with only a handful of years in the service; he did wear a nice suit and an expensive cologne though that Daniel figured must please some of the women with whom he came into contact. In contrast to what Daniel had been told and expected, Ward only skimmed over Daniel's version of events, asking the odd perfunctory question when there was a break in the flow of discussion, or when attempting to adhere to some prescribed agenda. He hadn't even bothered to test Daniel for radiation either, which Daniel had found unusual given the nature of Sieber's death.

In return, Daniel had been unable to elicit any kind of information, useful or otherwise from Agent Ward, the man being politely dismissive and unwilling to share anything pertinent to the case. Given the contrast in expectations and work practice between Washington and New York, this caused Daniel to wonder if there were conflicting agendas at play or if the guy was just a jerk in a man's world. The whole thing stank, and he was sitting in the middle of it. The meeting with Agent Ward closed with a sullen 'thank you', but no handshake.

Daniel decided to make use of his time as Simmonds had suggested so headed to Lenox Hill Hospital to see if he could uncover anything that the FBI wasn't sharing. Agent Ward wasn't the only one with questions, and there may be somebody there who was more amenable. He went directly to the receptionist at the entrance and showed her his FBI identification. He asked if there was somebody he could speak to concerning a death at the weekend. He was directed to the 5th-floor nurses' station.

Over the years, Daniel's experience with hospitals could best be described as painfully colorful, generally because, if he had the misfortune to be in one, it was because his job had put him there. He loathed the places intently, not out of intimidation, but rather a dread that had taken hold after he'd woken up in one, following a Luftwaffe bombing of Coventry in November 1940. The scars he bore were more than physical, and, along with the blood of 'innocents' on his hands, was the foundation on which he'd based his decision to move into a new line of work. In hindsight, he also considered himself lucky not to have been a transient resident of a hospital morgue.

He spoke to a nurse who looked as though she was nearing the end of a double shift. Unfortunately, she hadn't been on duty at the weekend, but through tired eyes, she checked the roster then called for Nurse Farley over the intercom.

Daniel had only to wait a couple of minutes before a young woman approached dressed in an angelic white uniform and light blue cardigan. Wisps of dark, brown hair escaped from beneath a starched, white hat. Judging by her appearance, she looked as though she'd been a new addition to the staff, having graduated from nurses' college (or wherever it was that women went to become nurses), the summer before. She was pretty, in her early twenties and, Daniel thought, still filled with the exuberance and dreams of youth, aiming to make a positive mark in the world. Even so, she stood more upright and became instantly more alert once Daniel showed her his credentials.

'Is there somewhere we can speak in private?'

Farley ushered Daniel into a small, vacant office behind the nurses' station where they each took a seat. Daniel started by asking for her version of events of Easter weekend. She began by detailing the days she'd been on duty.

'I started the first of a five-day rota at 7 a.m., Saturday.'

'So today is your last before you break again?'

She nodded, but added, 'I may have to come in for a few hours to cover for another nurse tomorrow, but I don't mind that.' She let out an endearing, little giggle, which made Daniel smile.

'I'm doing a follow-up on the death of Tomas Sieber on Sunday evening.'

A concerned and sympathetic expression fell across her face.

'Very sad.' She shook her head and composed herself by taking a breath and, unprompted, launched into her account.

'The Emergency Department had stabilized him to the point where he could be moved to a more peaceful location up here on the 5th floor. He'd been transferred to a private room on the ward sometime before my shift started. There was some excitement on the floor; after all, it's not often we have patients who are guarded by armed men. At first, we thought he was a celebrity. All the nurses who hadn't been cleared to treat him asked me all sorts of questions.'

'You mean only a few people treated him while he was here?'

She nodded. 'Two nurses per shift, there's usually between six and ten of us on duty per floor, depending on the day of the week. Professor Bamforth had overall responsibility for his care. We had to show Mr. Sieber's guards a special identification the FBI had provided us then sign in every time we went into his room.'

Unconsciously, she pulled up her sleeve and rubbed her arm gently with the palm of her hand. Daniel glanced down, made no comment, and prompted her to continue.

'He'd come through surgery on Saturday to repair some internal damage, which I believe had been minimal. As I said, I started my shift at seven on Saturday morning, so by the time I got to check on Mr. Sieber, it was about 7:45. Everything was normal, or as normal as it should be for a sedated gunshot victim. I updated his chart, left, and went about my other duties. Throughout the day, Nurse Kirkland or I checked on him and updated his chart. By the time my shift was over, we'd recorded nothing out of the ordinary. Mr. Sieber was just another recovering patient. Professor Bamforth doesn't generally visit his patients. He usually insists the junior doctors assess a condition and update him, but he had stayed in the hospital over the weekend and completed all the routine visits himself.'

Daniel made a mental note to check on the Professor, as he would Nurse Kirkland and the other shift nurses who'd been granted access to Sieber.

'OK, so you came back into work on Sunday morning. Had anything changed?'

Nurse Farley nodded. 'He'd started to lose his hair throughout the night. I remember that because I had to change his pillowcase before checking his vitals.'

'Did you find that unusual?'

'Not at the time. Patients can react differently to certain medications, so I thought it was just that. I noted it in the chart, but noticed the other shift nurses had reported the same hair loss during the night.'

She rubbed her arm again.

'You OK there?'

She looked down at her arm. 'It's a reaction to whatever it was Mr. Sieber had. They gave me Erythromycin to treat it and a topical cream for the itch.'

'Can I take a look?'

She offered her arm. Daniel inspected it and saw a deep, red rash that covered most of the inside of her forearm from elbow to wrist like a large cluster of hives.

'When did you start to get this?

She thought for a moment. 'Started on Sunday afternoon.'

'Who treated you?'

'Professor Bamforth. It was quite a privilege.'

'And what about Nurse Kirkland?'

'Everybody who came into contact with Mr. Sieber is being treated with the same antibiotic, although, I'm the only one with a rash as far as I know.'

'And how are you feeling?'

'OK, I guess. I was nauseous on Monday and Tuesday, vomiting both days, couldn't seem to keep anything down. I'm a little better today. Katie, that's Nurse Kirkland, is off until Saturday, so I don't know how she is.'

Daniel let go of her arm. 'OK, what happened next?'

'As the day wore on, Mr. Sieber's condition worsened to the point where we had to roll him onto his side to prevent him from choking on his vomit. He had tremors several times during the day, which worsened throughout the night, almost like he was taking a fit. I'd never seen a patient react to a gun-shooting like that before, none of us had. We were all quite worried. Other than what we pulled together, we didn't have any other medical records for him, so we tried to provide the best care without doing anything to compromise his recovery. The only thing we knew for sure was his blood type, B Positive.'

'You got that from the tattoo on his arm?'

'How did you know about that?'

Daniel gave her a queer look, which made her giggle again.

'I suppose you guys know everything.'

'I wouldn't be speaking to you if I knew everything.' Daniel smiled. He leaned back and looked away for a moment.

'What time did he die?'

'He was pronounced at 5:23 a.m. Monday morning.'

'So, you weren't present.'

She shook and bowed her head. 'I'd started to feel quite unwell by then.'

'How long have you been a nurse?'

'I graduated in summer of '51, so almost two years,' she said barely trying to hide her pride.

'And during that time, have you ever seen anything like this?'

Once again, she shook her head. 'Patients die all the time from complications due to surgery, or medication mismanagement, or just because it's their time. But, we generally discover the cause of death quite quickly.'

'We do know, though. Poisoning wasn't it?'

'Poisoning yes, but we haven't been able to determine what type, or at least if somebody has, they haven't told me.'

Daniel stood. 'OK, thanks for your time. You've been very helpful.'

He walked to the door and was about to leave when he stopped and turned back.

'Can you get me a copy of the register you had to sign when you went in to see Mr. Sieber?'

'Sure.'

She went out to the nurses' station and rummaged around a little, withdrawing a few stapled pages from beneath a stack of medical reports.

'The FBI took the original register, a hard-backed book, to aid their investigation, but we xeroxed it so we'd have a record.'

'Good thinking. Can you Xerox a copy for me?'

'It won't be as good as the original.'

'That's fine, so long as I can read the names.'

She disappeared back into the office, returning a couple of minutes later with a copy of the hospital's copy of the register. She handed it to Daniel.

'Last question, promise,' he said. 'Did you see or hear anything unusual while you were treating Mr. Sieber?'

Nurse Farley thought for a moment before shaking her. 'Nothing comes to mind.'

'OK. Thanks again. If you do recall anything, you can contact me at this number.' He scribbled on a slip of paper and handed it to her. He shook her hand and patted her arm. 'Keep taking the meds, OK.'

He reciprocated her smile and left.

Daniel took the stairs down to the lobby and felt the stresses of the morning ease as a hunger surfaced. He decided an early lunch was the best cure. He went across to a nearby payphone and dialed the same number he'd given Nurse Farley. Alona picked up on the first ring.

'FBI. Daniel Miller's office.'

'Sounds good,' he said. 'Very professional. Hungry?'

'Starving. I was going to order room service.'

'Don't bother, let's blow the FBI expense account on lunch.'

Alona laughed. 'Where to?'

He looked around and spotted a nice looking restaurant on the far side of the street.

'The Exchequer. It's on Park Avenue near the hospital. Drop whatever you're doing. I'll see you there in fifteen minutes.'

They hung up, and Daniel jogged across the road. He peered in through the window. It wasn't yet lunchtime, so the place wasn't all that busy. He went in and asked for a table for four; it was, after all, important to be comfortable while eating and thinking. He was shown to a table near the window that held a wondrous view of the passing rich folk in their Limousines.

Alona joined him shortly after. They each ordered soup and a sandwich which drew a frown from the waiter who passed no comment.

'What did you learn?' she said.

'I met with one of the nurses. She filled me in on the protocol that'd been put in place and the people who'd been allowed to treat Sieber.' He reached into his jacket. 'Here's a copy of the attendance registry. Run those names down against any FBI files you're allowed to see, but make sure you check on Professor Bamforth. From what I hear, he's top dog in there, and Sieber died on his watch. Sieber was guarded 24/7, so see if you find out who the agents were on his detail, try and get their profiles, too.'

Alona put the list in her bag. 'You're getting pretty good at this.'

'I'm probably missing lots, but it's a start.'

'I'll see if I can get a copy of the coroner's report and any other medical reports and charts for similar deaths at the hospital. We might notice a pattern. Maybe we could arrange for an independent evaluation, like a second opinion?'

Daniel agreed and turned to see the waiter approach with their order.

They ate in silence for the next few minutes, as the restaurant staff busied themselves preparing for the imminent lunchtime onslaught.

'A thought struck me,' Daniel said, wiping some crumbs from his lips. 'The nurse I spoke with was very young, only graduated a couple of years ago. Can you find out how old the other nurses are who were assigned to Sieber?'

STEPHEN FRANCIS

Alona nodded. 'You think they were hand-picked for a reason?'

'Maybe. If it were me, I'd have put somebody as important as Sieber in the care of my most experienced personnel. The hospital not doing that doesn't feel right.'

'Anything else?'

'I gave our telephone number to the nurse. She may call if she remembers anything, but I wouldn't count on it.'

'OK. What about Agent Ward?'

Daniel sighed and raised his eyes to the ceiling. 'A complete blowout. Flow of information went one way only.'

'We thought that might happen.'

Daniel snorted, and changed the subject. 'Did you get to see much of New York yet?'

Alona scowled at him. 'You had me cooped up in the hotel all morning, but the room does have more TV channels than I have at home, so it hasn't been an entirely wasted trip.'

'Glad to see you were productive. I'll bring you out to dinner tonight, somewhere fancy. We can take in some of the sights and sounds afterward.'

'Sounds lovely. I'll need to dress up for the occasion.'

Daniel fished some cash from his pocket and passed it across to her. 'We'll send the bill to the FBI. You done?'

She nodded, and they stood to leave. Daniel tossed some notes onto the table, enough to cover the bill with a tip to be remembered.

They headed out onto Park Avenue and stood on the path, as people milled around them.

Daniel looked south past Alona. 'Jesus, that's a long street. Wonder how far?'

'Nearly eleven miles.'

'How the hell do you know that?'

Alona turned back to him. 'I do my research, that's why you hired…'

Her eyes opened wide, and she lunged forward, grabbing Daniel by the jacket and pushing him back toward the restaurant door. Daniel fell to the ground, as Alona disappeared, replaced by the flash of a car that'd mounted the pavement.

When he got to his feet, the car had made its way back onto the road along with Alona who had been catapulted several feet into the air, landing several yards further down the avenue. Daniel ran across and knelt beside her but was afraid to touch her. Blood poured from her mouth and nose, her left leg in a grotesquely unnatural position. Her eyes were closed, and she wasn't moving or mumbling. He looked after the car, but it had disappeared, as a small crowd began to gather around them. One of the waiters ran out of the restaurant and knelt beside Daniel.

'I saw the whole thing,' he said. 'We're calling the hospital. It's only across the road, so they'll be here soon.'

His face turned ashen when he looked down at Alona, looking as though he might need an ambulance himself.

Daniel placed his hand on Alona's arm and leaned in close to her ear. 'You'll be OK. The ambulance is on the way, hang in there.'

The distant sound of a siren grew louder, as a deepening dread gripped him, and tears filled his eyes.

CHAPTER 25

LATER, WHEN DANIEL REFLECTED ON the events of the next few hours, all he'd be able to recall was a blur of rushing, white-coated medics, calling out instructions and repeating Alona's deteriorating vital signs. The ambulance had arrived within minutes of the incident and, after a brief triage by the paramedics on the street, transported Alona to Lenox Hill emergency department. Daniel couldn't wholly remember if they'd been panicked or merely prompt and efficient. He'd slid into the ambulance beside her and held her hand during the short journey, whispering words of reassurance that he wasn't sure she could hear. The paramedics had covered her with a heavy woolen blanket to help safeguard against shock, but Daniel draped his jacket on her to be doubly sure.

Once at the hospital, and after a concise examination by the on-call doctor, she'd been rushed to an operating theatre where she remained for the next nine hours.

Daniel called Ms. Walsh from a public phone in the foyer. As usual, she had been looking after Anthony while Alona was away. It had been a difficult, stop-start conversation that comprised few facts with a mixture of disbelief, alarm, concern, and some anger thrown in. He asked her not to say anything to Anthony until they knew more about her condition. They weren't due back to Washington until the following day, so there was no need to worry the child unnecessarily before then. Alona was to ring him later that evening as she always did, so Daniel said he'd make the call instead and let him know she'd been asked to support the FBI in the local field office, but that she'd call as soon as she could.

He also called Bradley Witten in Washington to let him know what had happened.

For now, Daniel drank coffee and paced the halls outside the operating theatre. He'd been surprised when Agent Ward showed up a few hours into the surgery.

'What do we know?' He shook Daniel's hand, placing his left hand on top like a preacher consoling the spouse of a dearly departed.

'Nothing. She hasn't woken up since she was hit and the doctors won't tell me anything. It doesn't look good.'

'How long has she been in there?'

Daniel checked his watch for the umpteenth time that afternoon. 'Just over three hours.'

Ward nodded and looked around. 'I'll see if I can find out anything more.'

He trotted away like a terrier that'd been given a small bone to bury, seeking somebody to bother only to return deflated a few minutes later, but holding a couple of cups of coffee. He passed one to Daniel, who swallowed back the one he had, discarding the empty in the trash. They took a pair of seats against the wall.

'Sorry for being a jerk earlier,' Ward said after a few minutes' silence.

Daniel, hunched over with elbows on his knees, the coffee cradled in his hands between, glanced sidelong at him.

'I don't get to work with consultants that much. I didn't know how to treat you or what I could tell you.' He looked across at Daniel. 'I hope you understand.'

Daniel did but didn't acknowledge it. He sipped his coffee instead.

'What happened?' Ward asked.

Daniel sat back in the chair and stretched out his legs. 'We'd just had lunch and were standing outside the restaurant.' He stopped. 'Next thing Alona throws me to the ground.'

'Then she was hit?'

'I didn't see it, just the car bouncing back onto the road.'

'Jeez. So the car mounted the sidewalk?'

Daniel nodded.

'And didn't stop? Did anybody see anything? What have the police said?'

'I haven't spoken to anybody, and the police haven't dropped by yet.'

Ward shook his head. 'I'll make a call and get somebody to take your statement so we can start to look for this lunatic.' He stood and swirled back the last of his coffee. 'I'll be in touch if I find out anything more. Let me know how she gets on?'

Daniel nodded. He watched Ward walk away and disappear into the elevator before walking to the nurses' station and asking for an update – there was none just like before. He resumed his seat and closed his eyes.

Waiting alone provides ample time to allow the mind to wander. Something had been niggling at the back of Daniel's mind for the last while, and it was here his thoughts had coalesced. Tomas Sieber had died while in custody, under circumstances which were considered suspicious by all. The man was most likely murdered to prevent him from disclosing his accomplices. Now, Alona lay in an operating theatre fighting for her life, her prognosis bleak. Were they connected? Daniel didn't believe in coincidences. He'd been with Sieber in the back of the ambulance after they'd sprung the trap at the Waldorf. It didn't take an enormous leap to believe that whoever had been behind Sieber's murder now wanted Daniel dead in case the deceased man had revealed anything while they were alone. The more Daniel let that stew, the angrier he felt himself becoming.

He stood and fired the cup into the trash, splashing coffee on the wall. He grabbed his jacket and headed for the elevator. He had to get away from the hospital to clear his head, try to put a check on his emotions. He stomped down the stairs, his blood bubbling. He stepped out onto the street and tilted his head back to breathe a lungful of New York City afternoon air.

He headed west along 76th Street and through the intersections at Park and Madison before crossing at 5th Avenue and disappearing into Central Park. The sounds of the city receded behind him the deeper he went until he could barely hear the car horns. He eventually came to the lake and found an unoccupied bench where he sat and stared across the still water at the vegetation on the far side. A handful of boats on the surface, their rowers enjoying taking their time, were in no rush to get or be anywhere. He snuggled into his jacket, his hands buried in his pockets.

Although mindful of Alona's wellbeing, and praying she'd pull through and make a swift recovery, his immediate concern was that if somebody had tried to kill him, then they might try again. He pressed his elbow against his side and was comforted by the hardness of the gun he felt there. He stole a glance to the left and right but saw nobody approaching from either direction. Perhaps, they thought they'd been successful, which comforted him somewhat, as it afforded him additional time to think things through.

As the afternoon wore on, the sun dipped below the multi-storied buildings on the far side of the Park, dropping the temperature a couple of degrees. Daniel's gaze followed the path of a gentle breeze as it fanned a succession of ripples across the water's surface. His thoughts wandered to Anthony and, for a moment, he wondered how the child would cope with the loss of his mother if it came to it. He tried to relate to his own experience. His parents, Catherine and Tom, had both died within a year of each other. But, he had been in his early twenties, so nature's law of succession had been followed, even if there had been nothing natural about the deaths themselves. Catherine had died from asphyxiation when she'd had an adverse reaction to a new spice she'd been adding to yet another of her experimental dishes. Tom had died after he'd popped out to lunch and a recently bombed building thought to have been made safe, had collapsed, burying him under a couple of tons of rubble. Although Daniel had mourned their passing, it had been at a distance, his absence enforced by events of the time. He shivered, feeling he was getting ahead of himself. Alona was a strong woman, who'd survived and outlived the National Socialist Party, an organization that'd been founded, and subsequently flourished, on a premise of fear and hate and an objective of eradicating people just like her.

A movement out of the corner of his eye caught his attention. He turned to see a man dressed in a long black, winter coat and matching fedora, tossing breadcrumbs to a gathering kit of pigeons. Although Daniel couldn't quite put his finger on it, there seemed something odd about the man's behavior, as though he wasn't all that absorbed in what he was doing, but rather more on his surroundings and the people in it. Daniel stared a moment longer before deciding he'd had enough fresh air, such as it was.

He headed back to the hospital, taking a circuitous route north up 5th Avenue under cover of the overhanging trees, their branches beginning to unfurl spring's colorful bounty. He crossed the road, stopping periodically to look into shop windows and glance back toward the Park's entrance. Although he couldn't see the man or anybody else who might be following him, he could sense watchful eyes.

He ducked inside a small delicatessen on 79th Street and ordered a chicken sandwich and tea, taking a seat at the rear of the shop facing the window. He watched the road while he waited, but saw nothing suspicious. Two men laughing at some joke they'd shared as they entered, ordered from the server behind the counter. They were both in their mid-twenties, fit-looking, and maybe a little too well dressed for this part of town. Neither of them looked at him as they sat at a table that had just become unoccupied.

Daniel could make out snippets of their conversation, something about the ineptitude of their boss and how he was more likely to get promoted (to keep him out of harm's way) than dismissed. The conversation flowed and grew louder as the men discussed and contrasted the qualities (or lack thereof) of other work colleagues. Daniel noted how the discussion seemed to dwell on the physical attributes of a young woman named 'Beth', who'd recently joined the company. At times, the diatribe bordered on the obscene which drew frowns from some of the other customers and members of staff.

Daniel went to the counter and asked for his order 'to go'. The server packaged it up, and Daniel left. He turned right and walked a short distance before stopping at another shop window. He looked back toward the deli. Nobody came out.

He walked briskly East, cutting down an alley after Park Avenue which took him to 78th Street where he turned left and then right onto Madison, stopping intermittently to check for a tail. He saw nothing. Even so, he still felt as though there were eyes on him, monitoring his progress back to the hospital. The deep-rooted sense of paranoia, which in his former line of work may well have saved his life, haunted him now.

A wave of panic swept across him as he drew nearer the hospital entrance. If somebody had gotten to Sieber who'd been surrounded by armed guards, then Alona would be easy pickings. And, who was to say they wouldn't finish her off first before they came after him again. He picked up the pace, hoping she was still in theatre and hadn't already been moved to the ward.

A few people stood in the foyer waiting on the elevator, so he took the stairs, three at a time, until he came to the 4th floor. He strode across to the nurses' station.

'Any update on Alona Peers?'

The nurse checked the register. 'She's just come out of the operating theatre and been taken to Room 407.'

Daniel looked around for a sign to indicate the way, so the nurse pointed.

'Down that way, second last door on the right.'

Daniel thanked her and hurried down the corridor, checking off the room numbers and glancing into each as he went. Up ahead, a doctor came out of the one toward which the nurse had directed him. Daniel slowed and placed his tea and sandwich on a nearby table. He opened his jacket, reached in, and took out the handgun before slipping it into the outside pocket. He approached the doctor.

'How is she?' He didn't take his eyes off the man.

The doctor looked up from a chart he'd been reading.

'Who are you?'

'Her partner.'

The response seemed to throw the man for a moment before he took Daniel by the arm and led him to a row of chairs outside the room. They sat.

'The operation went well, but it'll be some time before we know if there will be any lasting damage.'

'Damage?'

'She had several broken ribs, a pierced spleen, collapsed lung, and a herniated vertebra.' The guy made it sound like a shopping list.

Daniel said nothing at first.

'They sound like injuries from which she can recover?'

'Mostly, yes. The herniated disc is the problem. We can't touch it until the swelling goes down.'

'How long will that be?'

'A few days. We've given her medication to help speed up the process.'

'And what happens then?'

The doctor laid a hand on Daniel's arm and looked to him with sympathetic eyes. 'Then we see if she can walk.'

CHAPTER 26

IT HAD BEEN A PHONE call he hadn't wanted to make but, given Alona's condition, he had no alternative. During the conversation, Anthony had been inconsolable while Ms. Walsh had come close to tears several times. He had to comfort her as best he could from the other end of the line and wasn't sure he'd done a good job of it. She'd asked if she could bring Anthony to New York, but Daniel advised her against taking the young man out of his routine. Besides, Alona was still heavily sedated and wasn't in a position to welcome any visitors. Daniel promised he'd keep them updated with several calls each day until Alona would be able to ring herself.

And so, Daniel had stationed himself on the chairs outside her room, settling in for the night ahead. One of the nurses had given him a well-worn romance paperback that looked like it'd kept every member of staff company at one point or another. Although the subject matter didn't appeal to him, he flicked through the pages whenever he got bored or couldn't sleep. He read on and off, his eyes eventually feeling gritty and sore. It was the early hours of the morning when he eventually curled up his legs onto the chairs and dozed.

In the end, it had been uneventful except for one patient who required emergency treatment by a horde of medical personnel that'd caused quite a bit of commotion and another who'd passed away later that morning that hadn't. Daniel had slept fitfully given the makeshift bed, but then, he'd slept in worse places and harsher conditions.

After he'd checked the floor for anybody who looked like they shouldn't be there, he trotted down to the ground floor and bought himself a scone and tea in the canteen he found there, as well as a paperback that was more to his taste. He sat quietly outside Alona's room until the doctor had passed by during his early morning rounds. Her condition hadn't improved, which was disheartening, but then it hadn't worsened either, which he took as a positive.

Once the doctor and his entourage had moved onto the patient in the next room, Daniel nipped in to see her. He was wracked with guilt as soon as his eyes fell upon her. She lay on the bed, a couple of plastic tubes connected to her arm at one end and several elevated glass bottles at the other. The top of her head and both arms and hands were wrapped in newly applied bandages. What little he could see of her face was a kaleidoscope of bruises and treated cuts. Her breathing was shallow but regular. He approached the bed, pulling a wooden chair nearer. He sat next to her and gently cradled her hand between his. A surge of anguish swept over him, and he felt tears roll down his cheeks.

'I'm so, so sorry. I shouldn't have brought you here, not in the middle of an assignment.' He hung his head, the tears dripping onto the blanket. 'I've called Anthony and let him know you're OK. He wanted to see you, but I thought it'd be better if he waited until you were… awake….' He caught his breath and sobbed. 'That shouldn't be too long, eh?'

He ran his hand along her arm, almost afraid to make contact for fear of causing further damage.

'Agent Ward, the New York FBI fella, stopped by yesterday and asked after you. Maybe I was wrong in thinking he was an asshole. He's going to make some calls, try and find out if somebody knows something about the accident.'

He patted her arm. 'I'm going to stay with you a little while so you'll be safe. The staff here is great and taking real good care of you, so I guess it's up to you now.'

Daniel leaned back in the chair, closed his eyes, and sat in silence, cradling her hand, until a nurse came in to check on her. She took her pulse and temperature, listened to her heart rate and breathing, and opened her eyelids to check Alona's optical response. She made a note of what she'd measured and rehung Alona's chart on the end of the bed. She turned to Daniel before leaving.

'I noticed Ms. Peers has a tattoo on her left forearm. What is that?'

Daniel looked at her for a moment. 'She was a survivor from Auschwitz.'

She looked puzzled. 'Ausch…'

'It was a concentration camp during the war.'

'Oh.' She nodded. 'I saw a newsreel about those places a few years ago. Awful, awful places. Hard to believe what people are capable of doing to each other?'

Daniel didn't reply. He knew the kind of evil mankind was capable of perpetrating on itself.

The nurse shook her head regretfully and left the room.

Sometime later, Daniel heard the sound of footsteps in the corridor, drawing closer to the room. They stopped outside. He twisted in his chair and stared at the door. As the handle turned, Daniel reached into his pocket and gripped the handgun. The door opened slowly and noiselessly, raising Daniels hackles.

He was ready to pounce.

Agent Ward's head appeared from around the door. With a nod, he beckoned Daniel to join him outside.

'What's up?' Daniel rubbed his eyes with the palms of his hand.

'You look like shit.'

'You came here to tell me that?' Daniel could barely hide his disgust.

'I came here to let you know I'm posting an agent outside Ms. Peer's room until she's discharged from the hospital.'

Daniel looked at him for a moment. 'What aren't you telling me?'

'One of the nurses, a Kate Kirkland, who'd been treating Sieber, was found in her home this morning. A 22 caliber gunshot to the back of her head.'

Daniel's eyes immediately darted to the corridor beyond Agent Ward. 'Executed?' Suddenly more aware of everybody in his line of vision and, more importantly, what they were doing.

'It's too early to tell, but it looks like whoever was working with Sieber is trying to limit their exposure by killing those who came into contact with him. We've put a protective detail on all medical staff who attended him. Of course, it might just be a coincidence, but we're not taking any chances.'

'Including Nurse Farley?'

Ward nodded. 'We need to take you into protective custody too.'

'I'll be fine.'

'It's for your own good.'

'You think I can't protect myself?'

'I'm not sure, can you?'

'I've been doing this a long time.'

'And still, you were careless.'

Daniel scowled and felt his anger surfacing again.

'You had direct contact with Sieber. You were with him in the back of the ambulance.'

'So?'

'We believe the car that hit Ms. Peers was meant for you.'

Confirmation of his thoughts made Daniel grow numb. His head started to spin. Noises that had been loud and clear had suddenly become muffled and distant. He held out his hand and grabbed Ward's arm.

'Here, sit down,' Ward said. He moved Daniel across to one of the chairs. 'You need anything, coffee?'

Daniel shook his head. 'I'm fine.'

'This development has reprioritized Sieber's death within the FBI. It's top of our list now.'

'Right up there with hunting communists in Hollywood?' Daniel's head limply hung as he stared at the floor.

'Something like that.'

The two men sat quietly for a few minutes.

'The other agent will be here before midday. I'll stay with you until then,' Ward said. He checked his watch.

'No need. You probably have other things to do.'

'I do, but this is a direct order from Washington. Somebody down there thinks you guys are important.'

'Nice to be thought of that way, I guess. Will one agent be enough?' Daniel looked up at Ward to try and read the man's expression.

'Sure, it will.'

'What if he needs to take a piss?'

'He can use a bottle. Besides, we're rotating the shifts every four hours to make sure nobody loses concentration. If he can't hold his piss for that length of time, then he's in the right place to get it checked out.'

Daniel didn't acknowledge Ward's attempt at light-heartedness, continuing instead to stare at the floor.

The two men sat quietly for the best part of an hour, a trip to the men's room for each, an occasional passing comment, or a look in on Alona, the only disruption to their vigil. When the time arrived to hand over the reins to their relief, it was clear that both men hadn't wanted to be in the other's company, forced to do so by circumstance and perhaps, on the part of Agent Ward, a feeling of guilt. It was with a sense of thankfulness for both that Ward introduced the new guy to Daniel before taking his leave.

Daniel waited behind to brief the agent, a rotund, older gent who looked like he was counting down the last few years before retirement and also to allow Ward enough time to vacate the building ahead of him.

Daniel left as soon as he was happy that the new guy had no reason to leave his post; he'd even waited while the fella scurried off to take a leak. He jumped into a taxi and asked to be taken directly to La Guardia so he could catch a flight back to DC. He had questions and wanted to doorstep Agent Witten without giving him time to prepare his responses. He also doubted the FBI was as transparent about the case as they could be. To a certain extent, he understood that. But, he'd be letting them know in no uncertain terms that if they weren't prepared to share everything they knew with him, then he was going to take matters into his own hands, which was how he imagined it would pan out anyway.

If nothing, the FBI might be relieved if he could wrap up the case for them without having to stretch themselves in the process. They had relationships, some good some not, with other agencies and knew they'd need them in the years ahead, so it was logical to assume their preference would be to solve the case without burning any inter-agency bridges.

*

Shortly after 3 p.m. that afternoon, Morozov stepped out of his office on D-Street into the sunlight. He took a deep breath and turned right, taking the same route as before to lose the FBI tail – this was the first mistake he'd made since arriving in America.

He entered the same coffee shop and ducked out the back, crossing the same alley into the haberdashery store opposite. He stole a glance up and down Indiana Avenue, fixed his tie, and removed his hat before stepping into the same taxi.

Agent Ralph Crawford had drawn the shortest of short straws after he'd been assigned to sit and watch those who entered and, more importantly, left all the buildings on the north side of Indiana Avenue. He was parked near the corner of 7th Street on the right-hand side, which afforded him a relatively unrestricted view of all the building exits up as far as 6th Street. Sycamore trees lined both sides of the avenue, but thankfully their buds were a month or more away from fully opening and restricting his vision further.

He was a newcomer to the agency, having been selected for recruitment at the end of '52. A brief, but distinguished career as a 'windy city' flatfoot came to a close after he'd stumbled on a plot by Puerto Rican nationalists to assassinate then President-elect Eisenhower ahead of the '53 Inauguration. After a week's surveillance, Crawford had singlehandedly detained the four armed suspects and held them in custody while waiting for backup to arrive. The arrests and subsequent convictions were something of a media coup for Chicago PD, so accusations of 'lone wolf' behavior that might be leveled at the young man were easily forgotten, the authorities opting instead to award him with the Distinguished Service Award for an act of bravery above and beyond the call of duty. He'd gone to Washington and been presented with the accolade by President Truman. Shortly after, at the White House reception, he'd been approached by Special Agent-in-Charge Dubois from FBI headquarters with a request to serve his country at a federal level. With the potential for recognition and career advancement now at a national level, Crawford had jumped at the opportunity rarely given to such a 'green' law enforcement official. Images of chasing down and apprehending persons suspected of being threats to national security filled his imagination, and the glory that would follow seemed assured.

But, this had been the third day he'd been sitting in his car, watching the birds strut about, nibbling on the slim-pickings they found on the ground.

He tossed the newspaper he'd been reading on the passenger seat and poured himself a cup of lukewarm soup from a flask; the sandwiches he'd brought with him that morning, long since eaten. He checked his watch. He had less than two hours before he knocked off for the day, head home to prepare for another day of monotony.

And so, when a man strode confidently out of 'Sew & Tell' and into a waiting taxi, Crawford had to do a double-take. It all happened so fast that he wasn't entirely sure if the man was the Russian named Morozov. He watched as the taxi pulled away from the curb before deciding to throw the soup out the window and follow – better to be wrong than do nothing.

The taxi made a handful of left and rights, which Crawford mirrored from a safe distance before it pulled up outside Union Station. Crawford passed by slowly and pulled in a few cars ahead, checking his rear-view mirror to see if the passenger got out. He did. He watched, as Morozov, his right hand in a trouser pocket, strolled across to the station's entrance. Crawford was relieved now that he'd made the right decision to follow. He jumped out of his car and matched Morozov's pace.

Tracking him from the other side of the Great Hall, he spied Morozov making a bee-line for the bank of telephone kiosks at the far end of the vestibule. Crawford stopped at a concession stand and bought himself a Hershey's and another newspaper as Morozov ducked into one of the kiosks. He sat on a bench at a slight angle to his quarry, checked his watch, and opened the paper as though waiting on a train.

Morozov spent less than five minutes in the kiosk, but Crawford noticed he'd dialed two numbers. Crawford allowed the Russian time to leave the station. He waited for a minute or so until he was sure the man wouldn't return before calmly walking across to the same kiosk. A departing train rumbled away in the distance, the power of its engine resonating under and across the station floor. Crawford felt an excitement build that he hadn't felt since the previous year. He stepped into the kiosk and stared at the receiver for a moment before lifting it to his ear. He rummaged inside his coat pocket and pulled out a small card before dialing the operator.

'Put me through to 535-16702 please,' he said, when she answered.

A voice greeted him at the other end, a moment later.

'This is Agent Crawford from the DC office. Can you tell me what were the last two dialed numbers from this location?' He called out the kiosk telephone number and waited. The line crackled to life, and he jotted down two numbers. He hung up. He stepped out of the kiosk and went into the one next to it, to try the first number. The operator connected him straight through.

'Novosil Oil and Gas Exploration New York, how may I help?' The voice was unmistakably foreign and if Crawford was a betting man, probably Eastern European or Russian, but he was weak at identifying accents. He gathered his thoughts quickly.

'Hi, yes. I'm surveying oil and natural reserve companies operating in the United States, size, origin, location of head office, that sort of thing. Have you time to answer a few questions?'

'No. Too busy.'

The line went dead before he could follow up with another question.

He jotted down the company's name before going through the operator again to check the second number which he recognized as being local.

'Yes,' the voice on the other end said a hint of suspicion evident.

'I demand to speak with your supervisor,' Crawford said, mustering as angry a tone as he could without attracting attention from anybody nearby.

There was a pause on the other end.

'To whom am I speaking?' the voice said.

'To *whom* are you speaking? Who do *you* think you are,' Crawford said, beginning to enjoy the little pretense. 'You're speaking with somebody who has run out of patience with your organization's bullshit. I demand you pass me onto your supervisor immediately.'

'Perhaps, I can help,' the voice said. Initial suspicion had disappeared, replaced now by a mix of intrigue and mild annoyance.

'Indeed,' Crawford said. 'Who is this?'

'My name is Knox.'

Crawford paused. 'Is this Hecht's Department Store?'

'No, Sir, it is not.'

'Hmmm. Thought as much, you don't sound at all Jewish,' Crawford said, before snapping the receiver back into the cradle and making a note of what he'd learned from the two calls.

He went back to his car, wondering if Special Agent-in-Charge Witten would be still at the office. But, then, of course, he would. The man only ever left the building to be intimate with his wife, which was a rare enough event.

The drive back to I-Street was hampered by the crawling rush-hour traffic and by the time he had parked up and walked in. The office was practically deserted. He took the stairs to the 4th floor and knocked on his boss's open door. Witten waved him in, his head buried in some document. Crawford took a seat and waited.

'Well?' Witten said after some time. He sat back and rubbed his eyes.

Crawford recounted his story as Witten gradually sat upright as the tale unfolded.

'What is Novosil?'

'The guy said they were an oil company.'

'Find out more about them. What about the second number?'

'Local. I didn't recognize it. The guy who answered said his name was Knox.'

Witten said nothing for a moment, and Crawford wondered if he'd done the right thing in coming to him without having investigated further and providing additional information.

'Have you the numbers?' Witten said.

Crawford passed the card across, and Witten stared at it for a long time.

'OK. You check into Novosil. I'll look into this second number.' He nodded to Crawford, indicating he should take his leave. As he rose, Witten said, 'Good work today. Might be the break we were looking for.'

Crawford couldn't help but smile, his grin widening the further away he got from Witten's office.

CHAPTER 27

Daniel stopped off at Ms. Walsh's apartment to check on Anthony before he went back to his place. He'd bought him a 100 piece jigsaw puzzle of the Statue of Liberty half shrouded in mist, which he hoped would act as a distraction. Anthony was thankful as always whenever Daniel gave him a gift and seemed to have gotten over the initial shock of his mum being in an accident. Daniel had told him she was doing well and responding to her treatment, which brightened the kid up a little more. He scuttled off to his bedroom to get a start on the puzzle, just as Ms. Walsh came into the living room with a pot of tea.

'How is she really doing?' she said, her tone hushed.

'Hanging in there. She has a lot of internal injuries that will take time to heal, but she's getting stronger each day which is something. She's a tough woman. I think she'll pull through.'

Ms. Walsh appeared unconvinced by Daniel's optimism, so he felt compelled to provide a little insight into why he believed what he did.

'She had a hard time during the war. She survived some of the worst abuse and cruelty I've ever seen and came out the other side smiling. This'll be a walk in the park for her.'

'She never told me what happened to her during the war.'

'I think she prefers to keep that part of her life private, maybe even try to forget it ever happened.'

'Anthony once told me that she sometimes wakes him up at night, screaming. He's never asked her about it. I think he's too afraid.'

Daniel sipped his tea and bit into a biscuit. 'Maybe he should say something to her, although maybe he's a little young for that sort of conversation.

It might do both of them some good.'

The pair sat in silence for a moment before Ms. Walsh spoke.

'I've seen the tattoo on her arm, you know.'

Daniel said nothing.

'She tries to keep it covered, but sometimes her sleeve rolls up, and there it is.'

Daniel watched her.

'It's from one of those camps the Germans ran during the war, isn't it?'

'It'd be better coming from her,' Daniel said.

Ms. Walsh nodded sympathetically but looked forlorn. 'Mr. Walsh thinks she was in Auschwitz.' Her eyes focused on Daniel, who took time to answer.

'She was there in the early part of the war before they moved her further east.'

Ms. Walsh shook her head. 'And that's what she survived.'

Daniel placed his cup on the saucer. 'I have to be getting away. I've some work to do. Thank you for the refreshments.' He smiled, stood, and gave Ms. Walsh a comforting hug. 'Alona knows Anthony is in safe hands with you so that'll definitely help.' He walked to the door. 'I'll stop by before I go back to see her, we can pray I'll have some good news by then.'

The short trip home was a blur. The taxi driver had tried to engage in idle chitchat about the upcoming baseball season but gave up after a couple of minutes of disinterested grunts. Daniel passed him the fare and climbed the steps to his apartment. He opened the door and stepped onto a folded piece of paper. He picked it up and read a couple of times what'd been written, before checking his watch and jogging back down the steps, a tingle tickling his stomach as he scanned the street for another taxi.

It was late evening, and traffic was minimal with most of what was around heading west across the Potomac towards the Virginian suburbs, leaving Daniel an open road towards Maryland. The cab pulled up outside 'The Friendly Bean' café twenty minutes later. Daniel stood on the pavement, looking up and down the road, as it pulled away. He looked through the window and spotted a large man sitting near the back.

As he entered, the man stood gingerly, favoring one leg over the other. He moaned, holding his hip, and gestured for Daniel to join him. Daniel turned his chair away from the table, so he had a view of both the door and the man.

'The waitress will be locking up in a moment which will afford us some privacy. I hope you don't mind?' the man said.

Daniel didn't reply.

'You should try the scones. They're really good here,' the man continued, 'Alona loves them. Can I get you anything?'

'A reason as to why I'm here, maybe.'

The man nodded, the pain of unhappiness appearing on his face for the first time. 'I was saddened to hear of her accident. Alona holds a special place in my heart.' He patted his chest gently.

'Funny, she's never mentioned you. Come to think of it, I don't even know who you are.'

'Who I am doesn't matter, but if you'd like to call me something, maybe Gerald will suffice.' He shot Daniel a questioning look.

Daniel didn't bother pursuing it.

Gerald signaled to the waitress. 'A cappuccino and a scone for my friend please.'

Daniel held up his hand. 'Nothing for me, thank you.'

Behind him, the waitress shrugged to herself.

'Aren't you getting a little ahead of yourself?' Daniel said.

'How so?'

'We hardly know each other, and now we're 'friends'?'

'I feel like I've known you all my life.'

'That's' disconcerting.'

'Understandable, given what it is you do, or rather 'what you did'.'

'Do I need to reach for a gun?' Daniel fired the questioning look right back.

'Only if you feel threatened.' Gerald's eyes sparkled. He bit into a half-eaten scone. 'I really can't tell if it's the scone or the jam. They make their own you know, and although the strawberry season was last autumn, it still tastes as fresh in spring.'

'What do you want?' Daniel said. He was tired of the verbal preamble and needed to move things along.

The man's face hardened. 'I want to help you, or rather, I want to help Alona, and I have information which will do both. But, it's action that's needed, and swift, if we are to put things right.'

'We?'

'Yes. We have a common goal and, as it happens, a common enemy.'

'I'm listening.'

'I received a phone call this afternoon from an acquaintance in New York. He'd been tailing a Russian named Zorin Sokolov. The surveillance didn't quite work out as planned. As you're no doubt aware, operations in the field can sometimes take on a life of their own. Something as simple as sitting in a parked car, staring at the front door of a café can be compromised by numerous external factors. Suffice to say, my acquaintance became momentarily distracted and lost the Russian he was tailing.'

'And this helps me how?'

Gerald smiled. 'It helps you because of the person he saw emerge from the café after the Russian had left.' He paused to take another bite and marvel at the scone again.

'Go on.'

'He recognized the man, but couldn't immediately place the face. I suppose we each meet so many others through the course of our lives that even for a fleeting moment, we can be forgiven for not remembering every name and circumstance of the encounter. Anyway, he did eventually recall the name, but only after his photograph had been distributed to every law enforcement agency in the tri-state area after you'd shot him in Times Square.'

Daniel leaned forward. 'He recognized Tomas Sieber?'

Gerald nodded. 'My friend had been an MP during the war and had the opportunity to meet many individuals, some more despicable than others, of course. It transpires that Mr. Sieber had been captured by the Americans in the first week of May 1945 and held for several days where he was interrogated many times as was the protocol of the time. As was also a sign of the times, paperwork got shuffled, and the man was moved from a detention center in Holland to well… nobody knows where.'

At least this corroborated the FBI's story on Sieber, but Daniel wasn't about to let an opportunity to learn as much as he could slip by. So, he played dumb.

'Are you saying he just disappeared?'

'Of course. You look shocked.'

'That he disappeared? Not really, a lot of people went missing back then, the war proved beneficial for those who sought to take advantage of the ensuing disorder. The fact that he resurfaced is troublesome.'

The pair fell silent. Daniel watched as Gerald buttered another piece of scone. He didn't know who the man was, where he'd come from, or what his intentions were. But above all, he didn't trust him. All he could be reasonably sure of was that his name wasn't Gerald. However, he did seem to have a heartfelt interest in Alona's wellbeing, which tipped the scales of trust ever so slightly in his favor

'I think I will have that coffee after all,' Daniel said.

Gerald motioned to the waitress.

'Several questions spring to mind,' Daniel said.

Gerald wiped his fingers on a napkin and placed his hands on the table in anticipation.

'How did Sieber escape Europe after the war? Why did he come to the US now? Who helped him do what he did? Who gave him the information and tools to carry out his assignment? Who killed him? Who tried to kill me and ended up injuring Alona? Why did any of this happen?'

Gerald nodded. 'I don't have definitive answers to all of those, but I can infer some based on what I learned from the second phone call I received this evening.'

'Maybe you should tell me about that then?'

'Indeed.' He grew quiet, as the waitress placed Daniel's coffee and scone on the table. When she was out of earshot, he continued.

'A man named Nikita Morozov was followed from his place of business at Ternopil Research Limited to Union Station in Washington. Once there, he made two phone calls. The first was to Novosil Oil and Gas Exploration. Do you know who works there?' Gerald shot Daniel a sidelong glance, a sparkle in his eyes.

Daniel shook his head.

'Mr. Sokolov.'

'The guy from New York?'

'Yes.'

Daniel hunched forward. 'And Morozov's second call?'

'I cannot say for reasons of internal security, but the matter is being dealt with by the relevant people.'

Behind them, the waitress quietly busied herself, tidying up after the day's trade and preparing for the following morning.

'A review of phone records from the Union Station public telephones over the past week reveals a number of calls to Novosil O&G.' Gerald sat back and looked at Daniel, whose mind was working hard at connecting the dots.

'Who do they work for?'

Gerald shook his head. 'That's not as important as what they're doing, which is another matter being dealt with by the relevant authorities. If you want answers to the other questions you've asked, then all roads appear to lead to New York.' Gerald chuckled at his paraphrase. He reached inside his jacket and withdrew an envelope.

'Here are the pertinent details. Home and work addresses, and photos of both Morozov and Sokolov.' He slid it across the table.

'What am I supposed to do with this?' Daniel asked.

'Whatever you feel is necessary.'

Daniel stared squarely at Gerald's impassive expression. He polished off the last of the coffee and picked up the envelope. Standing, he looked down at the man. Gerald was shabbily dressed, with thinning, grey hair. He looked tired and older than his years, but Daniel could see an inferno burning brightly behind his rough exterior.

'You haven't tried the scone?' Gerald said.

'Another day, perhaps.' Daniel headed for the door.

*

Michael Valent made his way to a small, private hanger at Washington National Airport. It was shortly after 8.30 p.m. The sun had set more than a half-hour before, and the ensuing twilight cast an eerie blue hue across the fields and intertwining runways. The scent of freshly cut grass drifted in the warm air, strangely putting Valent at ease. Sieber had been taken care of, Knox had seen to that. So, any link between the three of them had been erased. There were, of course, hundreds of more Nazis who'd escaped the Allies via the Vatican ratline that he and Knox had helped create and utilize, but he felt sure that none would reappear; they too wanted nothing more than a peaceful existence beyond the world's gaze. Now, it was time for him to return to Italy. What he'd come to do had been accomplished. There was nothing left but to live out his remaining days, drinking the wine his vineyard produced while enjoying the view from his veranda of the rolling countryside; a little slice of heaven on earth that he'd carved out for himself.

The taxi dropped him off at the security gate away from the main passenger terminal. He gave his name to an old guard who raised the barrier and allowed him to enter. It was a short walk to the hanger where Leon Knox stood waiting beside a 6-seater Beechcraft S50 Bonanza, a cigarette dangling from the corner of his mouth.

'You probably shouldn't smoke around these things,' Valent said.

Knox grunted an acknowledgment and stubbed the butt out on the floor.

'Plane is prepped and ready to take you to Toronto. From there, you'll be able to pick up an international flight to the destination of your choice.'

Valent walked around the aircraft, rubbing his hand across the surface. 'Doesn't look like it can make the distance.'

Knox smiled. 'Granted, she doesn't look like much, but she has a range of over 1,700km. It's less than 600 to Toronto.'

Valent frowned. He disliked people who used the feminine to describe inanimate objects, almost as though women were only as good as the tools men used for their pleasure. Decades of Vatican life had taught him to be respectful of both sexes equally, even if it wasn't practiced at the Holy See.

'I suppose its best that I leave with a minimum of fuss, away from prying eyes.'

'Ever since the shenanigans in New York, the FBI has agents stationed at every point of entry and exit to the States. Best be safe than sorry.' Knox looked at the plane. 'Refreshments are on board, tea, coffee, sandwiches, and a selection of beers I thought you might enjoy.' He looked hopefully at Valent.

'I don't touch alcohol while flying, but thank you for the courtesy all the same.' He held up his bag.

'Max will store that for you,' Knox said, motioning to a man who'd emerged from the cockpit. 'He'll be your pilot this evening.' He looked up at the pilot. 'How long will it be?'

Max, a clean-shaven young man in his mid-twenties, shrugged. 'About two hours, depending on headwinds.'

Valent handed his bag to the pilot and turned back to Knox. 'I didn't think international flights left this airport.'

'They don't, but my position has some benefits. Besides, this is a private flight. The rules around filing a flight plan are somewhat more relaxed.'

Valent extended his hand. 'I presume this will be the last time we will meet.'

'I imagine so. Take care, old friend.' Knox shook Valent's hand, warmly.

The older man climbed the steps and slipped into the aircraft, choosing to sit at the rear of the plane so he could stretch out and maybe catch up on some sleep before they landed in Canada. He buckled up and settled in, as the engine came to life. The plane taxied onto the runway.

Out of the corner of his eye, he saw Knox wave, but he didn't return the gesture, his gaze drawn instead to the food basket that had been positioned in the aisle next to him. He reached across and took a 'turkey and stuffing' sandwich. It was sure to be dry, so he poured himself a cup of tea to help wash it down.

By the time the Beechcraft had reached cruising altitude, Michal Valent lay dead in the back of the plane, bubbles of white froth dribbling onto his blazer. He never knew if it was the food or the drink that had been laced with cyanide. In fact, it had been both for Leon Knox wasn't one to gamble with another man's predilections.

CHAPTER 28

IT WAS A BRIGHT, AIRY morning and workers in their thousands waited impatiently at intersections the length and breadth of Manhattan for the lights to favor their progress before scurrying along the island's pavements towards their destinations. Not so for Daniel. He'd been standing in a bookstore on Broadway, pretending to read the blurbs of some of the latest bestsellers as he kept a close eye on the entrance to Novosil Petroleum and Gas Exploration.

He had arrived before dawn, watching from outside when the owner had appeared soon after to complete a stock-take before opening up for the day. They'd struck up a conversation where he'd told her he had flown in from Cleveland for an interview that morning but was a few hours early. She'd kindly invited him in out of the cold and even gone to the trouble of making him a mug of coffee.

The previous evening, Daniel had reviewed the material given to him by Gerald. He now knew who the major players were and understood how Sieber, Morozov, and Sokolov had been connected. He considered passing on what he'd learned to the FBI but believed that, if Gerald possessed the information, then it was likely they had it too. He wondered if they'd purposely kept him in the dark, or if they hadn't gotten around to telling him, or worse, they were still trying to assemble the pieces of the puzzle and hadn't yet made the connection.

It was, he felt, part of a larger game unknown to him, and one in which he was merely a pawn. Of course, he always knew the bit-part he played in any agency game, but on this occasion, Alona had been critically injured through, what he considered to be, their inaction. He also believed, perhaps erroneously, that they would allow the Russians to pursue him as per their original objective – the hunter becoming the hunted, in the hope of catching them red-handed. Any criminal action perpetrated by a foreign agent on US soil might then be used as a greater bargaining chip when it came time to deal with other matters. He wasn't about to allow himself become bait as had von Braun. And so, the time had come to take matters into his own hands. He would strike first and dispense the only form of justice the players of this game fully understood.

It was getting close to 9 a.m., and Daniel hadn't yet seen Zorin Sokolov arrive at Novosil. Included with the information supplied by Gerald was a note, saying that Sokolov was on a 'watch list', but with the increase in foreign influence that threatened to undermine the 'American Dream' (not to mention the rise in domestic crime), the FBI was being pulled in every direction imaginable. And so, those on 'the list' weren't always under the level of observation required to monitor and prevent the perpetration of a crime.

Daniel understood the dilemma, which was another reason for him setting in motion the sequence of events he'd planned that he believed he could better control. Decisions had to be made to prioritize resources, but he wondered what might be more critical than a Russian oil company employee working in downtown Manhattan right under the sniffing nose of McCarthyism. He also wondered if any foreign influence was perceived, actual, or fabricated. In the underworld of global intelligence and espionage, reality was frequently invented to suit the agenda of the day.

'Can I get you anything else?' the bookstore owner asked.

Daniel turned and smiled. 'Nothing, thank you. I appreciate you letting me in like this.'

She waved him away. 'What sort of a Christian would I be to allow a man remain on the sidewalk, exposed to the elements?' She looked at the book in his hand. 'The Silver Chalice. Have you read Costain before?'

'No. Number three in the New York Times bestseller list though. Must be good.' He glanced out the window and glimpsed a man who matched that in the photo provided climb out of a taxi and enter the office across the street. Sokolov had arrived. Daniel turned back to the bookstore owner.

'I'll take this for the trip home.' He walked with her to the cash register and passed her a few dollar bills. 'Thanks for the coffee. I feel bright-eyed and bushy-tailed. All ready for my interview.'

She beamed. 'Good luck today. Maybe you'll stop by again if you get the job.'

Daniel smiled politely and left.

He walked to the intersection of Broadway and 19th and crossed to the other side, keeping an eye on the other pedestrians as he walked towards the oil company's entrance.

The building was a large rectangular structure, like most of the others in Manhattan, of perhaps twenty stories. Daniel ducked in and scanned the company directory pinned to the wall opposite an unattended reception desk. Novosil shared the 6th floor with three other companies.

He took the elevator and got off on the 7th, double-backing down the stairs to the floor below. He checked the door for an alarm – there was none. He opened it carefully and peered cautiously along a new, heavy piled carpeted foyer that had large, glass doors on each of the four walls. He walked in and across to the door with Novosil etched in bold translucent writing. Pushing through, he was confronted by three more doors, with the one on the right bearing the name of Mr. Zorin Sokolov. The other two bore names he didn't recognize, and he doubted anybody worked in them. The place had a musty, disused smell as though doors and windows had rarely, if ever, been opened. The carpet was old and stained, with a slightly threadbare path leading from the entrance to Sokolov's office.

Daniel stepped lightly across to the middle of the three doors and listened.

There was no sound from the other side.

The door opened inwards when he twisted the handle. He popped his head around. Four filing cabinets lined one wall while the only illumination came from two windows with lowered Venetian blinds that gave the room a dismally depressing, almost oppressive quality.

He pulled the door shut, took one look at the other office door on the left, and decided it too was probably empty. He turned back to Sokolov's door.

He walked across and gave a slight cough before knocking firmly. A male Russian voice bade him enter, but Daniel had detected a moment's hesitation in the response.

Daniel marched in a stern expression on his face. Sokolov rose from behind his desk; a worried look etched on his face. Daniel stuck out a hand that Sokolov shook on instinct; seemingly unsettled.

He was a young man of slight, but muscular build. His shaved head was almost hairless, giving the impression of baldness. The faint odor of alcohol and sweat lingered in the room, but Daniel couldn't tell if it was from the man himself.

'Morozov sent me,' Daniel said in Russian. 'He's asked me to get a full report on your activities of the past two weeks.'

Sokolov took a step back. 'I do not know what you mean. Morozov has not said anything to me about this.' He swallowed hard; the mention of Morozov rattling the man further. 'I spoke with him only yesterday afternoon and told him everything, exactly as it happened.' He took a breath. 'Who are you anyway?'

'Leonid Skoch.' Daniel patted his pockets as though searching for identification. 'Left it in the car,' he muttered to himself. 'You know what Morozov is like, always wants to double-check the facts before reporting back to Moscow.'

Sokolov stared at Daniel for a moment before his face softened. 'Can I offer you anything?' He gestured towards a seat opposite.

Daniel unzipped his coat and sat down. 'No, thank you. It's warm in here.'

'It has been cold recently, but I must regulate the heating as the weather improves,' Sokolov said.

'So, you were going to tell me about the German, one less fascist to worry about, eh?' Daniel said.

Sokolov tapped the desk but remained quiet for a time.

'Is everything alright?' Daniel fired him a questioning look.

'I find these circumstances highly irregular.'

Daniel's face hardened, but he nodded. 'Yes. These are turbulent times for the Motherland, but the things we do in the present will help achieve success in the future. I'm sure you agree?'

He looked around the office – a desk with a phone, two small piles of paper, and a mug that held pens and pencils. A single filing cabinet stood off to one side. The walls looked recently painted, a dark orange, no doubt to reflect the spread of communism.

'I am sure there will be promotions as a result,' Daniel said, once he'd taken it in.

'I do not do this for personal gain.'

There was a mix of agitation and uncertainty in Sokolov's voice, and he actually seemed offended. Daniel had to restrain himself from laughing – bloody fanatic.

'None of us do. Still, it's nice to be appreciated. Helps motivate those whose dedication to our cause might waver. We are, after all, only men. So, Sieber?'

Sokolov leaned back in his chair and sucked gently on his lip for a time before he spoke. 'The longer his assignment went on, the more his eventual capture was inevitable. As you know, we had hoped the Americans would have killed him; they can sometimes be impetuous.'

'But sadly, not on this occasion. Indeed, it would have saved us quite a bit of trouble had they pulled the trigger themselves.'

Sokolov shrugged. 'I sent Gavlov to the hospital, and he poisoned the man.'

Daniel recalled that had been the name on the third office door, the one he hadn't checked. 'And how did he get past the security?'

Sokolov leaned back in his chair, and Daniel could feel the Russian's eyes scour him, his confidence appearing to rise.

'Through our contact within the American intelligence community.' He dragged out the words as though uncertain if he were to speak of such things so openly.'Perhaps, I will call Morozov and confirm he has sent you.'

Daniel nodded.'If you must. But, he's a busy man and will not welcome the intrusion.'

'He will be pleased that -'

There was a knock on the door before Sokolov could finish the sentence. He checked his watch.

'Late again,' he said quietly to himself.

Before Sokolov could say anything further, the door opened behind Daniel.

'I apologize for being late Zorin.'

'This is the third time this week,' Sokolov said. He looked at Daniel.'If he wasn't so good at his job, I'd have sent him back to Moscow long ago.' He looked back at the other man.'They would know what to do with you, eh, Gavlov? Probably send you to a Gulag if you were lucky.'

'Yes, Zorin...'

Daniel sensed a pause in the man behind and heard footsteps approach. He followed Sokolov's eyes, moving between him and Gavlov, who drew up alongside him. Daniel turned to see the man's mouth open slowly. Gavlov's eyes bulged. He pointed at Daniel as he shouted.

'You!'

Daniel leaped to his feet, grabbing the phone with one hand and a pencil with the other. In one fluid motion, he slapped Gavlov on the side of the head with the phone before diving across the desk at a stunned Sokolov, who hadn't moved. Daniel landed on top of him and, consumed by rage, jammed the pencil into the man's neck piercing his windpipe. Sokolov flailed helplessly, his hands barely impacting on Daniel's arms, as he reamed a large hole in the Russian's neck, inflicting the maximum amount of damage. By the time the pencil snapped, Sokolov lay gurgling on the floor, his head and back soaked in an expanding pool of blood. Daniel stood over him, staring into his eyes as the man's life left him.

He turned back to Gavlov, who had collided with, and knocked over, the filing cabinet such was the force of the blow to his head. Daniel checked for a pulse. There was none. He moved Gavlov's body to one side and righted the filing cabinet – if he couldn't get anything out of either of the Russians, then maybe the documents they stored might hold some answers.

He spent the next thirty minutes sifting through the files in Sokolov's office, before going next door and scanning the documents stored in the filing cabinets he'd seen there. He found hundreds of files. Requests for information, requests for quotes, and responses to tenders for many US government initiated natural resource projects. He felt sure a more thorough analysis would yield that the company had never once been successful in any of its bids. As expected, there was limited information on Sokolov, Gavlov, or any other Russian contacts.

He found nothing on Morozov.

He tried the door of Gavlov's office and found the room bare except for a phone on a desk and a small stash of unused notepads and pens. He checked the drawers and found a slip of paper with a scrawled address in lower Manhattan. He put the paper into his pocket.

He went back into Sokolov's office and tried the phone which, miraculously, still worked. He dialed the operator and asked to be put through to the FBI New York Field Office. While he waited to be connected, he surveyed the two bodies on the floor, his eyes lingering on Gavlov a little longer. Although both men were equally culpable, it'd been Gavlov who had murdered Sieber and given his reaction at recognizing him, appeared to be the one who'd been tasked with killing Daniel. A glimmer of satisfaction sparked inside, pleased that some measure of retribution had been exacted for what had befallen Alona.

Daniel was already on his way to La Guardia by the time Agent Ward showed up with half the New York Field Office in tow.

CHAPTER 29

A MID-SPRING HEAT WAVE ENVELOPED Washington in temperatures that allowed the most daring and frivolous to discard their overcoats, even if it was only a temporary respite from the cold. That was in contrast to the glacial atmosphere that swaddled Yuri Karatsev's office in Ternopil Research Limited on D-Street.

He had received word earlier that morning of the deaths of his comrades in New York which, he'd been informed, were being treated as homicides by the investigating authorities. As yet, there were no suspects. However, as both victims were Soviet nationals, (and nothing to do with the fact they were on somebody's watch-list somewhere) the FBI was leading the investigation. With support from the US State Department, the Kremlin was being kept apprised of any progress made through the Canadian Consulate in Moscow which, in these times, acted as an intermediary between the two nations.

Legal representatives of Novosil had been dispatched from Moscow, but it would be many hours before they arrived, and by then the Americans would have taken copies of everything the New York office could offer up. It was, of course, a pretense and, although it could not be proven, the Americans knew Novosil was a front for ongoing Soviet covert activities in their country. Although the dead men had been well trained, Karatsev prayed neither of them had been foolish enough to leave any documentary evidence of their endeavors, or worse, anything that might disclose the locations of other agents stationed in other cities across the country. Anybody so named would be rounded up, corralled, and questioned, until the Soviet government intervened. Agents would be deported and placed on a diplomatic blacklist that would be shared among the western democracies, thereby ruining years of hard work and forcing the Kremlin to recruit and train a new brood of spies above and beyond those currently being bred.

Of course, if the FBI found nothing, which was also likely, then the worst it could do was increase its surveillance on those suspected of being anybody other than those whom they claimed to be.

That, he could deal with.

The Americans were, after all, new to the intelligence and counterespionage arena and still had so much to learn, which was in contrast to the Soviets who had decades of experience. Even so, as part of his crackdown, Hoover had directed his cronies to test all government employees for 'loyalty' and investigate educators, union officials, and the stars of Hollywood whose sympathies lay beyond American borders. So, the FBI already had its hands full, investigating the crimes of paranoia that'd taken root within its borders.

Karatsev swung his chair around to face the window. He stared blankly at the building across the street, tapping his fingers on the arm-rests. After a time, he rested back his head and closed his eyes.

Of course, he shouldn't dismiss the possibility that the deaths of Sokolov and Gavlov might well be just 'one of those things', completely unrelated to any activities in which they were engaged – but that was a fool's hope, and he knew better than that. Not only were both men highly experienced spies and trained killers, but Gavlov, in particular, had, on more than one occasion, exhibited psychopathic characteristics that had made even him wince. It was doubtful that both men were subdued and murdered by persons who were not similarly trained.

And that's what worried him.

He had to consider the very real probability that those suspected of espionage in America were now being hunted and eliminated just as they had done with the Nazi scientists. In a way, he had to admire the directness of this approach, as successive Tsars and governments in his own country had been removing traitors, opposition leaders, and their followers by this method for centuries. Several questions swirled around his mind, the most pressing being: who was doing the hunting now and why were the Russians in the New York office targeted first? Whatever the answers, while important, they were not as critical as the third question that followed: who was next? Increasing security for his personnel embedded in America had become his number one priority, and he'd already made several calls to initiate additional protective measures. But, this was not without its consequences. Everybody knew that increasing security attracted unwanted attention while hampering further their ability to do their jobs effectively. That said, it was a small price to pay in the short term to ensure the Kremlin's objectives were met in the long term.

He stood and moaned, placing his hands on his lower back and stretching. He walked out of his office, careful not to catch the eye of any of his staff who he could feel watched his every movement, and into another further down the corridor. The seat sighed as he sat. He looked squarely at Morozov. 'You have to leave.'

'I was thinking the same.' Morozov placed a pen on the note pad in front of him.

'You're the only one connected with the New York office. If the link is found, you'll be exposed, which focuses the Americans on this office. I cannot allow that.'

'Will you be coming with me?'

Karatsev shook his head. 'I need to ensure we consolidate our efforts here with as little disruption as possible. We still have much to do.'

For a time, the only sound in the office was that of an electric fan buzzing away in the corner and the odd clacking of a typewriter from the pool outside.

'I've made arrangements through diplomatic channels. Your flight leaves at 9.15 p.m. You'll return when this has blown over, so you may leave your belongings in your apartment if you wish. All you'll need is your passport.'

'I have that here.' Morozov slid open his desk drawer and took it out. 'How long will I be away?'

'Difficult to say without further information. The Kremlin is working with the Canadians who have already made representations to the US State Department.' Karatsev looked away, momentarily distracted, his thoughts wandering to the memories of his two comrades.

'I would rather stay.' Morozov said.

'I know, but we need to ensure we accomplish our long term objectives and, of course, ensure your safety.' He smiled.

'And what about you?'

Karatsev laughed. 'I'll be fine. I've taken precautions.'

Morozov pushed his chair back and separated the blades on the Venetian blind to peer through. 'They are well hidden'. He turned back.

'They are experts, hidden in plain sight.'

'All I see is the window cleaner and the paperboy.'

'There are others.' Karatsev winked at the younger man and stood. He paused, taking in the room before returning to his own office without offering a handshake.

*

It was after seven when Simmonds and Witten gathered at a conference table. They'd been on the phone most of the day with various government agencies and officials, discussing the events in New York. Now it was the turn of Special Agent Ward who was on point at the Novosil office.

'Bring us up to speed Jeffrey.' Witten leaned in over the speaker, supported by his crossed forearms.

'We've confiscated every shred of documentation we found in here. It's been boxed-up and shipped-out for a thorough analysis off-site.'

'Do you need more men?'

'Not until I know more about what we have, but having glanced at some of the files, we will need more accountants. There's plenty of business material to sift through which is outside our area of expertise.'

Witten glanced sidelong at Simmonds. The older man had remained staunchly impassive throughout the day. Ward's briefing did nothing to change that.

'What about the bodies?' Witten said into the speaker.

'The coroner finished with them a couple of hours ago. He released them to the morgue where they'll remain until somebody comes to claim them. Might be a representative of Novosil or the Soviet government, I don't think there's much of a difference. One thing's for sure; it won't be either of the dead guys' relatives, neither of them had any relations in America.'

'Cause of death?'

'Initial indications show Gavlov died of blunt-force trauma to the head, a single strike on one side followed by a collision with the corner of a steel filing cabinet, looks like the telephone was the weapon.'

Witten coughed to stifle the laugh he felt coming on, inappropriate perhaps but he couldn't help himself.

'Sokolov died by either asphyxiation caused by blood entering his windpipe, which then seized up, or exsanguination due to the wound he received to his trachea. Looks like the murderer used a pencil.'

Witten half-opened his mouth, unable to get any words out, his eyes wide in disbelief. Simmonds spoke for him.

'Did Miller do this?'

There was a pause on the other end. 'He didn't say when he called, but this has all the hallmarks of a trained assassin. I'd be able to give you a better answer if I knew more about him.'

Both Simmonds and Witten exchanged knowing glances, but neither chose to enlighten Agent Ward further.

'He may simply have found the two victims as they were and reported it,' Ward added.

Simmonds closed his eyes and shook his head.

'Thanks for the update, Jeffrey,' Witten said. 'We'll keep these calls going three times a day as discussed. Let's make sure the information keeps flowing right through the weekend.' He hung up the receiver.

'Miller?' Witten said.

'Of course.'

'But why?'

'Who knows, maybe revenge for Ms. Peers.'

Witten shook his head. 'How did he find out?'

The question drew a wry smile from Simmonds. 'Because he's better connected than we gave him credit. He probably gets the same intelligence we do, maybe more and better for all we know.'

'So what, he strolls into Novosil's office and kills two Russian nationals by way of retribution?'

'It may not have been his intention. He may have gone on a fishing trip, and when events took a turn, he had to act.'

'And leave us with two dead bodies and a political shitstorm?'

'Dead non-nationals and political shitstorm are not mutually exclusive. They are very much a part of our business. We need to manage the situation properly.'

Witten watched Simmonds and knew the older man's mind had already moved on to damage limitation, diversion, and blame if it was required.

'What do we do about Knox?' he said.

Simmonds put a finger to his mouth.

'And if Miller knows about his alleged involvement?'

'We keep an eye on Knox for now, but we don't get too close. We don't want him to become aware of what we know. He's a suspicious and careful man by nature. It wouldn't surprise me if he's already taken measures to distance himself from the Russians. Although, I wouldn't be too upset if anything foul should befall the man.'

Witten acknowledged the order.

'And nothing on Miller?' Simmonds said.

'Nothing. The phone call to Agent Ward was the last we've heard from him. He hasn't even shown up at the hospital.'

Simmonds ran a fingertip across on eyebrow. 'We have to assume he committed these murders. I want to try and bring him in before somebody else does. We also need to know if he took anything of relevance that might aid us in the future.'

'I'll have agents issued with his photograph and deployed to airports and ferry terminals immediately, but we may have already missed him.'

'That's a possibility, but you also forget who we're dealing with.'

'You think we'd be wasting our time?'

'Definitely. But no harm in doing so, we might get lucky.' Simmonds stood. 'I'm going to see the President. He's requested a daily briefing each evening until resolved.'

'You need anything from me?'

'Stay by your desk in case I've to call. You may not have anything more to add, but Eisenhower will want the very latest update.'

He walked out of the room, leaving Witten to organize what he now knew would be a fruitless manhunt.

CHAPTER 30

THE TWO KGB AGENTS IN the downstairs lobby of the Ternopil offices on D-Street were anything but innocuous, and Daniel immediately knew that they were a protective detail assigned to one of the Ternopil employees once news had filtered back of the deaths of their comrades in New York. At first, he thought they were FBI or CIA, but the fact they were sitting like they had broom handles up their asses, told him they were on the clock and ever watchful. After a cursory scan of the vicinity, he counted three more in various disguises outside the office and presumed others had hidden better.

In fact, it made his job a little easier. He had no idea how many employees were at the company but, given its location in the heart of downtown Washington, he suspected it was more than the paltry two in Novosil. Gerald had told him that Morozov was the link between Novosil and Ternopil, so it was a sure bet that the two goons in reception would accompany either Morozov or somebody of even more importance when they left the building, so all he had to do was wait and follow them when the time came.

He'd walked through the front door of the building opposite, a multi-story that was managed by a landlord who leased various floors to several companies in some sort of entrepreneurial incubator project. As it happened, the receptionist there barely batted an eyelid as he breezed past; no doubt well-practiced at ignoring the many strangers who happened by. Besides, she was putting on her coat and getting ready to go home and looked like she wasn't overly concerned with having to deal with another guest at the end of a busy day of not dealing with other visitors.

He made his way to the second floor and found an empty office with a window view of the street below. He pulled across a chair and began his vigil.

Nothing much happened for the first two hours, apart from an increase in pedestrian and vehicle traffic to choking point as the city's workers emptied of their offices. Before too long and, almost as soon as it had begun, traffic slowed to a trickle which made it easier to maintain watch on those entering and leaving Ternopil.

It was just after 7.30 p.m. when a car pulled up outside. Both Russian security guards discarded their newspapers and walked out, looking up and down the street. One of them opened the rear passenger door. A few moments later, a guy fitting Morozov's description joined them on the path and jumped into the car like he was diving into a foxhole under enemy fire. He wasn't carrying anything, not even an overnight bag. The two Russians joined him, one in the front passenger seat, the other, besides their charge. At first, Daniel thought the guy might be heading home for the evening like the rest of the city, but his instinct told him otherwise. He hurried down and outside, looking east along the street. The car was stopped at the lights at the intersection with 6th Avenue. He hopped into his rental and pulled away from the curb before coming to a stop four cars behind Morozov.

Once he'd made it through the junction, he glanced behind to see if he was being followed – he wasn't. After tailing the Russians for a few minutes, he noticed a second car up ahead hanging a few cars behind the first. While other cars turned off or joined the line of traffic, it mirrored the route the first car was taking. There were only two possibilities: the Feds, resuming their surveillance, or KGB, offering protection. It didn't matter to him. Having identified them, he knew he just had to give them a wide berth, also. Both cars ahead took a meandering route around eastern Washington, past The Capitol before sweeping west onto the 14th Street Bridge. Once across the Potomac, they headed south along the George Washington Memorial Parkway which all but confirmed Daniel's hunch that the Russian was making a break for it. Daniel continued south towards Alexandria as the cars took the exit for Washington Airport; he double-backed after a couple of miles and headed for home.

He suspected the FBI would have his apartment under surveillance by now and so he parked in the alley behind his apartment complex. He scaled the wall and ducked into the house through the back door.

Once inside, he grabbed the small holdall he'd used for his Oregon and Nevada trips, having already replenished it with enough clean clothes and toiletries to last him a week. He edged cautiously towards the window and peered out, spotting a parked car a little further along on the other side of the street, its occupants making no attempt to camouflage their presence. He slipped into his bedroom and opened the wardrobe. He placed his hand on the base and, with a twist of his wrist, removed a false bottom, revealing a safe he'd had installed into the concrete floor. He flicked through the passports he kept there before settling on two. He grabbed an envelope marked 'State Bank Notes', took out a handful of high denomination Rubles and shoved them into his wallet. He secured the safe and floor before taking a heavy woolen, waist-length coat off the hanger. Carrying it along with his holdall, he left by the backdoor.

A little later, he crossed the Potomac on Arlington Memorial Bridge, skirted the military cemetery, and drove along Washington Boulevard. He passed the miniature cities of Falls Church, Merrifield, and Fairfax before heading south on Centreville Road towards Manassas. The trip took just under an hour.

Once there, he headed directly for Manassas Regional Airport and booked a flight out of Virginia to Portland, Maine, which was scheduled to depart at 7.22 a.m. the following morning. He checked into a cash-only, no-questions-asked motel nearby, and settled in for the night.

He didn't spot anybody resembling federal law enforcement at the airport when he arrived for the flight the next day and so was reasonably confident that if the authorities were looking for him, they either weren't overly concerned with his capture, or their manpower didn't stretch beyond airports in the larger cities.

A low-pressure system was sweeping in from the Atlantic, so it was a bumpy ride to Portland which, thankfully, only lasted ninety minutes. As soon as he disembarked, he went directly to flight bookings and bought himself a seat on a DC-6 to London. It wasn't due to depart until 2.10 p.m., so he killed the few hours by strolling up and down the city's main street, browsing the antique stores he found there and grabbing a club sandwich and a pot of tea at a small café.

Even though it was the middle of April, a few inches of snow still covered the city- winter's dying breath laid for all to see. He was relieved he'd brought his heavy jacket, although he thought he'd only have needed it once he'd reached his final destination.

He spent the remaining time in the departure lounge, nursing a refilling coffee cup while reading a copy of the Bangor Daily News.

CHAPTER 31

THE SUN HAD LONG DISAPPEARED beneath the imposing Moscow skyline by the time Nikita Morozov ambled through a grand and aging building at Staraya Square, home to the Soviet Politburo and the Central Committee of the Communist Party. In the near-deserted edifice, his casual footsteps clicked sharply, echoing loudly no matter how softly he tread. His hands behind his back, he walked along a dark and musty corridor past enormous, ornate, gold-framed paintings of Soviet leaders of yesteryear, their lifeless eyes thoughtful, yet ever-watchful as indeed they had been before death had taken them. With each step, he struggled to contain a growing smile of smugness and increasing confidence.

Despite the deaths of two of his comrades which hadn't been his fault, he'd done well. His master would be pleased.

He came to a stop outside a richly stained, wooden door near the end of the passageway. He knocked and waited for a response. He stole a glance along the way he'd come to ensure he hadn't been spotted – not that it mattered. Although the corridor appeared empty, he knew that in this place above all others, spies lurked, their allegiances changing with the shifting political sands. Behind him, a portrait of the recently deceased Comrade Stalin stood as though guarding the office to which he'd been summoned. The faint smell of paint lingered, the portrait a recent addition to those gone before.

The command came, and Morozov entered. He closed the door behind him and without welcome, nestled into a comfortable wing-backed chair, and faced his superior.

Oleg Petrov, one of a generation that had fought and survived two world wars and the purge sat at the opposite of the desk, his lips pursed, his beady eyes washing over Morozov. He stared for longer than was required by a man asserting his dominance. A crack appeared in Petrov's lips as the foundation of a smile eased Nikita's sudden discomfort.

'I am happy to have you back, comrade.' Petrov's smile grew wider. He took off his glasses.

'It's good to be back.'

Petrov settled back into his chair and, tilting his head as though in wonder, twisted his glasses playfully in his hands. He nodded.

'The work you have done has been splendid. Your regular feedback on Karatsev has been invaluable to our cause. Our boss is delighted with the outcome.'

Morozov rubbed his sweating hands gently on his trousers and returned the man's smile. 'Will it be enough to turn the tables in our favor?'

'With every day that passes and the evidence we amass, I grow more confident of a positive outcome. Beria will not last much longer, I guarantee it.'

Morozov grinned. Even though Stalin's corpse was still warm, the struggle to seize power within the Kremlin had ignited a little over a month ago. And, to the silent annoyance of many, Lavrentiy Beria was the man in charge – for now. Unknown to him, a covert action was in progress to depose the new leader, an action in which both Morozov and Petrov had delighted in being willing participants.

Petrov stood and walked across to a small drinks cabinet and poured two glasses of vodka. Morozov thought it a stereotypical act. It was a celebratory shot that he would now enjoy having missed it immensely ever since he'd finished all that he'd taken with him to America. Petrov passed him a glass.

'To your namesake,' Petrov said, holding his glass aloft. He swallowed the shot in one go.

Nikita did likewise and felt a warm surge bathe his chest. Oh, how he'd missed it, the taste of home, the taste of victory.

Petrov poured a second into each glass. 'Karatsev will soon return, and when he does, we will have gathered enough information to sway the remainder of the Presidium and finally put our First Secretary under arrest. After that, Beria's trial and execution will be a formality.' He knocked back the second glass and let out a gasp of delight.

Morozov held the vodka to his lips but hesitated.

Petrov eyed him. 'You seem concerned?'

Morozov knew he had to choose his words carefully, or he too might end up facing a firing squad. 'Merely saddened.' He bowed his head, cradling the shot glass in his palm.

'How so?'

'For the death of our comrades.'

Petrov remained silent for a moment before replying. 'Unfortunate as they were, their deaths will ensure a brighter future for us all. Ever since Comrade Stalin's death, Beria's craving for power has become insatiable. He was always dangerous, but now, I fear, it will consume him completely, and he may become impossible to control. Like a lit match in a dry forest, we must extinguish him before his inferno engulfs us all.'

Although Morozov knew this to be true, the deaths of Sokolov and Gavlov had hit him harder than he thought they might. They had been more than comrades. They had been friends. An even though they'd grown up in different parts of the country, the three men (among others) had been plucked from the thousands of men and women willing to offer their lives in service of the Motherland. They had been whisked away to an unknown location where they'd undertaken an intensive training regime, learning all there was to know of the new enemy, its organizational structure, its way of life, the forces that drove its economy, its beliefs, its ideology, and most importantly, its weaknesses.

Then, they'd been dispatched.

And, even though the Americans had learned of his two friends' activities through the despicable actions of another as yet unknown party, the events of the past week had proved timely and, in fact, advantageous. Blame for their discovery and demise would be apportioned, adding yet another nail to Beria's political coffin.

Morozov looked up at Petrov and, nodding firmly, knocked back his drink to honor his dead friends.

'Mark my words,' Petrov said. 'Khrushchev will be our leader before the year is out. He will not forget what you have done to help put him there.' He laughed. 'It wouldn't surprise me if you never have to leave our homeland on assignment ever again. You'll probably end up with a comfortable and prestigious position within his new administration.'

'As will you, dear friend,' Morozov said.

'Perhaps, perhaps. Now, you must leave quietly. I have reports to imagine and create.' He laughed again. 'Make sure nobody sees you as you go.'

Morozov set the glass down on the desk, stood and, without exchanging pleasantries, left Petrov's office.

He slumped in the back of a state-owned limousine as it arrowed its way along the broad avenues and empty streets of Moscow; it was dark after all, and a curfew had been imposed. Neither he nor the driver spoke throughout the journey which pleased him as all he wanted was to crawl into bed and emerge from beneath the covers whenever the mood took him. Petrov had rewarded him with a few days off which, in truth, he deserved. He'd watched Karatsev, an ally of Beria, ever since his deployment and reported back to Petrov at least once a week, more if the circumstance warranted. If he were kind to the man, he'd have said Karatsev had performed his duties adequately but seemed to not fully understand the seriousness, importance, and scale of the operation of which he'd been placed in charge. And although he'd mentioned on more than one occasion how he missed the Motherland, Karatsev had grown soft. He had appeared to enjoy the trappings and frills of the American way of life that had come with his posting. What had irked Morozov most however was the man's obsession with golf and the compulsion to let everybody in Ternopil know how his swing was improving, what score he'd posted, or how many birdies he'd made during any given round – whatever the hell they were. Above all, it was this he could not forgive, for he hated the game almost as much as he did the Americans.

The car swung gently to the right and made its way along a pebbled driveway.

Morozov sat forward and looked at the outline of his home (a mansion on the outskirts of Moscow, inherited from his father, who'd been a high-ranking Stalin sycophant), silhouetted against the dim glow of the city's lights. An excited tingle sparked within him, and suddenly he couldn't wait to get inside and remind himself of what he'd missed these past few years.

The driver came to a stop and helped Morozov to the hall door with his bags.

'I'll be fine from here,' Morozov said. 'Come back at 7 a.m. on Thursday.' He fired the driver a look that said 'and not a minute sooner'.

Once inside, he dropped his bags in the hallway and stood, listening to the quiet darkness. An overwhelming feeling of contentment washed over him, and he sighed, long and deep. He was home.

After a few moments, he made his way to the drawing-room on the right. He pulled a box of matches from his pocket and began lighting a row of candles on the mantelpiece. But, before he lit the last, he stopped. Something was out of place. He tilted his head and sniffed the stale air. A voice broke the silence.

'Nice place.'

Morozov spun around, his knees flexed, his arms outstretched, his body prepared to defend itself.

A man sat cross-legged in an armchair in the furthest corner of the room, cloaked in shadow, his features intermittently visible whenever the flickering candles allowed. He held a brandy glass in one hand and a gun in the other.

'Who are you?' Morozov said. His tone a mix of outrage and fear in equal measure.

The man looked neither happy nor sad, his expression vacant, his eyes dull yet hard and unwavering. 'That doesn't matter.'

'Who sent you?' Morozov's voice grew louder and sharper as anger began to triumph over terror, and adrenaline took hold. 'Beria? Or one of his cronies?'

A quizzical look passed across the man's features for a fleeting moment, before blankness returned. Only then did Morozov notice the scar, faint as it was, etched on the unshaven face. The man shook his head.

'The internal politics of the Soviet Union doesn't interest me.' The man paused. 'Not anymore.' A smile appeared and evaporated in less time than it took to take a breath, his face hardening, his stare solidifying. 'I'm here to right a wrong.'

Morozov stood upright and moved his hands toward his pockets.

The man tutted. 'Hands were I can see them, palms facing me.' He raised the gun slightly higher to emphasize the point. Morozov acquiesced.

'What do you want? Money? I have plenty. My belongings? You can take it all.'

The man sat motionless for a time, seeming to neither inhale nor exhale. He sipped his drink. 'I want what's most precious to you.'

Confusion reigned in Morozov's mind before he realized what that meant.

Without diverting his eyes from Morozov, the man placed his drink on a small table next to the armchair. 'You understand and play the game well. But, I'm afraid, not well enough. You overstepped your responsibilities in America, and that caused some to become upset.'

Morozov listened carefully to the accent. The man's Russian was excellent, but he wasn't from this place. And not from America either, of that, he was sure. He searched his mental archives but couldn't quite place it. In the end, he decided it didn't matter. The man had come to do a job and, for the moment, held the upper hand. Morozov straightened and stepped slightly to his left to remove the shadow he cast that partly covered the man. In the weak luminescence radiating from the candles behind, he regarded the man from toe to tip.

The man's clothes were well-worn, shabby even by proletariat standards. He wore scuffed, dull boots with under-soles caked in damp mud,

Morozov only now noticing light shoeprints left on the brightly carpeted floor from the hallway to the drinks cabinet and finally to where the man sat. A gentle shiver rippled through Morozov's body when he realized there was nothing remarkable about the man, nothing that would distinguish him from anybody else in the country. He felt his throat tighten and mouth become dry.

The silence between them seemed vast, filled only with endless uncertainty.

Although a rising star in the Politburo, Morozov had never been to war and had never faced the prospect that he may not return. His training had provided ample opportunity for others to point weapons at him in mock situations designed to prepare him for some future showdown. Thinking back, it didn't matter how much training one received; nothing could adequately prepare you for an occasion where the training was required. It was well known that nobody ever really knew how they would react when the time came. Some remained calm, others crumbled, most behaved somewhere between those extremes. His breathing was regular, he didn't feel himself sweat, and although his heart rate was elevated, it wasn't beating a retreat out of his chest. Morozov was secretly pleased with how relaxed he felt now that his time had come to be tested. However long it would last, would be determined by the man with the most power and he knew that just because someone held a weapon didn't necessarily mean they held all the cards. All he needed was a moment to turn the tables.

'America? I've just returned from there.' Morozov smiled. 'I'm in the oil business.'

'So I've learned, but it's your other business I'm more interested in.'

Morozov feigned bewilderment, his outstretched palms rising slowly, imploring protest. 'You must have mistaken me for another?' He smiled, but the man's scowl immediately put paid to the hope that that was indeed the case. His mind drew a blank, bereft of another idea save the obvious.

'OK. Well, I don't know what you believe I'm guilty of, but if you're here to kill me then get on with it. I'm a busy man.'

The man stood slowly and took a couple of steps nearer Morozov, raising the gun to head height. Morozov saw the man's finger tighten on the trigger and wondered which he'd experience first, the bullet burrowing a path through his skull or the sound of the explosion deafening his ears as the hammer pounded the back of the casing. He glanced past the barrel to the man's face. Instead of detecting a change of heart, the man's eyes fluttered involuntarily. His face creased and without warning, he sneezed.

The opportunity had presented itself, and Morozov wasn't about to let it slip from his grasp. He summoned the remaining energy in his weary body and sprung forward. Charging the man, he grabbed the underside of his hand and pushed upwards, a shot rang out, the bullet tearing into the ceiling.

Both pairs of hands grappled for control of the gun acutely aware of where the barrel was pointing, each man straining ferociously against the other, their eyes locked together in a burst of hatred. Morozov attempted to plant a knee into the man's side, but it had been anticipated and parried by a defending leg. As both became briefly unbalanced, they collapsed to the floor, each man's hands gripping the others, refusing to surrender and relinquish control. They rolled around the floor and on top of each other, swearing incoherently, bumping into the bottom of the sofa, their legs ricocheting against the chairs and table.

Morozov tried to wrench the gun away but found the man's grip had somehow tightened. With every twist, pull, and push, he could feel his energy-sapping away. Despite his desire to prevail, he knew he was losing the battle; the scarred man was gaining the upper hand. He had to at least level the playing field, and that meant disarming them both. In desperation, he summoned every ounce of strength and smacked both their hands off the sofa leg.

The gun sailed through the air and disappeared into the relative gloom of the hallway as the man cried out in pain. Morozov smiled. He'd heard something crack, perhaps he'd been lucky, and the man had broken a bone. Morozov managed to sit on top of the man and began raining punches on his head. Some found their mark, several cuts appearing on the man's face, but remarkably, most were deflected by defensive moves that Morozov hadn't seen since his training.

Unfortunately, it was Morozov's surprise that tipped the balance in his would-be assassin's favor.

Daniel immediately recognized Morozov's lapse, felt the lessening of the blows to his face and arms, and realized he could turn the tables once more. With Morozov half-sitting, half-standing over him, he drove his knee into the man's crotch from behind. The Russian shrieked, his face screwed in agony as he fell to his right, clutching his groin. Daniel leaped to his feet and set upon his prey, grabbing him from behind. He leaned back, exerting a chokehold he knew he could keep indefinitely but wouldn't have to. Morozov's arms flailed at Daniel's arms and face desperately seeking purchase to alleviate the pain and restore his rapidly depleting air.

As with the punches thrown, his thrashing and flapping slowed as the life drained from him. Amidst dribbles of snot and spit, Morozov breathed his last few shallow breaths before his lifeless body slumped to the floor.

*

It was 5 a.m. on the nose when Alexsander Figner and Felix Kaplan set out on the last patrol of their shift at the Kremlin. Their route, as it had done all night, would take them south along the Kremlin Wall from their sentry point directly opposite where Kazan Cathedral once stood before Stalin had it demolished, past the 'Cathedral of the Intercession of the Most Holy Theotokos on the Moat', or 'Saint Basil's' as it was more commonly known, down to the Moskva River. They would stand to attention for precisely one minute, before retracing their steps north to be finally relieved by the morning crew. Although they knew their duty to be largely ceremonial, it didn't preclude them from maintaining an austere discipline.

It was still dark, and the bluish hue that preceded dawn was a good fifteen minutes away yet. The overnight temperature had been below zero and would not move into double digits even when the sun did eventually show itself. The ground underfoot was icy, but the men were used to it, having trodden the same path many times, over the past few months.

They started their march with a glacial northern breeze at their backs, knowing it would freeze them on their return. It took just under twenty minutes to get to the corner of the southern wall which followed the contours of the river westward. They waited the requisite length-of-time before turning around, bracing themselves against the wind that bit into their uncovered faces.

The sky was clear but now brightening, enabling them to see farther than when they had made their first pass. They marched past Saint Basil's, now on their right, for the second time, and followed the wall's lineation as it kinked northwest. Up ahead, they could just about make out the grand outline of Lenin's Mausoleum on the left. But, as they drew closer, they spotted a dark shape lying on its steps. The two men didn't look at each other until they were no more than thirty yards away when it became apparent it was a body.

'Чертовски пьяный,' Figner muttered – *'bloody drunk'.*

They were almost upon the man when they noticed the garrote. They rushed across, Kaplan bending down to check for a pulse as Figner tried desperately to remove the steel cable that bit into the man's neck, drawing a circle of blood that had seeped onto his collar. Pinned to the man's chest was a fluttering slip of paper with one word – 'Убийца' – *'murderer'.*

'Sound the alarm,' Figner said

Kaplan hurried away toward the guardhouse, scrambling as his feet tried to gain purchase on the ice, his rifle swinging loosely in one hand while the other held his hat in place. Figner stood and scanned Red Square and what he could see of the streets on the far side that entered the merchant's quarter of Kitai-gorod. He saw nobody.

*

Daniel was only a few miles from the border by the time the authorities identified Morozov's body. On this occasion, he'd gone north into Estonia and to the small city of Parnu where he had secured passage to Sweden aboard a fishing vessel whose captain was a fervent nationalist with dreams of one day making it to America. The only other usual member of the crew was his son, but the good captain had left him behind on this trip. Few were to be trusted on this side of the Iron Curtain.

The Baltic Sea lived up to its name, calm yet bitter, forcing Daniel to spend the journey watching for the lights of Stockholm to appear on the horizon from the relative warmth of the cabin. They wouldn't stop there, but would instead moor in the harbor of the small fishing village of Nynäshamn a little farther south. From there, he'd take a train north to Stockholm and hop-scotch several flights back across the Atlantic.

He thought back to his last trip out of the Soviet Union a little over a month ago. He never imagined he'd have returned to the country so soon. He'd killed again, three agents in as many days, yet he felt no remorse. Those men had understood the perils of their profession and known their lives may be cut short at any moment in service of their Motherland. As the boat knifed through the waves, and his destination became ever nearer, he felt a growing sense of satisfaction. No 'innocent' had died at his hand this time around. He wondered if, despite rigorous planning, destiny had a role to play in pre-determining a course of action that he was powerless to prevent. He regretted every one of those killed, but they'd been necessary victims and perhaps, necessary in the grander scheme of things.

EPILOGUE

HE HADN'T BEEN SURPRISED WHEN the call to retreat had eventually come. And, although disappointed, Karatsev was somewhat relieved as he roamed through his Washington home one last time – he wouldn't return. Everything he needed, and indeed owned, had been packed into large containers and delivered to the airport where it was being loaded on a plane destined for the Soviet sector of Berlin. Anything no longer required had been destroyed and the remnants carefully disposed of by professionals. Following the death of comrades Sokolov, Gavlov, and now Morozov, orders had been issued from the Kremlin. Activities in America were to be scaled down until the KGB could better determine, and make provision for, the security concerns of its American operation. As a consequence, many of the more high profile operatives were being recalled to the Motherland where a review and overhaul of KGB campaigns, not only in America but across all western countries, had already commenced. He hoped for redeployment to another mission, but feared a harsher outcome, as his bosses usually opted to make examples of those who failed.

And it didn't matter which way he looked at it. He had failed.

Maintaining and enhancing the integrity of the American mission had been his sole responsibility, and with wholesale evacuations underway, his fate had been, he suspected, decided. He wouldn't be consulted, nor his views considered in whatever plans would be concocted within the confines of the Kremlin and Lubyanka. That would fall to younger men, with fresh ideas. Although he doubted the wisdom of implementing change without invoking institutional memory, he knew mistakes would be made again. But, those decisions were neither his to make nor worry.

He looked around the living room one last time, running his hand across the back of his favorite cushioned seat that faced east, the unobstructed view through a large window of the sparkling Potomac and thousands of miles beyond well beneath the horizon, his homeland. He felt an overwhelming sense of happiness swaddle him, and he smiled. Whatever anxiety he'd felt before, had now subsided.

He turned and walked toward the door.

Outside, he handed his briefcase to one of the four security agents assigned to him. The man, a burly giant with scarred fists the size of watermelons, placed it in the limousine trunk and opened the rear passenger door. Karatsev slipped inside, as the man scanned the grounds.

The vehicle eased along a short, tree-lined driveway, slowing down when it came to the bottom of the incline. A security guard opened the gates, and the car glided out onto the road, heading for Washington National.

*

A crowd of almost 28,000 had packed into Griffith Stadium for the afternoon's game between the Senators and Red Sox. With only two games played, it was still early in the season and, despite both losses to the Yankees, there was a general feeling of optimization among the partisan home support. Last year's mid-table finish had been adequate, but the fans hoped for better this time out.

As had been the case for every weekend home game since he'd returned from the war, Thomas Mitchell took his seat four rows back from 3rd base. He held a program in one fist and a hot dog that he wouldn't eat in the other. It was a mostly symbolic and superstitious act, performed to curry favor with the sporting Gods. Mitchell didn't know who they were or even if they existed for that matter, but for one hundred and fifty-four games every year he worshipped them, nonetheless.

The Senators took to the field, charging from their dugout to the cheers of the excited congregation. The basemen tossed a ball between them to shake away any pre-game nerves before Boston's lead-off hitter got to stand at home plate.

'Hey Eddie, how may walks you gonna get today?' Mitchell shouted.

Eddie Yost, the Senator's 3rd plate baseman turned around and came up to the fence, a huge smile on his face. 'I might hit one out of the park just for you. How'd you like that.'

'You only hit twelve homers last season, so I guess I'd be pretty damn impressed,' Mitchell said, drawing laughter from the nearby supporters.

Eddie feigned hurt. 'Sometimes, I don't know if you come here just to annoy me.'

'I guess you'll never know.' Mitchell held up the hotdog, offering it to the deities as Eddie trotted off to get on with the game, the crowd settling in for the next few hours.

Somebody sat in the seat next to Mitchell as he watched the flight of a fly ball to left field for an easy out.

'I heard Mickey hit one out on Friday,' the person said.

Mitchell didn't react but kept his eye on the next batter, making his way to the plate. 'Sure did.'

'You see it?'

'Can't make the weekday games. Some of us have jobs to go to.'

'If I didn't know you better, I'd be hurt by that.'

'You don't know me at all.'

'Touché.'

They watched the 2nd batter ground out to shortstop.

'How'd you find me?' Mitchell tossed the uneaten hotdog into a nearby trashcan.

'You're not the only one with contacts.'

'That sounds ominous.'

'You shouldn't be concerned. I only came to let you know how Alona was getting on.'

Mitchell turned toward Daniel. 'You look well. Been away?'

'Took a trip abroad, found it refreshing.'

'Relaxing?'

There was a pause. 'I'm relaxed, now that I'm back.'

'No place like home, eh?'

'So they say.'

A third out and the teams swapped places with the Red Sox taking to the field at the bottom of the 1st.

'So, Alona?'

'She's doing well.' Daniel said.

'Out of the woods?'

Daniel nodded. 'Been through worse. She's a strong girl.' He changed the subject. 'I heard the Russians have pulled out.'

'Is that a statement or a question?'

'Bit of both.'

'Some are gone, others remain.'

'And the Feds know who's still here?'

'They know what they know.'

'Ambiguous.' Daniel glanced across at Mitchell, who'd stood to applaud a base-hit to right field. 'Do you know more?'

'More and less. Depends on what the topic is.'

'Jesus, you're evasive.'

Mitchell said nothing for a moment. 'Did she get the flowers?'

Daniel smiled. 'Nice touch. The corn poppy. She was wondering if she could make opium from them.'

It was Mitchell's turn to smile. 'Took me an age to find them. They don't bloom until late spring.'

'She knew that and appreciated the sentiment.'

'When is she getting out?'

'Looks like the end of the month. Doctors advised against flying, so I'll drive her back. I'm sure she'll want to thank you for the flowers in person.'

Mitchell sat back and stared at the back of the seat in front.

'You OK?' Daniel said.

'Sure. Just realized I've arrived at one of those life's crossroads.'

'You've a choice to make?'

'Always have choices, some impact more than others.'

'And this?'

Mitchell grunted. 'This is a whopper.'

The Senators left two men on base at the end of the inning before Daniel patted Mitchell on the thigh.

'I'll leave you to the game. Never could understand it, anyhow.' He stood and disappeared down the exit tunnel.

For the next two and a half hours, Mitchell watched the rest of the game his mind wandering absently. He wondered if this would be the last time he'd visit the old Stadium. The secrets he carried would benefit many individuals, and so he debated whether he'd have to change his routine and disappear. He'd become complacent over the past few years, especially with Alona. He admired her and respected her steadfast spirit, but over time he'd told her things about himself that should have remained private. And although she wasn't to know if he'd spoken untruths, it may have jeopardized his existence.

He remained in his seat long after the last Red Sox batter was out in the 9th. He stood and, as the sun set behind him, took a last look around the field for the day and left, still unsure if he'd ever return.

****

'Thought I'd catch you up with what's been happening on the case.' Daniel waited for a response at the other end of the line.

'Sure,' Collins said after a moment. The delay was probably less than a second but felt like an age every time either of them spoke. 'Looks like you've been busy?'

'So, you heard?' Daniel said.

'We get the newspapers out here too.' Collins chuckled. 'Had your very own gunfight right in the middle of Times Square.'

'Exaggerated in print, I'm sure. Looks like you can wrap up the murders of Otte and Lenz. We've been able to tie Sieber to their deaths, along with Hasse's in Oregon and a few others on the east coast.'

'That is good news,' Collins said. 'Ain't nothin' like a solving a case.'

The line went quiet for a time.

'How're things there,' Daniel said, not wanting to say goodbye and hang up on the guy.

'Busy as usual.'

Daniel thought he detected a hint of resignation in the Sheriff's voice, but it may just have been the poor quality of the line.

'Been thinkin' 'bout givin' it all up,' Collins said. 'I'm gettin' too old to run around the desert, tryin' to catch the bad guys.'

'They're not all that bad.'

'Hmm. Some of the bozos that're flyin' in these days are a real handful and gettin' worse by the day. It's a young man's game these days. Maybe you wanna come out here, take over for a bit?'

'Are you making me an offer?'

Collins laughed out loud. 'You kiddin' me? I need a Brit out here like I need a scorpion down my pants. Be safer for both of us if you stayed over your side of the country. I might come visit you though, never been to our nation's capital before. You could show me around?'

'Just let me know when you're coming,' Daniel said. 'I'll make myself scarce.'

Collins laughed then sighed. 'See you round, kid,' Collins said, and the line went dead.

*

Special Agent Ward had been summoned to FBI headquarters in Washington to provide a face to face update on the investigation into the murders of Sokolov and Gavlov. There were no new developments, but he got a sense that Simmonds and Witten hadn't cared too much about apprehending those responsible. Sure, they had their suspicions and one name, in particular, was prominent in their small suspect pool, but as their surveillance workload had decreased following the recent Russian retreat and a nod from the top to move on to pastures new, they appeared content with letting the indiscretion slide.

'How is the analysis of Novosil's documents going?' Witten asked.

Ward blew out hard. 'Slow. Preliminary indications are that these guys were never serious about winning business in the US. Looks like they were a front for the KGB as we suspected. The accountants are still going through them, but any money they made came from overseas shell companies whose origins we're still trying to uncover. This could take years.'

'And the company?'

'They've terminated the lease with the landlord, vacated the premises, and gone back to Russia.'

'Just like Sarov, Koshki, Elaur, and Ternopil,' Witten said. 'We're getting reports from all over of Soviet companies moving their operations out of the US.'

'Which is a shame. They won't be so easy to spot next time they set up.' Simmonds said. He took some notes and closed his notebook. 'And Ms. Peers?'

'On the road to recovery.'

'Excellent news. We'll require them both in the future.' He turned toward Witten. 'They weren't properly set up for this sort of assignment as a first outing. Perhaps, you can assist them, so they don't make the same mistakes again?'

'Babysit them?' Witten said.

'Implement some measure of professionalism. We need to be sure they are well prepared for whatever we throw their way. Working out of their apartments isn't appropriate. Help them acquire suitable premises. Something close, but not too close.' Simmonds looked at Ward. 'You can go back to New York and continue the investigation into Novosil. It's the only company whose documents we have.'

Ward rose, shook hands with both men and left.

Once the door was closed behind him, Witten turned to the older man. 'And what about Knox?'

'As before. We keep doing what we're doing.'

'Watching and building a dossier for later use.'

'Precisely. No point killing the hound if it can be trained by a new master.'

*

Despite the surveillance countermeasures he'd employed, Leon Knox had an increasing sense of being followed as he drove the interstate to Maryland. He'd had a feeling of being watched for more than a fortnight and, even though he hadn't noticed anything obvious, he hadn't been able to shake it. Eventually, he'd put it down to paranoia brought on by the sudden departure of some of his Russian contacts. Although it paid to be suspicious, he knew he couldn't allow it to consume him to the point of paralysis. All he could do was trust his training and instincts to prevent him from doing anything reckless.

It was an enchanting late-April evening. The air was calm, and the sky a spectacular kaleidoscope of color as the sun gave up on the day. Summer was just around the corner, the air warm enough to allow Knox to take off his jacket and lay it on the seat next to him. He stopped at a convenience store and bought himself a soda before making the last leg of his journey into Johnstown.

He drove through a residential area with rows of brightly-painted bungalows set back from the roads by equal-sized patches of freshly-cut lawns, the scent of which dispersed a soothing effect across the neighborhood, allowing the community to forget its ills at least until the following morning. He slowed to a crawl to avoid colliding with the hordes of children who were playing on the road, enjoying the last of the weekend before school the following morning. He pulled up next to the curb and took his keys from the ignition. Rolling up his sleeves, he stepped out of the car and sauntered, hands in pockets, across a blackened and saturated lawn.

He stopped at the edge of a debris field where a house once stood, his eyes scanning the wreckage for any signs of its basement and the secrets it once held – everything was destroyed, and a sense of calm came over him. With the death of Tomas Sieber and the subsequent evacuation of several high profile Soviets from all across the country, he'd put in place a series of protective measures designed more for self-preservation than anything else. The first had been the elimination of a ghost from his past (he still didn't know where the pilot had dumped Michal Valent's body), the second was the destruction of his arsenal of records from the war. Although tortured by it, he'd decided it would be better to be ignorant of certain facts rather than run the risk of drowning under their burden should they be discovered.

He stepped cautiously into the rubble, careful not to fall through into the cellar, but it appeared as though the crew he had employed had done their job effectively. The smell of burnt timber was strongest closer to the center, but he couldn't detect the whiff of whatever accelerant had been used. Of course, once the investigators ruled the fire as an accident, a tidy insurance claim would make its way to him via a shell company.

He retraced his steps across the lawn, wiping his scuffed shoes on the grass as he went and slipped back into the car. He pulled away from the curb, leaving the secrets he'd destroyed confined to the past as ashes.

*

I'd never been in an airplane before. I was so excited that I had to go to the bathroom lots of times. I was told it would be a short trip, but Ms. Walsh came with me, anyway. She said I was too young to go on my own. I was happy about that because I like her and I like the funny things she does when I stay with her. I didn't know why my mum was in the hospital or why she was in another city. Big people don't tell me a lot. If it was up to me, she'd be coming home, but then I don't even get to pick out what I eat for dinner, Ms. Walsh does that. Most of the time she gives me food I like, but sometimes it's yucky. But, she did let me pick out what tee-shirt I wore every day. That's something that mum never does. Now that I was allowed to wear what I wanted, I was going to tell mum that that'd be the way it'd be from now on – and I wasn't kidding.

Ms. Walsh told me I'd get a hard-boiled sweet before the plane took off but that I wasn't to eat it until we were up in the air. She said it would help my ears. I didn't have anything wrong with my ears, but she didn't explain any more after that. I held the sweet in my hand and waited for her to let me know but, to tell you the truth, I nearly forgot I had it as soon as the propellers started turning. Ms. Walsh let me sit in the seat beside the window so I could watch the land whoosh by – and boy did it. I squeezed my hands into two fists so tight I thought I'd break the sweet, but when I looked it was still there, and my hand was all sticky.

I had a coloring book in case I got bored because I didn't know how long we'd be up in the sky. I hardly had time to open it because a woman in a nice uniform gave me as much soda as I wanted for the whole time we were up in the air. She had a nice smile at the start of the trip but wasn't smiling at the end. I don't know why. Maybe she felt the same way I did when the plane was coming down. I thought I was going to get sick from the plane bumping around so much, but I didn't. I did go to the bathroom when we got into the airport. I felt much better after that.

Uncle Danny was there to pick us up in a big, black car with a driver. He's not really my uncle, but I call him that because it's easier and Mum said it would be rude to just call him Danny. There was a woman with him. She had a red hat that didn't sit straight on her head. She was pretty, I guess, I don't really know. I don't really like girls that much. Uncle Danny told me I'd change my mind about that when I got older. He's usually right about a lot of things, but I was pretty sure he was wrong about this.

The driver seemed to know exactly where he was going, which was good as nobody said anything to him the whole time. We just talked about the airplane trip and the hotel we were staying in that night. I'd never stayed in a hotel before, and I wondered if I'd be as excited as I was about the airplane. Uncle Danny said there was a TV in my room and it had lots of stations, more than I've ever seen. I couldn't wait to see that.

In no time at all, the car came to a stop and Uncle Danny got out. He talked to the driver for a bit, and then we all got out. Uncle Danny took our bags which was a good thing as my arms would have fallen off if I had to carry mine.

Then we went into the hospital.

It was a really busy place, more people than I'd ever seen in my whole life. Uncle Danny and the woman with the red hat went first, and we got into an elevator.

'Press number 3,' Uncle Danny said. He pointed to a wall that had lots of buttons with numbers that went from one to eleven.

I did, and the doors closed.

I felt my stomach drop for a second and then catch up with my body. When the doors opened, the corridor was different than when we'd gotten in. Uncle Danny stepped out, and we followed him through lots of corridors that all looked the same. I'd have definitely gotten lost if Uncle Danny hadn't been there.

Finally, we came to a doo. He asked me to open it and look inside.

I did.

Mum was sitting up in a bed in the room. She was awake, but she looked tired.

'Come here, you little rascal,' she said to me, leaning forward and holding out her arms.

I've never been so happy to see my mum ever, and I didn't know why it had taken so long for me to see her. She looked perfectly fine to me, and I should know. I'm an expert when it comes to looking after my mum.

ACKNOWLEDGMENTS

ALL TOLD, IT TOOK A little less than five years to write 'An Act of God'. And when I say it like that, I wonder what the hell I was doing all that time. But that's not the whole story. You can't just dismiss five years of sporadic toil in a couple of lines – it's far more complicated than that. You see, once the elation of publishing 'Into The Lions' Den' had sub-sided, a few chapters of novel number two, this novel, followed swiftly on. I was, after all, on a roll. I'd set myself a target – get the next book out within a year. And I had the whole thing planned to minute detail, too. Allowing for multiple redrafts, editing, and the usual promotional build-up to launch, I'd calculated how many words I'd have to write each day. I was set.

Or was I?

Within a fortnight of punching the keyboard, I found myself im-mersed in a period of ponderous reflection and subsequent dismay. I mean, I always knew how I'd start AAoG, even had a rough idea of how it would end, but it was the sticky middle, those damn 80,000 words that were the problem. I walked a lot. I drove a lot. Ideas were born, they grew, they festered… they died. It wasn't writer's block (at least I don't think it was). I simply couldn't piece the story together; I couldn't make it fit.

And then, in an explosion of subconsciousness, I wrote the entire first draft of 'An Act of God' in a single month. It was a March, as I recall. I spent the next couple of weeks redrafting and editing before shipping the not-so-finished work-of-art away to a battery of beta readers who had the arduous task of 'taking me to task'.

And while I waited, I toyed with other ideas, novel number three, for instance, along with ruminations of another series of novels featuring Daniel's yet-to-be-born grandson.

But, I hadn't been left to dawdle too long before feedback began to pour in. At first, you dread it, fear the thoughts of reviewing the reviewers through squinted eyes because they were sure to call me out for what I was. A con and a hack who had just wasted both his time writing and theirs reading this turd of a novel. Surprisingly, it wasn't nearly as bad as I imagined. Reaction spanned a broad spectrum were the truth, no doubt, lay somewhere in the middle.

And so, my first thank you goes to those foolhardy souls who stuck their necks out and offered their opinions - AAoG is much better because of them.

I'd also thank Andrew and Rebecca at Design for Writers who worked tirelessly on the cover and printed matter formatting, trying to make sense of whatever ridiculous ideas I proposed – I hope you like the result.

Lastly, and by far, my biggest thank you goes to my wife, Joan, and not for the reasons you might think. Throughout this entire process, she has listened to the ramblings of a tortured soul pontificating of plot holes and the intricacies of publishing and promotion. However, over the past few years, she has given me, without comment, something more precious – her time. And it is for this; I will be eternally thankful.

Lightning Source UK Ltd.
Milton Keynes UK
UKHW041841251119
354234UK00002B/76/P